The Malachi Mysteries

Wellington's Story

By

Sue Lowe-Lauri

Bright Pen

visit us at: www.authorsonline.co.uk

Acknowledgements

I would like to thank Dawn Miller for showing me around the Evelina Children's Hospital and Dr Sanjiv Nichani, Consultant, for showing me around the Paediatric Intensive Care Unit at the University of Leicester Hospitals NHS Trust and explaining the symptoms of a coma.

Thanks also to Cath D'Alton, The Drawing Office, UCL Department of Geography, University College London, for producing the maps of London; to Rob Sones for the use of the photo of Catherine Booth (Image Copyright R Sones; this work is licensed under the Creative Commons, Attribution-Share Alike 2.0 Generic License). Also thanks to Philip Jackson for the use of the photos of Mozart and Queen Elizabeth, the Queen Mother; and to Tom Good for work on some of my images. All the other images in the book are the copyright of the author.

The photo on the back cover shows the Children of the World statues, created by Frederic Lanovsky, outside the main entrance to the Evelina Children's Hospital, London.

Thanks also to my family and friends for supporting me through the whole process.

This book is dedicated to my boys, all four of them.

About the author

Sue is married with three boys and lives in a Cambridgeshire village. She graduated from Oxford University with a BA (Hons) in Chemistry and spent her early career in the IT industry in the City of London. Whilst being a full-time mother to her boys she studied for a degree in Mathematical Sciences with the Open University. With her family Sue enjoys sport and music. This is her first novel.

Chapter One

"Tea's ready!" Liz yelled up the stairs to Rory and Sarah again. "Why don't they ever come down the first time?" she moaned.

"That's teenagers for you," Mike, her husband said, laughing. "Don't you remember those days?"

"I suppose so," she sighed resignedly.

Eventually a loud banging noise signalled Rory's arrival as he leapt down the stairs two at a time, whilst Sarah descended in a more ladylike fashion, being careful not to smudge her newly-polished nails. Soon, with all the food dished out onto plates, the Wheeler family were sitting round the table having their Sunday meal after a day relaxing on Oriental Bay Beach in Wellington, New Zealand. This was their special time as a family. All of them had enjoyed indulging in their favourite sport of one sort or another and now here they were tucking into a succulent joint of lamb, the children's favourite roast. All homework was up to date, uniforms ready for the start of the week and Mike and Liz were looking forward to sharing their future plans with Rory and Sarah.

"Why don't you tell them?" Liz murmured to Mike as she passed him the gravy.

"No you," Mike pleaded.

"Tell us what?" Sarah interjected, her hearing as sharp as ever.

"OK, OK," Mike said. "Here goes – your mother and I have been offered the chance to spend some time in Europe over the winter vacation, probably June, and we thought it would be a fantastic opportunity for us all to go and have a really exciting adventure."

"It's going to be the trip of a lifetime," Liz added as she reached across to the sideboard for the brochures. "Your father has worked very hard for this – a month's sabbatical – and we've decided that we should explore our roots and spend the time in Europe. I've spoken to your head teacher and she has authorised the extra time off school. What do you both think?"

Rory was stunned. Although the holidays were still weeks away, already his group of friends were planning how they would spend their free time away from prying parents and annoying brothers and sisters. He was fourteen now and he and his mates were determined to do their own thing during these holidays. He felt robbed – how could his parents do this to him?

"Well – I don't know about Sarah but I'm staying here and that's all I've got to say on the matter," and with that Rory stormed out, slamming the door so hard behind him that the glasses in the sideboard rattled. He ran upstairs and threw himself on his bed, face down, trying not to believe what he had just heard.

"Great – so what do we do now?" Mike sighed and looked in desperation at Liz.

"Look, just explain it all to us in detail and I'm sure Rory will come round."

As ever, at twelve years old, Sarah was the peacemaker and off she went to talk Rory into coming back downstairs to give their parents a chance to talk through more of the details with them.

Once he understood the timescales and that they were being allowed time off school, Rory began to feel a lot happier with the idea of spending the holidays visiting places they had only seen on TV and surfed the Internet about. He could see some advantages after all – a trip to the Theatre of Dreams perhaps, shopping in Hamleys to get the latest games, and he supposed it would be good to see where the Queen lives. He began to realise that there could be a lot in it for him if he played his cards right. And his friends would be so jealous that when he came back he would be the real cool dude of his gang. Oh yes, this wasn't such a bad idea after all, and he could see that his parents were really excited about the trip. Sarah seemed as taken with the plans as he now was and soon the two of them were shouting louder and louder to get their views heard as to where they should visit.

"Hang on there!" Mike exclaimed. "Now, we need to do this sensibly so what I would like you both to do is make a list of places you want to visit and things you want to do in order of preference and we'll try to fit in as many of them as we can. We want to make this a fantastic trip for us all so it's important we have an equal say in the plans."

His Dad was being quite reasonable, Rory thought, as he and

his sister went off to research the Net to get a better idea of where everything was in Europe and to make a proper plan.

***

"Girls – it's time to go, hurry up, I don't want to be late again." Boudicca was at her wits' end. She and her daughters had to be at the Wellington Arch in half an hour and the girls were still deciding what to wear.

"Look Mum, in our day we had no choice so we are just making up for lost time," Camorra explained, as she and Tasca swapped outfits yet again.

"No-one is bothered about what you look like, they just want us there on time," their mother reasoned as patiently as she could. Back in 60AD they were lucky to have a new winter and summer cloak each year but now, nearly 2000 years later, fashions had been revolutionised and who could blame her teenage daughters for wanting to indulge in the latest trends. Boudicca often thought back to what their life would have been like if she had married that Roman emperor, Gaius Suetonius Paulinus. A life living in Italy would have been amazing but totally against her principles. She had been right to support her husband, King Prasutagus. Perhaps taking her own life and that of her daughters was a bit extreme but here they were in the 21st century having been returned as Malachis to inhabit her glorious statue and do good for the human race. Not many people get that chance and she wasn't going to lose it because her daughters made them late for the summit meeting.

"I'm going now so if you're not ready you'll have to make your own way there," she yelled up the stairs, just as Camorra was putting the finishing touches to her lipstick. "At last," Boudicca sighed. "And do you have to wear so much make-up?" She really should try to be more patient and understanding with her daughters and relax a little. After all they only wanted to fit in with the current styles. She could hardly blame them for that.

Boudicca herself liked to dress stylishly but in a very classic and understated way and so was sporting her usual black work suit with the subtlest of make-up, all cleverly designed to look as

3

though she had achieved her look effortlessly. You'll just annoy Victoria again, she thought, but who cares. I'm doing this for me and no-one else. And so, with Camorra and Tasca looking suitably trendy, Boudicca and her daughters made their final preparations for the meeting.

"This is going to be interesting girls," she mused as she started to explain the process to her daughters. "The chiefs and their deputies of each of the London zones are being briefed for the forthcoming annual contest between the Malachi zones for the title of Supreme Malachis of London. We are going to agree the rules and regulations for this year's event. I don't suppose there will be many differences compared with previous years but there may be the odd variation as the result of the post-match analysis of the previous contest. Just make sure you are polite to Victoria, you know what she's like when it comes to manners."

Tasca reminisced about the last occasion and hoped that she could be more influential this time. She remembered then that all she could really do was help out when her mother needed an extra pair of hands. What would be really cool was if she could foresee calamities and initiate Malachi responses herself. Camorra, being a year older had been allowed some freedom to work on her own the last time so she was banking on being able to take some more initiatives. Her mum would need to convince Queen Victoria, their chief, that she should be granted some responsibilities, but she was reasonably hopeful. As long as she and Camorra behaved themselves at the meeting and sat in the background they would probably get their way.

Meanwhile, Boudicca was thinking about who would be there; obviously Queen Victoria, chief of her zone – the southern zone (the Meridion Zone) – of which she, Boudicca, was deputy. Then there would also be Nelson, chief of the western zone (the Occidental Zone) and Queen Anne, the chief for the eastern, Oriental, zone. They in turn would be accompanied by their deputies: – Dwight Eisenhower (Ike to his friends) and William Gladstone. The six of them formed the so-called inner circle of London Malachis, with Victoria being the overall chief. She was contemplating the fact that humans had no concept of the reality of Malachis, in other words 'angels'. Of course, they are written about in the Bible and some people claim to have seen them but humans have no idea what they really are. Just as well she thought – they would never accept the idea. It was best to let them imagine or believe in coincidences that happen in their lives as being purely accidental with no relation to any external force whatsoever. That way Malachis could have a lot more fun and influence in real life. Of course, Malachis were totally dependent on humans for building and maintaining their statues so that they could come back to Earth, albeit in a different persona, and make differences to the lives of the human race. And, furthermore, you could only return in this fashion if your statue had been built after your death.

She felt sorry for Elizabeth I. She had been such a fantastic leader in her time but couldn't return as a Malachi as her statue in Fleet Street was built when she was still alive, making it against the Malachi regime. It was this same rule which also denied Queen Charlotte Malachi status. Boudicca had a lot of time for Queen Victoria though, the longest reigning monarch, and she actually enjoyed working with her. Even though Victoria had had a reputation for being stern and uncompromising in her real life, she had softened somewhat since she had become a Malachi and now she was actually quite reasonable and even managed to balance her two roles quite well. When she needed to be in overall charge she had the command and respect of her fellow Malachis and equally when she assumed the role of chief of the Meridion zone she did not use her absolute authority to give her zone any unfair advantages. She even let Boudicca have a free reign with the rest of their southern cohort of Malachis and the deeds they could perform. Nelson was a good bloke too. Of course, he had the big advantage of a bird's-eye view over most of the capital but he was a good delegator and she knew that Dwight had an excellent working relationship with him.

On the subject of Queen Anne, however - what a problem she had been. What with all her health problems and her fondness for the intoxicating substances. Now, it was all well and good for Anne to complain to Queen Victoria about Boudicca's own penchant for opiates but she had been brought up on them and the doses were minimal compared to what addicts take these days. No, Boudicca was clear on that score. Also, it went without saying that she hadn't let Camorra and Tasca near the stuff. Queen Anne really had to sort her problem out or the whole Malachi regime would get a bad name.

The three of them grabbed their coats and bags and let themselves out of the portal. They were some of the few Malachis who had a proper door to their abode. Queen Victoria had done Boudicca proud when she had commissioned this fantastic monument to her and her daughters. Boudicca was also lucky that her statue had been built to incorporate her chariot and her two favourite horses. This way they could escape the city and enjoy fabulous days racing around the countryside, and from time to time they would even venture up to her old home in East Anglia. At least that part of the United Kingdom hadn't changed that much, compared with the capital, London. There were still plenty of open spaces in the Fens although there was much more water now than she remembered.

Once clear of the portal they made their way along Birdcage Walk and Constitution Hill to Hyde Park Corner, now home to the Wellington Arch, the Malachi conference centre. As they went past Buckingham Palace Boudicca noticed that Victoria had already left for the summit as her statue had dimmed. Good, Boudicca thought, Victoria must be getting everything set up, so things should go relatively smoothly.

***

Queen Victoria had arrived at the Wellington Arch in plenty of time to get the meeting organised. It was so much harder as a Malachi without all her ladies-in-waiting that she had had in her day but she supposed that the independence was more progressive and at least it showed that she was capable of managing on her own. Boudicca and her two girls would be here soon, she thought. Camorra and Tasca were little madams having been brought up in a fairly lawless society all those years ago but having coped with invasions and the torture they had been subjected to, actually they had come out of it quite well. In fact, Queen Victoria thought, there was little difference between those Fenland girls compared with today's youth – they had the same brash, self-confidence about them. Boudicca had done a good job as a working mother and Queen Victoria admitted she was really grateful she had her as her deputy for the Meridion Zone as she was so decisive and pragmatic. Boudicca was able to rally the other Malachis into action and the two of them complemented each other really well.

"Now, where am I going to sit everyone?" Victoria mumbled to herself as she marched into the conference room. She loved this monument but had been saddened in her real life when it had to be moved from the Palace to Hyde Park. Now, however, it was the ideal place to convene her senior Malachis. She knew that the present occupiers of Buckingham Palace wouldn't appreciate the disturbance that a Malachi meeting could make.

"We'll just sit with our deputies around this round table. That way, as there are only six of us we can be next to each other," she decided. Victoria only hoped that Queen Anne would be sober this morning and not whingeing and whining the way she usually was. If only she would put up and shut up she would probably be a lot happier in herself – it was all this self-pity Victoria couldn't stand. She had a certain sympathy for her old colleague Gladstone who was the Oriental's deputy and who had to cope with Anne's foibles.

Victoria was particularly well prepared for this meeting. She had printed the copies of the agenda, and drafted the terms of reference for this year's contest. She knew there would be some negotiation over the details but she felt that in overall terms they would satisfy the chiefs and deputies.

The last contest had been a bit of a fiasco with terms of reference that she thought could at best be described as blurred and at worst as non-existent. "This year it will be so different and everyone will have to toe the line. We'll have regular review meetings to assess progress systematically and we'll have someone to keep the scores from each zone but, of course, they will keep each other's scores and not their own. The other major difference is that we will have a theme. Finally, each Malachi can only use a maximum two skills at any one time. That should stop Malachis like Florence Nightingale and Baden-Powell trying to do everything themselves."

Victoria glanced around the table checking off all the necessary items were in place. "Right, that looks fine. I've just got a few minutes to go over my introduction." Victoria wandered over to the magnificent panoramic window and went through her script in her mind. After the third run-through her thoughts drifted. As she looked down onto the people below she wondered who the humans would be who would benefit from this contest. She hoped it would be a complete cross-section of society (she sounded just like a politician, she thought) so that they couldn't be accused of bias.

***

Meanwhile, Nelson was collecting his papers and getting ready to meet Dwight Eisenhower. He liked the general – they were two of a kind. Dwight Eisenhower had made a good elder statesman in his time and Nelson marvelled at the fact that he was still so fit. Nelson had taken quite a few years, once he had returned as a Malachi, getting used to his statue in Trafalgar Square. Things were a little easier once the lift had been installed. Before that he hardly went anywhere unless he really had to as he couldn't bear the thought of the long climb back up all those stairs. One alarming aspect was the aeroplanes that kept flying around up in the sky. Once humans had started using them for transport his world had changed completely. Not only did he have all that human activity scurrying away down below him, he also had these flying metal tubes with wings which roared almost as loudly as his own lions. At first they always took him by surprise and he would duck instinctively as soon as he heard them approaching. He eventually came to realise that the humans would be pretty stupid to get their calculations so far adrift that he would be in danger of being flown into and soon began to feel more at home with these machines, even anticipating who the pilots would be at any given time. He tried waving at them but of course they never saw him.

Once the lift had been installed Nelson felt much more inclined to fulfil his Malachi purpose. His particular strength was guiding, with his secondary one being strengthening. Whenever he could he would look for opportunities to guide humans onto the right track but if he was too late then at least he could give them the strength they needed to get themselves out of trouble. Of course, Dwight's speed was his main attribute, with delivering being his secondary strength. Between the two of them they made a good team and they could always draw on the strengths of their western Malachis to support them if necessary. He remembered the time when he and Florence Nightingale had to deal with an accident on the London Underground. Guiding the humans back out of the subway tunnels had been mostly down to him, whilst the ambulance service had to thank Florence Nightingale for all her work with the injured. No, they weren't a bad bunch really, in his zone; some of them just needed a bit more practice. He wasn't sure what he should do with Sigmund Freud though – he was always analyzing and questioning every decision he and Dwight made and trying to relate things back to their mothers! I mean, honestly, he thought, he should just get on with the job!

"Anyway, enough of this reminiscing," he decided. He had arranged to meet Dwight on Piccadilly, just outside the Ritz, for a quick briefing and catch up before going on to the Wellington Arch. Should he go in casual or be a bit smarter? "Oh, what the heck," he decided as he pulled on his favourite cord jacket which was hanging on the top of the banisters. "This will do. It's not as if we're meeting anyone special, only royalty." He quite liked the modern fashions of the 21st century – at least he didn't have to wear hose; socks were so much cooler and he loved the baggy trousers as he didn't have to breathe in every time he stood up as he used to do in his day. "Right then, have I got everything?" Nelson did a quick check around his home. He never liked leaving any lights or appliances on as it was so high up he didn't think any human would be able to spot smoke spiralling out at the top should there be a fire, only the pilots of course and they wouldn't quite know what to make of it. "Safest is bestest," he muttered as he got into the lift and pressed the down button. Gosh, that was fast! he thought as his stomach leapt up to his head. "I bet Ike trumped it," Nelson said as he staggered out of his portal and almost fell into the square.

The fountains were on and the square was full of tourists.

Nelson loved days like this, a warm summer's day, happy groups of humans milling around, climbing all over his lions, taking photos, what could be better? He noticed Napier was out and about. Quick, he thought, he mustn't see me otherwise he'll start quizzing me as to why he didn't get selected. From what Nelson had heard, Napier had been a bit too free and easy over in India and had taken a few too many liberties. Yes, Nelson acknowledged, the objective had been achieved but at what cost to human life? He was and still is really pally with Byron so at least they've still got that friendship to fall back on. Nelson turned the corner just as Napier was about to call out to him and he made his escape.

Ike was already at the Ritz by the time Nelson arrived. He was window-shopping all the beautiful watches and jewellery in the shop front.

"Hi Ike," Nelson said, as he approached. "How's it going? Are you ready for this? Got any feedback from Roosevelt?"

"Fine thanks, and yes Franklin and I were chatting this morning. He can't foresee any major problems. Florence Nightingale will be her usual self and Charlie Chaplin and Shakespeare are both up to speed with their parts. We are a bit bothered about Napier and Byron but as long as they are kept at arm's length we should be able to cope. Then it's a matter of bringing the others along as and when we need them. They are a good team on the whole. And I've been keeping my fitness up as I can see we'll be relying on me for my speed." (In fact, that very morning Ike had done another session around Grosvenor Square, with Franklin timing his laps as he pounded the pavements.)

"OK, good. I don't know what the theme is yet. I think Queen Victoria has got a few we need to review and then we'll agree on one this morning. Basically the rules will be the same with a few minor variations. I'm looking forward to this – I like having excuses to get down to street level and get involved with the people. Working with the other Malachis is good too."

Nelson felt really upbeat about this contest. He was confident that his team of Malachis could cope with any set of circumstances they would need to help out with.

"Oh, by the way, you haven't been interfering with my lift have you, only it descended at quite a pace just now?" Nelson asked Ike.

Ike looked away, trying not to let Nelson see the smile on his face. "I don't know what you mean," he replied, innocently.

And so the two of them continued along Piccadilly, both lost in their own thoughts, quite at ease in each other's company. It's the journey that is the important thing and not the end result, Nelson thought, as he reassured himself. At least, that's what Scott and Shackleton were always reminding him.

As they came round the New Zealand memorial they heard a shriek. "Just stop having a go at me. Leave me alone and just keep your thoughts to yourself for once! Just remember I am your chief – you have no right to speak to me like that!"

"Oh no," Ike muttered to Nelson, "it's Anne and it looks like she got out of the wrong side of the bed, if you get my meaning!"

And sure enough Queen Anne and William Gladstone were having their usual shouting match at the entrance to the Arch.

Gladstone pleaded with Ike and Nelson for moral support. "Look, chaps, can't you explain to her that if she lets us down again then there is only one thing for it – she will have to reconsider her position as chief."

"I am perfectly aware of that, thank you, Gladstone," Anne shouted back. "But if you don't mind, I would like you to know I haven't touched a drop this morning, yet; although if I have to listen to you for much longer then I'll be driven to it. In any case, who else would take on the role as chief of the Oriental Zone with you as deputy?"

"I know that both John Wesley and Edith Cavell would jump at the chance so I shouldn't worry about that. In fact they are just waiting to grab the first opportunity they can," Gladstone retorted.

Gladstone and Anne were at each other's throats again. Gladstone could not abide Anne's secret habits and only wished she would pull herself together or relinquish her role. Anyway, now was not the time to be arguing. They had a mission to accomplish and so Gladstone reluctantly muttered the briefest of apologies and allowed Anne to pass up into the conference room.

"Here we go again," Ike whispered ironically to Nelson. "If they carry on like this we won't have too much trouble from the Orientals as they'll be too preoccupied with these petty tiffs."

"Yes but we can't let it distract us either," Nelson retorted. "Come on, let's go and see if Boudicca and her lovely daughters have arrived yet."

Chapter Two

All four of them ended up sharing the same lift. There was a frosty silence as they sped up to the conference room and spilled out into the sumptuous surroundings.

Ike loved this place, as he loved England's entire heritage. Where he came from the oldest buildings were only a few hundred years old. He loved the plushness of the English state apartments, the proportions of the rooms, the richness of the paintings. No wonder the rest of the world was just a little bit envious of Britain.

Where are those gorgeous girls, he wondered? Ike had a bit of a soft spot for Camorra and Tasca. They reminded him so much of his own granddaughters. I'm sure they give Boudicca a hard time and she has done a brilliant job with them, but they have hearts of gold underneath all that sassy front.

Just then the lift door slid open and, lo and behold, in came the three warrior women, as Ike called them.

"I hope we're not late," Boudicca burst out, as they almost fell into the room.

"No, no, you're fine; the others have only just got here too. Now girls, I hope you've been helping your mother this morning. She's got a busy time ahead of her so the more you can do to help the better," Victoria said as she greeted them.

Camorra and Tasca looked at each other with raised eyebrows and rolled their eyes. "Yes, Ma'am". They sauntered over to the coffee table where Ike was already doing the honours.

"Coffee for you two?" he asked as he reached for a cup.

"Oh, yes please," they replied in unison. "And Ikey, none of that decaf rubbish for us – we need pure caffeine in our veins at this time in the morning, besides we're not used to these modern chemicals."

Ike was only too pleased to give them what they asked for. "Biscuits?" he asked, knowing what their reply would be this time. "No thanks, just an apple for us."

Boudicca took the opportunity of having a quiet word

with Victoria. She wanted to make sure that their views on the forthcoming contest were aligned and in particular she wanted to make sure that Tasca could take part, at least have a minor role this year.

Anne and Gladstone took their coffee and sat down at their allotted places around the conference table. In spite of her outburst earlier, Anne actually felt quite serene this morning. She'd slept really well and her legs had loosened up with her now daily stroll around Paternoster Square. Unbeknownst to her rival, Gladstone, she had actually started to realise that all this gin and high living wasn't doing her body any good, and had done some research on the newfangled health remedies that were so popular now. She'd overheard Prince Charles talking about homeopathy and although she was very sceptical as to how miniscule amounts of anything could have such a dramatic effect, she had thought there must be something in keeping one's body in good shape. "I mean," she had argued to herself, "I need more and more gin to have the slightest effect on me, these days, rather than less". And she also had nothing but admiration for people who regularly pounded the streets around her.

After watching all shapes and sizes take to the streets she had decided she would give it a go herself and so, having researched the Internet, she had set herself on an intense programme of walking and healthy eating. It was going to take some time, she'd warned herself, to get into any kind of decent shape and she really had to want to do it for herself. Over the years she had had the odd setback but having lost several stones and been able to control her drinking to primarily social events she was feeling really positive about life, for the first time in centuries. Now she just had to convince William Gladstone that she should stay as their chief. She didn't want him to know about the fitness programme though, and she was too proud to admit that she had had a problem back in the old days. Gladstone never noticed what she wore so it had been easy to downsize. Basically she still wore the styles she'd worn in real life, the plunging necklines and full skirts on dresses with waists; she'd just taken the waists in bit by bit over the years as she'd needed to. She thought Gladstone's eyesight wasn't what it was either.

She looked over at the other end of the conference room. Victoria and Boudicca were deep in conversation, no doubt discussing tactics. She was quite envious of their relationship – seemingly so different, they nevertheless had a strong bond between them. Anne thought that it was probably because they had both suffered from losing their precious husbands in tragic circumstances. In spite of the huge gap in years between them they were actually very similar in the way they approached life, although Boudicca was far more decisive and was able to stick to the decisions she made with consummate ease. She was a born leader but didn't particularly like the limelight, which was something Victoria was used to and so in this respect they worked well together. Also, Boudicca was so lucky to have her two daughters by her side. That was due to Thorneycroft, the sculptor of her magnificent statue on the Embankment. She couldn't complain though. Anne loved her own statue, especially the location. She could look down Ludgate Hill at all the City workers hurrying and scurrying to their modern offices. Before all the developments she had a much better view along Fleet Street and on a good day she could see Nelson enjoying his prominent spot in the middle of London. Compared with some of the statues of her fellow Malachis she had been looked after very well. She often heard the grumblings of the half–Malachis, or busts as humans knew them as, along Threadneedle Street – they could only act as observers and had no recognised Malachi powers. They had actually gone on strike recently and stopped communicating for a month. None of the full Malachis had seemed to notice though, but she supposed they had felt better for it! Anne didn't think they would have much to do in this latest contest because of that, although she must remember to bring that up as a clarification point at the end of the meeting just to be sure. She probably had more than her fair share of half-Malachis in her zone and she needed to know what their boundaries were otherwise she could be at a distinct disadvantage.

Gladstone was already flicking through the agenda and associated papers. He hoped Victoria wouldn't have a go at him this morning. Their relationship hadn't improved that much over their Malachi years but at least he felt he could tolerate her now. I suppose I've mellowed with age, he mused. He knew how much more time she had for Disraeli compared with when he had been Prime Minister, but now he must put that out of his mind. They were here in the 21st century as Malachis for a purpose and with his strong sense of duty to his country and fellow men he crossed his legs, had a sip of coffee and settled down to concentrate on the tasks ahead of him.

The agenda didn't look too burdensome this morning. There were one or two regular items to be sorted out first but the main item was 'the event'. He and Anne had had some discussion over their preferred tactics, but he hadn't been sure at the time how much Anne was taking in. "We'll just have to do our best with what we've got," he said to himself resolutely, and at that point the others came and took their allotted seats around the table and the meeting began.

***

"Thank you all so much for coming, and for getting here so promptly." Queen Victoria opened the meeting and everyone fell silent as she dealt quickly with items one and two on the agenda.

"Now let's get down to the real business of this morning."

The anticipation was palpable as each of the chiefs and deputies waited anxiously.

"We've got a couple of ideas for the theme of this year's contest with a third that has been suggested by Mr Charlie Chaplin." Victoria looked around the table to see if she could read the reactions of her colleagues as she summarised the case for each one.

The table fell silent as the serious business got underway. Victoria was very authoritative and professional in her presentation giving a full and detailed breakdown of all the options, whilst the others gave the ideas their full attention. Gladstone was impressed – he hadn't seen Victoria in this mode before, she was acting more like a politician than a monarch – and surmised she must have learnt something from himself after all those years as Prime Minister. Gladstone weighed up the options in his own mind as Victoria went over them in fine detail. There were three proposed themes: Prime Time, Prime Number and the one suggested at the last minute by

Chaplin was Prime Mover. The rules of the contest were quite clear: any Malachi moment had to reflect the chosen theme and each moment could be redeemed by only two Malachis using only two of their skills. The results would be recorded by a half-Malachi, the one nearest the scene, and they would also be accounted for independently.

So far so good, Gladstone thought, we all seem to be in agreement, and he glanced around the table. Nelson and Ike were nodding and looked fairly confident about the prospect and Boudicca and the girls seemed quite happy. But what was the matter with Anne? As he looked to his right she was grimacing and seemed to be in a lot of discomfort. She's not with us on this – I may well end up looking after the Oriental Zone on my own, thought Gladstone, despairing. How could Anne let him down now?

Little did he know that she was suffering from the most excruciating bout of cramp in her right calf, but there was no way she was going to admit this to him. She reached down surreptitiously and tried to massage the offending muscle. It must have been the run she had done that morning – she hadn't warmed up properly before she had set out and she was now paying the price.

"Let's just go over the minor details and then we'll take a vote on the overall theme," Victoria was drawing to an end and all were listening intently.

Eventually Victoria concluded, "So – who votes for Prime Time? This means that any Malachi moment must be performed during a prime hour. Don't rush all at once. Any takers?

"Second is Prime Number. This means that the moment can take place in a location associated with a prime number. So, for instance, the house number must be prime, or the postcode.

"Thirdly, Prime Mover?"

Nelson looked around the room and could see the expressions on his colleagues' faces. He surmised that no-one was that impressed with the idea of these themes. We'll be better off just having the traditional contest, he thought, this will only complicate things and the rules are pretty complicated as it is.

"Look, I don't want to put a spanner in the works, Victoria, but don't you think the idea of a theme gets in the way of what we are trying to do here? I mean, why don't we put the theme idea to one side at this stage and concentrate on the overall objectives?" Nelson spoke out as persuasively as he could whilst at the same time hoping that Victoria wouldn't take offence. She had obviously put a lot of thought into these themes and the last thing Nelson wanted to do was cause a massive upset. He could see the others nodding slightly in agreement and figured he had hit the right note.

"Oh, thank goodness for that!" Victoria exclaimed. "You have absolutely no idea how much sleep I've lost worrying about these wretched little themes when all along all I wanted was a traditional contest like we always have."

Ike broke the tense atmosphere by laughing his head off.

"Oh, you English!" he joked. "You are so bothered about not offending each other! That's sorted then – no theme and all the extra details we've already discussed."

Boudicca was thankful to have Ike's grass roots pragmatism in the group. He's right, she thought, we can be so concerned about other people's feelings that we never say what we really feel; unlike these brash Americans who just call a spade a spade and take the consequences.

With the atmosphere returned to normal they spent the rest of the time clarifying the details once and for all and then checked their diaries for the precise timetable for the next few days.

"Very well," Victoria summed up, "the contest starts on Monday, so good luck to everybody!"

And with that the zone chiefs and deputies gathered up their belongings, tired but full of ideas to take back to their teams.

Chapter Three

Over on the other side of the world, the Wheeler family had spent several busy weeks organising flights, hotels, and all the fine details of their future trip to Europe, whilst at the same time making sure that their house and menagerie of animals would be taken care of in their absence. Rory's and Sarah's friends were naturally really jealous of them but had been appeased with promises of presents and mementoes from the trip.

The flight over to Europe had gone without a hitch and most of the arrangements had worked out. They spent their last afternoon in France, before flying into London for the culmination of their trip, lying on a private beach on the *Promenade Des Anglais*. Sarah had loved being able to ask for drinks to be brought to their sun loungers on the beach but regretted the fact that she had discarded her jellies when she was ten. Those little rubbery sandals would have been perfect for this beach. Every time she wanted to go and cool off in the glorious flat Mediterranean Sea she had to brace herself for the most tortuous three metre walk she had ever taken as the large, round pebbles dug into the soles of her feet leaving them bruised and battered. So much for the elegant swagger into the water – it was more a case of trying not to fall over and just get to the water's edge, taking as few steps as possible, and start swimming as quickly as possible. Not the entrance she'd planned. But at least she'd made up for that in the evenings. Strolling around the old town in her skimpy sun-dresses showing off her golden tan was her idea of heaven.

Rory, meanwhile, had spent most of the last day swimming in the water, messing around on a pedalo and up in the air attached to a paraglider. He'd saved up for this experience and had made his Dad stand on the beach videoing the whole trip.

All four of them were looking forward to their last meal in France before the adventures that were lying in wait for them in London.

***

Boudicca was glad to get back to her comfy sofa and put her feet up. It had been a tough meeting. Victoria had negotiated well on behalf of the Meridions and Boudicca had broadly supported her. She didn't agree on the new penalties that Victoria had managed to wangle through but she would just have to make sure they didn't incur any along the way. The main thing was that Victoria and the others had allowed Tasca a supporting role in the outfield so that should keep her out of mischief while Camorra had been promoted to fourth lead.

"Thanks, darling – that's lovely," she sighed as Camorra brought her a glass of the most divine white wine. It wasn't bad this stuff from the New World, better than they had managed to produce in East Anglia in her day. "Are you and Tasca OK to sort out supper? I'm exhausted."

As the two girls started to prepare the meal in the kitchen Boudicca began to relax as she felt the cold, white nectar slowly find its way down her throat and into the pit of her stomach where it began to relax all her jitterbugs from the day's events. She looked around her home and felt the most enormous privilege at having been allowed to return as a Malachi. She couldn't quite believe that she had this pad to live in with her precious girls. What would Prasutagus think of all these mod cons? He had been a real traditionalist, insisting on open wood-burning stoves, thatched roofs and skin cloaks. What would he make of the granite worktops for instance? I mean, back then it was just lying around but nobody thought of using it as a food preparation surface as they do now. And the limestone floor tiles which seem to be everywhere these days. A few tons of dried grasses sufficed for us and we could replace it as soon as it got too grubby. Nowadays, though, recycling is the name of the game. You can hardly throw anything away without feeling a tiny tinge of guilt as you rack your brains to see if you can reuse, recycle, re-give the item. No wonder people these days look so careworn and troubled. Even the basic everyday activities have to have a thorough profit and loss analysis conducted before they can do anything. But she loved the variety of food, clothes and entertainment of this modern lifestyle and was glad she was having the opportunity to experience it after all these years.

With her mind slowly reverting to its normal speed and her limbs beginning to lighten with the demands of the day drifting away from her she allowed her conscience to wander aimlessly amongst the remaining thoughts as she tried to relax. The cries of the street seller just outside her home faded as the aromas from the kitchen wafted into the living room and took over her senses. She loved being able to look out onto the Embankment and River Thames below her. There was plenty of activity on the water with boats and barges still chugging back and forth up and down stream. The London Eye was on its continual journey as it rotated its passengers round and round. What a feat of engineering that was, she marvelled. One of these days she'd take the girls for a ride on that, she promised herself, and with that she closed her eyes and drifted into semiconsciousness.

**

It was 6:30pm and the doors were closing. Jack gathered up his briefcase, made sure his season ticket was in his pocket and easily accessible and with some relief headed for the Tube. It had been quite a day: meetings all morning and then the disciplinary right at the end of the afternoon. Alison would be furious if he was late again. He'd promised he'd be home early tonight to help with bedtime. He'd have to phone her on the way and hopefully he could pick up some wine and flowers at the station as some sort of peace offering. His feet ached and his head throbbed. He walked as quickly as he could along Victoria Street, a route he'd been taking for the last six years since he'd joined one of London's smartest department stores as Principal Buyer for ladies fashions. He loved his job but some days it could be exhausting, especially like today, he thought, as he hadn't even had time to stop for lunch. "Oh why don't people move more quickly and just get out of my way?" he said to himself, as he weaved around the tourists who didn't have a care in the world. They didn't have to get a train in a hurry like he did. Nearly there, he thought, as he sped down Bridge Street. He rounded the stall in front of Boudicca's statue and raced down the

21

steps to the entrance to Westminster Tube and then his world went blank.

***

Boudicca jumped up with alarm, her peaceful reverie suddenly broken by a loud bang on the back door.

Oh no! What was that? she wondered, as she dragged herself to her feet and stumbled over to find out the source of the disturbance.

"It's OK, Mum – it's only a guy who's slumped down against the door. I think he might have fainted," said Tasca as she peered out of the rear window.

"Right," said Boudicca. "This could be your initiation act. Now – how do you think you could help him? What particular skill could you use to get this chap back onto his feet and able to get on with his journey?"

Boudicca had seized the opportunity to show Tasca what being a Malachi was really all about. It was all very well to go off to these meetings, discuss and agree things and come back home full of good intentions but it was another thing altogether to perform the deeds that were required of a true Malachi. But, of course, the actions all depended on your own particular skills and Tasca had not been blessed with too many human life years to have honed her expertises. She just had the basic skills for a girl of her age.

Well, let me see, Tasca thought, as she went through the panoply of possible skills she could use. With the state the guy was in she thought hard. She only had a couple of options: she could give him strength to get himself out of the situation he was in or help deliver him from it herself.

"I know, I'll make him put his head between his knees and remind him that he's got a bottle of water in the bottom of his rucksack that he should drink to rehydrate himself and get his blood pressure back to normal."

"Good," said Boudicca. "Now go outside and see if it works."

Tasca let herself out of the portal which involved a tricky

22

manoeuvre as Jack was slumped partway across the entrance. She knew both her mum and sister were watching her every move and she tried to think back to the training sessions she had gone to which Florence Nightingale had given last winter. She just had to get this right otherwise she wouldn't be taking part in the contest.

The trick was to make the guy do what Tasca wanted him to do without him realising anyone was helping him. She focused in on his brainwaves and soon connected. That was a good first step.

"Now Jack," she said, very gently, "you need to lean forward, very slowly, no harsh movements and sit up slightly. That's good, and now just put your head between your knees."

Jack sat up and began to wheeze.

"No, no – that's not what I said." Tasca realised that she hadn't been clear enough. "KNEES," she repeated carefully and slowly.

Jack grabbed at a pile of leaves in the corner.

"No – **KNEES**," she insisted.

This time Jack seemed to understand and leant forward whilst at the same time Tasca gave the instruction for him to remind himself that he was carrying some water with him. With that, he had enough sense and energy to scrabble around in the bottom of his bag and retrieve the said bottle. Soon he was standing up and, ruffling his hair and feeling very confused, he took a step down towards the entrance to the Tube station. "How peculiar," he muttered to himself. "I could have sworn someone helped me back there but there is no-one around. It's a good job I remembered the water I had – probably been there a week but it seems to have done the trick. Now I hope I haven't missed my train." And with that Jack disappeared into the bowels of the Underground, and wondered how he was going to explain that to his wife when he got home.

Tasca looked up at her mother and sister looking down at her through the upstairs window as she made a thumbs-up sign to them.

"Well, how was that?" she demanded as she strode back into the living room. "Mission accomplished, wouldn't you say?"

"Well, it was OK in the end but you did have a couple of false starts," retorted Camorra, smugly.

"You must get your intonation correct, otherwise you really don't know for sure what the humans will do. At least this was a

23

fairly innocuous case. So yes – well done. Not bad for a first attempt. Also you must remember to send out clear messages."

***

Dusk was approaching as the two Malachis crept towards the cabmen's shelter. They had been using this one for years because it was in a busy road and always well stocked with tea and light refreshments. Set on the bottom of Northumberland Avenue just by Embankment Station it looked like an abandoned caravan with no wheels rather than the cabbies' café it was and had been since its inception in 1875.

"George, good to see you." Charles held out his hand and shook his friend's in their customary greeting. "Cup of tea?"

They went inside the shelter and helped themselves. It was just after closing time and the cups had been left to drain.

"Now what do you make of the rankings then, Charles?" George had been furious when they had been debriefed by Nelson after the summit meeting and had been told that he wasn't eligible to take part in the contest because he hadn't accumulated high enough scores since the last. How dare Nelson decide! What did he think he's been doing in Greece all those years ago?

"Look, calm down." Charles tried to remain calm himself but inside he too was pretty annoyed. Like George Byron, Charles Napier had squandered his Malachi years swanning about the capital and not paying any attention to the plight of Londoners and so had failed to achieve his objective targets set by Nelson and Eisenhower after the last contest. "You never know what's going to happen during the actual contest and there are always the peripheral jobs that need doing. You may get a call about one of those."

"I don't think I'd demean myself to stoop so low, but let's stick together on this – eh? Remember Greece back in 1822?" George reminded his friend.

How could his old ally, Charles, ever forget those heady days when he was Governor of Cephalonia? Byron had been a good friend to him then so it was only right that they stuck together at this time. After several cups of tea and a good moan the two men felt much happier. The other Malachis in the Occidental Zone who hadn't qualified were David Livingstone, Captain Scott and the Queen Mum so they weren't the only ones out on a limb. Both the men hadn't done so well on the guiding tasks as they should have done given their previous experience, and the Queen Mum was still a novice having only returned to earth recently when her statue had been unveiled by her daughter.

Chapter Four

Earlier that afternoon Nelson and Eisenhower had called a meeting for the Occidental Zone in the old cottage in Soho Square. They had bought themselves a takeaway snack and wandered into the square itself where there was more room for them all. Finding a relatively quiet and shady spot in the north-west corner they sat on the grass and concentrated on the rules for the forthcoming contest. Most of them had been quite satisfied with what was to be expected of them. They each knew their two key strengths which they would have to use; they understood the need for independent counting and were happy with the idea of using the half-Malachis for this purpose. Of course, the normal laws were to be followed, i.e. no harm to come to people which was caused solely by a Malachi action, and so on. The senior Malachis in the group understood their extra responsibilities and Shakespeare and Florence Nightingale had been particularly proud to be designated the senior officers for the competition.

"We'll have to keep an eye on Byron and Napier," Florence muttered to Will, under her breath. "They don't look happy that they won't be active this time. They are going to have to re-do their second training course now to get their skills up to speed. We should expect some rumblings from them I think."

"You're right, Flo, as usual. I'll have to get de Gaulle to do some spying, he'd like that. We can't afford to lose the contest just because they aren't happy. I'll also make sure Scottie does something useful by keeping his eyes open." And with that Will Shakespeare and Florence Nightingale had a final chat with Nelson and Ike to work through the finer details of their strategy.

The other Occidental Malachis stood around chatting, catching up on the latest Malachi gossip.

"Did you know both Camorra and Tasca will be involved this time? They could cause some chaos if Boudicca isn't careful!"

"She'll have to keep them away from Byron – he has a soft spot for young ladies."

"Did you hear about Edith and Newton – what an unlikely friendship!"

So it went on as the light dimmed and the square emptied as the people made their way home.

Nelson and Ike decided a swift half or three were in order and retreated to their usual haunt, The Mason's Arms, just down the road in Maddox Street. As they were approaching they noticed a young girl was being pestered and jostled by a couple of rather unsavoury types.

"Listen – I've already told ya, I've no more money. You'll have to wait until tomorrow."

"No, girlie – that's not good enough. You either go with us now back to our place or I take this," and with that the taller chap pushed the girl back and tried to grasp the gold necklace from around her neck.

Oh no you don't, Nelson thought, as he stirred up a pile of dust and debris on the pavement. The swirling particles flew straight in the man's eyes and caused him so much pain he staggered back, rubbing his eyes trying desperately to relieve them of the agony.

"Quick! Run!" said Ike to the girl, who wasn't sure what had happened but had the sense to make her escape whilst she could. "And you two – freeze!"

"It's good to get the practice in when we can," Nelson joked to Ike, as they watched the men stare in disbelief at the fleeing girl, unable to move as they were temporarily disabled by the two Malachi.

"Now, Ike, what are you drinking?" Nelson said as they strode into the pub.

***

Anne and Gladstone had been quite civil to each other as they made their way back along the Strand. "Let's convene a meeting in the morning, Will," Anne proposed. It wasn't that late but Anne wanted to do another workout before she ate and went to bed and knew that if they had a meeting tonight time would run out.

"Ok – will you get the word around then? We'll meet at the Monument at 10 in the morning. Does that suit you?"

"Yes that's fine, thanks. Goodnight."

Anne left Gladstone to open his portal, hidden amongst the wreaths at the bottom of the plinth. She had another mile to walk as she continued along the Strand, then Fleet Street and up Ludgate Hill to St Paul's. She had put her trainers on this morning under her dress so that she could power walk home. The evening was drawing in as Anne set off. She had a routine to her training with the first five minutes walking normally, followed by a sharper ten-minute session building up to a further ten minutes of really striding out with arms pumping and her breathing in time with her legs. Building the rhythm up in this way provided her body with a gradual warm-up and meant that she didn't put any undue strain on her ageing muscles. Wow – she felt good now, and as she marched up Ludgate Hill. She wished she had been able to share this experience with her old friend Sarah Churchill (before they had fallen out) – they would have had lovely walks at Blenheim Palace. "Anyway, time to warm-down now," she said as she approached her monument. It was still really busy with commuters rushing to their stations or bus stops to make their homeward journeys. She activated her portal just as the bells of St Paul's were signalling the start of evensong. This was her favourite service and as she pulled off her trainers she looked forward to relaxing in a warm bath, closing her eyes and drifting off to the sound of the choristers' voices as they sung in total harmony to the beautiful accompaniment of the organ.

The next morning the Malachis in the Oriental Zone assembled as planned. They were very fortunate to have the use of the cellar in the Monument, all tastefully refurbished. Anne remembered when she was a little girl coming to watch as the first stones were laid. She'd only been a baby when the Great Fire ripped the heart out of the City of London in 1666 and soon after that she'd been sent to France to live with her grandmother so that she could receive the best medication for her dodgy eye. She returned just in time to see the great unveiling of this tallest, free-standing column ever built at that time. Everyone was singing the praises of the brilliant architect who had designed this and many other buildings in the City of London. Of course, Anne had had the privilege of meeting him when he'd visited Paris a few years earlier and so naturally was one of the

28

honoured few who were allowed up to the viewing gallery. The views had been magnificent then but now the landscape of London was completely different. Mercifully, most of Christopher Wren's designs were still standing but around them had been shoehorned in a multifarious array of office blocks and outlandish buildings. "I mean to say," she muttered scornfully to herself, "Chris (as she liked to refer to him) would never have designed a tower to look like a vegetable, and a gherkin at that. I can't remember eating those in my day. I don't know – the modern architects of today," she sighed. "And we always built our buildings to last, not like the Millennium Dome. What a waste that would have been if that had been removed as per the original plan soon after the turn of the century. And what about the Olympic Stadium?" She sincerely hoped that would be a building worthy of the greatest of British architects.

The group was ready and waiting as she entered the basement. This was where the science lab was set up all those years ago when Britain was at the forefront of science research. Now the Malachis had refurbished it into a very comfortable assembly room.

John Wesley, Isambard Brunel and Edith Cavell were huddled in a corner pouring themselves some coffee.

"Morning all," Gladstone said as he breezed in. "Good to see you all here. Let's get started. I just want to run through the main criteria for this year's contest and then I'll take questions. Anne – do you have anything to add?"

"No," Anne replied, feeling a little bit relieved that Will had taken charge for this meeting. He was good at this sort of thing, whereas Anne tended to get a bit tongue-tied.

"Right then – here we go. The competition will be in three phases each lasting a day. You can use two of your key strengths for any action. And only two of you can be involved at any one time. A slight change this year is that the half-Malachis are going to do the counting. This way we involve them but also keep the counting independent. And finally, events cannot be engineered by us – we can only react to events. Any questions?"

Will hoped he'd explained everything clearly enough. Naturally, though, there would be queries along the way and there was the opportunity for the three zone chiefs to review the situation from time to time.

"Yes – just one," butted in Newton. "Out of interest, who will be the senior team leaders?"

"I propose Isambard and Edith," Gladstone replied. Isambard Brunel and Edith Cavell grinned at each other. This was what they had been hoping for. "Any objections?"

The others were quite relieved their names hadn't been mentioned as Isambard and Edith signalled their acceptance of their roles to the group with a nod of the head.

All the Oriental Malachis seemed quite content with the rules of engagement. They'd been assessed at the quarterly training session earlier in the year and knew their strengths and weaknesses. Some had even earned more strengths, which was a rarity but well-deserved in these particular cases.

"I'm a bit nervous about the whole thing, I must admit," whispered Gandhi to Newton. "I mean, I just want a peaceful life and I'm not happy about interfering with the natural course of events."

Newton was reassuring. "Look, mate, you just look for situations where people need to find their inner strength and leave the other things to us. You can always count on Edith to get stuck in and Brunel will always look for a practical situation. Besides, we can't predict what we'll have to deal with and if you don't feel comfortable with anything just give one of us a shout."

Gandhi was slightly happier with Newton's response. He also knew that Joseph Priestley just down the road would be a good support. With the lovely, peaceful squares they resided in there was sure to be someone in a state of turmoil who had come to the gardens to try to calm their nerves. He'd seen so many people, for instance, who had relatives in the nearby hospitals who were very sick and needed some quiet, contemplative time. They would be the ones he could help, Gandhi thought, now slowly beginning to look forward to the days ahead.

Chapter Five

Victoria and Boudicca were making their way back from their zone meeting. It was nearly lunchtime and they'd decided to stroll into Kensington Gardens. They'd had a successful meeting. All their Malachis had been really positive about the contest and had arrived at their centre, the cabmen's shelter on Pont Street, on time and with renewed enthusiasm. A month earlier they had held a retreat at the Battersea Power Station where they could have plenty of space and freedom to practise their particular skills and also to do some team building. Victoria and Boudicca recognised that they had some strong characters in their zone and unless they had taken the advantage it was likely that they would be fighting each other rather than working together for the good of their zone. Prior to this, Cook and Columbus used to argue over who had been the most intrepid explorer. Of course, Columbus claimed this title and insisted that if it hadn't been for him then James Cook would never even have ventured to Canada never mind the South Pacific. But Cook was quick with the retort that hadn't Columbus thought he'd reached the western coast of the East Indies – and so on. Oh, what on Earth are they arguing over this for? Boudicca would wonder. She had a thing about Italians and didn't have much time for Columbus. He was so self-conceited, and vain as well, always putting forward *la bella figura*, a typical Italian bloke. Anyway, nowadays, in part due to Byron's daughter, Ada Lovelace, the world had such things as the Internet, sat nav and street view, and people were making journeys to outer space. "Now Columbus, did you ever think of going there?!"

A couple of the other Malachis had also really benefited from the weekend away, and had built up their self-confidence. Mozart didn't believe he could do anything other than compose and play music. What he didn't realise was that his music was incredibly popular these days and appealed to a huge cross-section of society. Furthermore, people were familiar with some of his most famous pieces even if they didn't immediately recognise them as being composed by him. Victoria had been really good with him, giving him lots of encouragement and little by little he had developed some of his other skills so that he was reasonably competent at quite a few.

Catherine Booth, on the other hand, had needed to improve her stamina. She had been fine on the quick-fire tasks but when confronted with one which required more sustained thinking and determination she often went off the boil at the last minute and then lost control. Baden Powell had given her a couple of one-to-one mentoring sessions so she was much better at lasting the course. With Emmeline Pankhurst and Christopher Columbus assigned the roles of zone seniors, their team was prepared and ready to go.

They walked past Harvey Nick's and then turned west along Knightsbridge. Victoria wanted to pay her respects to her beloved Albert at his memorial. He'd been offered the chance to become a Malachi some time ago but hadn't taken it up yet. Victoria was trying to persuade him but he still didn't feel ready for the 21st century. So much had changed and he liked the traditional Victorian way of doing things. He wasn't sure he could adjust to the pace of life at which these modern people had to live.

Boudicca sauntered off ahead giving Victoria the privacy to speak to Albert in peace and quiet. A doubles match was being played on the tennis courts. "Oh, I wish we could have played that in my day," she sighed, wistfully. "It looks like a great sport and being out in the open air – just my thing. The girls would have loved it too. I wonder if we'll be called to Wimbledon this year – it would be good to get Murray out of a spot of bother with Federer if the chance arises." And, dreaming of fit sportsmen and tanned bodies, on she strolled to the Diana Memorial Fountain.

Now there was one hell of a character, she thought to herself, as she remembered the brief but glamorous life the one-time nursery nurse turned wife of the future king had led. She had had the media at her beck and call and it was a complete tragedy when her life had been cut short so suddenly in Paris.

She continued to the café where she sorted out sandwiches and juice for herself and Victoria and positioned herself in the full sun at a table on the terrace whilst she waited for her friend to join her.

As she sat there, soaking up the warmth from the sun and breathing in the scents of the flowers planted in tastefully arranged beds, she watched the children playing at the water's edge.

"I don't think you really want to be doing that, do you?" She focused on the little boy, Peter, who was reaching out to grab hold of his sailing boat which had been buffeted away from the shore and was heading towards the middle of the Serpentine. If he stretched out much further to retrieve his toy he would be in the water, no doubt about it. Boudicca could see his mother was deep in conversation with the waiter and wasn't going to notice her son's predicament in time. "I must get that young lad with the hoodie to do something," she decided, as she spotted the only person nearby who could possibly be called upon in time to prevent a terrible accident.

"Yo, my man, what's up?"

Boudicca had made Rudi take out his mp3 player from the pocket of his jeans to select a different track whilst he strolled past the toddler, his hand outstretched towards the water. Peter was so taken aback at the sight of the teenager bending down to see what was going on that he let out a long, piercing scream.

"Is this what you're after?" Rudi stepped out of his trainers and quickly strode out into the water. "Phew – that water's cold, but I love your vehicle," he said as he grasped the boy's boat, gave it a quick dry down on his hoodie and started to hand it back to the toddler.

At that moment Peter's mother came running out of the café and onto the terrace having immediately recognised her son's cry.

"Just what do you think you're doing?" she yelled at Rudi. "Give it back this minute!"

"Hey man, I'm just saving this boy's life. He could have had a nasty shock if I hadn't come to his rescue," Rudi explained.

Boudicca focused all her thoughts on Tina, Peter's mother, and tried to make her see sense. Rudi had actually saved her son from falling into the water to retrieve his boat. Now, can't you see that not all young people are self-centred and ignorant? And she focussed her thoughts into Tina's mind.

Tina felt herself do a double take. This was not what she was expecting – young lads wearing hoodies are things to be avoided at all costs aren't they? She and her close circle of friends from the mums and tots group were always insisting that their boys would never be allowed to wear such clothes, listen to such music and speak in that trans-Atlantic, disco-speak. So how come this one had done something for which she would be eternally grateful? Boudicca continued to get her thought waves into Tina's subconsciousness and gradually she felt her change her point of view.

"Oh – did you rescue his boat?" Tina replied hesitantly, not wanting to lose face and still wanting the teenager to know where he stood in the hierarchy of things.

"Sure did, Lady and so if you don't mind I was just about to give it back," Rudi was indignant. "In fact, I was going to ask him to show me how it works." He had a much younger brother himself and actually quite enjoyed playing games with him, as long as it didn't interfere with his music-time.

"Oh, er, all right then. Peter – what do you say to this kind gentleman? He rescued your boat and saved you from falling in."

"Tanks, much," Peter faltered, obeying his mother. "Want a go?"

"Sure thing, bro," Rudi answered as he knelt down at the water's edge, a new friendship forged.

"Well – would you believe it?" Tina muttered to the waiter. "You just can't take anyone for granted these days, can you?"

Boudicca smiled and took a sip of her juice.

"What are you looking so smug about?" Victoria asked as she pulled her chair out and joined Boudicca at the table.

"Oh nothing – just putting the world to rights, that's all!" Boudicca replied, and as she looked across at the water's edge Rudi, Peter and Tina were deep in conversation about which flavour ice cream they would choose.

***

The Duke of Wellington was reckoning up. He was in his statue in Hyde Park, and had been given the honorary position of Counter of the Malachi Contest. This took him back to his army days when he was in logistics and he had to determine the precise requirements for his battalion to wage war against Napoleon. Oh, the minute detail he had to deal with then and all just using a pen and paper; all those lists and figures and columns of numbers. He was quite relieved he had the use of a laptop now. He'd already set up a spreadsheet and so it was just a matter of itemising the Malachis, their actions and scores and he'd soon know which zone was the victor.

Now the question of how the scores were going to be communicated to him was still something he had to work out. It had already been established by the senior committee that the half-Malachis were going to be the independent observers and counters which was fine, but how were they going to report to him? Wellington was musing on this problem as he started to set up the spreadsheet with the names of all the Malachis from each of the zones that Victoria had given him. He could see from the list that not all the statues were occupied. "Of course only those who are called to be Malachis return to this Earth," he mused. Then the solution came to him. "That's it – we'll have a reckoner from each zone responsible for tallying another zone's scores. That way we get some independence. I know that there are one or two Malachis who aren't going to be taking an active part in the contest for one reason or another. This will give them an alternative but equally important role."

Wellington was feeling very satisfied with himself for thinking up this rather neat solution.

"Now – I think I'll nominate Charles I from the Meridion Zone to track the Orientals, Henry Havelock in the Oriental Zone to track the Occidentals and we'll have Napier, for the Occidentals, to monitor the Meridions. But there's a slight snag with this idea – neither Havelock nor Napier have their own horses. I'll talk to George IV and Haig – they won't mind lending them their mounts for the duration of the contest. They'll only be needed at the end of each day and they could probably do with a good canter. That should keep everyone happy. Of course, I shall have to run this past Victoria but I'm sure she'll go along with it. Oh, and I'd better have a session with the three counters and brief them on their roles. They can then communicate to their teams of static observers." And with that Wellington carried on completing his spreadsheet.

He rode over to Trafalgar Square, rounded up Charles I, Sir Henry Havelock and Sir Charles Napier and then the four of them cantered over to Richmond Park. This gave the horses a good workout and was the perfect spot to have a quiet discussion. The park was looking at its best – the roses were in full bloom and the air felt so clean it was as though you were breathing pure oxygen.

Charles was particularly pleased Wellington had chosen this park to ride to. After all, it was down to his own efforts that the park became the Royal Park it is today. He knew he had upset a lot of people when he denied them their claim to common grazing on much of the land and introduced deer to the park for hunting. But look what he'd done to recompense them – and he'd built the wall to keep the deer in. Nowadays, of course, people didn't remember that far back and took the park for what it was – a fantastic public park full of interesting fauna and flora with a large open space for Londoners to escape to from the hurly burly of city life and spend time appreciating nature. And sure enough, even at this time of day, there were plenty of people doing just that. It was just a shame they'd had to drive here!

They tethered their horses and sat down outside Pembroke Lodge. Wellington outlined his expectations and ran through the rules of the contest. Charles and Henry were more than a little relieved to be given this prestigious role. Neither had relished the actual contest that much but they were still more than happy to be involved in this way. Wellington noticed that Napier was slightly hesitant about the prospect. He probably feels that he should be more involved but he didn't quite cut the mustard at the pre-training session, Wellington thought to himself.

"Now, as for the counters themselves, each of you will have to ride round your allocated zone and get the results from the half-Malachis each day and then feed them into this spreadsheet. I must say I find the Web incredibly convenient. I've set up a website giving each of you access to the zones you are counting for, so all you have to do is enter the numbers on-line and then I'll do the overall reckoning. Is that clear?" Wellington explained.

"Seems fine," replied Henry. "But I'm sure we'll be able to resolve any questions we may have as we go along. I'd just like to say thanks, Arthur, for asking me to perform this role. I won't let you down, you can be assured of that."

"Well – that's OK old chap. I know you'll do a good job, that's why I asked you," Wellington replied. "So – who's ready for a canter?"

And with that they rounded up their horses and set off around the park, all happy at the prospect ahead. Napier still felt slightly uneasy. Was he betraying Byron by accepting this role? He would have to wait it out until he saw Byron next.

This was the final piece in the jigsaw. The three zones and their teams were in place and the annual Malachi contest was about to begin.

Chapter Six

Now, after they had explored every square inch of Europe, or that's how it seemed to Rory, here was the Wheeler family making their way from Nice to London Heathrow. Rory couldn't wait to see the new terminal building. He was fascinated by modern engineering structures and since he'd been a toddler was always modelling bridges, towers and anything else he could with bits of Lego and Meccano.

Sitting back in his seat, having had an uneventful flight, Mike turned to Liz and asked, "So, darling, what has been your favourite part of the trip so far?"

"Well, I loved Italy, especially Rome and the Coliseum but I have to admit that my favourite place has to be Nice. So nice!" she joked. She was feeling relaxed and rested after their last three days soaking up the sun in the South of France. Their budget had been stretched to the limit and they had been very careful to allocate their funds according to priorities. But there was one promise which Liz was determined to hold Mike to.

"We will come back to Nice won't we?"

"Sure," Mike replied.

"And we will stay in the Negresco, won't we – for our silver wedding anniversary?" Liz continued.

"Oh – well, I'm not sure. That depends." Mike said, semi-seriously.

"On what?" Liz demanded.

"On whether you're still my wife then!"

Liz gave him a playful tap. "You rotter!" she said, laughing.

"Cabin crew, 10 minutes to landing," the pilot's voice interrupted them over the intercom as they started their descent. Soon the airport was in sight.

"Wow," Rory exclaimed to Sarah, "just look at that!" He was enthralled by the planes, jumbos and Lear jets that were laid out below him.

Sarah muttered, "Very nice," as she kept her nose in her book, and having been oblivious to the change in aircraft noise as the landing gear descended.

Eventually, after all the rigmarole of landing and a long wait to get through passport control, with Rory getting ever more frustrated, the family found the baggage reclaim station for their flight. It was 11 o'clock in the morning and after the flight from Nice all Liz wanted to do was to get settled in their hotel and grab a power nap. Forty minutes would do it, she reckoned, before they started exploring the most fantastic capital in the world. She hadn't been back to London since her student days, nearly eighteen years ago, she thought with a deep longing – oh, the parties they had enjoyed then. She blushed as her memories came flooding back. What had she been like? It was as well she had met Mike just in time who had tamed her free spirit and was happy to start their married life in her home country all the way on the other side of the world. She couldn't believe Mike had agreed that they should spend their first night in London in the Ritz! What an experience that would be for them all.

She was brought back to reality by Rory nearly ramming a trolley into the back of her ankles. "Look out, Rory!" she exclaimed. But by now she was nervous, she always hated this part of flying: watching the suitcases and bags of every shape, size and colour being spewed out on to the snaking belt which seemed to delight in raising her levels of anticipation to breaking point as more and more bags appeared but never one of theirs. The hassle there would be if a bag went missing would be unimaginable. It had happened a couple of times many years ago but fortunately before the children were born. Imagine the tantrums if Sarah's hair straighteners went missing or Rory's Barcelona football shirt he'd bought at the Nou Camp went astray, never mind being without her own essentials and clothes.

"There's one of them." Rory had spotted the large one he and Sarah shared and he lugged it off the belt and heaved it onto the waiting trolley, being carefully guarded by Sarah, who miraculously was still oblivious to everything going on around her as she continued to devour her book.

"And there's Mike's."

Where was her case? She was just now beginning to get anxious and start to go through all the items in her bag, totting up their value for a possible insurance claim. Why does it always happen to me, she thought, with no valid reason behind that thought at all. She turned round to check yet again that the other two cases were safely on the trolley when the next she knew Mike was heaving her coffin off the belt.

"What have you got in here?" he demanded to know.

Liz breathed a huge sigh of relief and replied, "The kitchen sink – what did you expect?"

Eventually the four of them made their way through customs and out to find a taxi which would take them to their final destination, London, the best capital city of the world, according to Rory, where they would spend the next few days having the most fabulous time of their lives.

***

The taxi was making good progress as they made their way into central London. The rush hour was over and the roads were relatively quiet. After their first night in the Ritz as a special treat for them all, they were booked into the Novotel near Lambeth Palace. Possibly not as grand as the Ritz but still in a fantastic location for all the sightseeing the family was planning to do. They had driven in along the Westway and now the taxi was cruising down Edgware Road and approaching Marble Arch.

"Look kids." Mike was pointing out various landmarks as they negotiated the busy roundabout. "That's Oxford Street up there – Sarah's Mecca – and soon we're going to be going down Mayfair, one of the most expensive streets in the world."

Rory and Sarah remembered the street names from endless games of Monopoly. Rory had always imagined himself as a property tycoon. Maybe one day he'd be buying and selling hotels on this street, he wondered. These last few days are going to be seriously cool, he thought, and he amused himself by going through, for the fortieth time, the list of things he was going to do during their last few days in Europe.

"It was the Ritz you said, mate, wasn't it?" the taxi driver shouted from the front.

"That's right," Mike replied. "We could do with a taste of luxury for one night after all the rushing around we've been doing."

"Just up here then and soon we'll be there."

They had stopped at the traffic lights at the bottom of Park Lane. Liz could just make out the tops of the columns of the New Zealand War Memorial. This was on her 'to do' list. Her great-grandfather had given his life for freedom and democracy in the Second World War fighting for the Allies and she had promised her grandmother she would pay her respects to him at this new memorial. Rory was more interested in the sculpture on top of the Wellington Arch, with the chariot, angel and horses in full flight. "Wow, look at that Sarah, don't you wish you could ride in a chariot like that, way up above the streets, looking down on everyone? What a feeling that would be!"

"Don't be so fanciful, Rory. Your imagination always gets the better of you," she replied, looking forward to pampering herself in a luxury bath filled with all the bottles of bath gel get she could get her hands on.

"What the..."

Crash! Bang!Crash!

Rory and Sarah, sitting on the pull-down seats in the cab with their parents on the rear bench seat, had been looking at a message on Sarah's phone when suddenly the whole world erupted. Rory had never heard such a cacophony of noise and terror in his whole life. Tyres were screeching, people screaming, bags flying, cars crashing into each other.

The taxi had been shunted from behind with the force of a tsunami and the impact had driven them into the back of a stationary bus. Rory and Sarah were thrown against the glass with such force it sounded like gun shots, whilst Mike and Liz were held in place by the effective seat belts.

It was mayhem. Pedestrians were jumping back out of the way, cars were skidding into each other and the Wheelers didn't know what on Earth was going on.

Just a few yards away Wellington had been busy grooming his horse when he saw it all happen in slow motion. Why hadn't he noticed the build up of traffic earlier? Then he might have been able to prevent the accident or at least steered the car into the wall at the side of the road. But no – he'd been too preoccupied with Copenhagen, his horse, and hadn't anticipated the crash. All he could do now was see if he could help out with the aftermath.

"Come on, old boy, we've got to do something. Let's go!" And with that he jumped up into the saddle and the two of them took an almighty leap over the wall, landing in the middle of the carnage, and tried to assess the damage.

From what he could make out it would appear as though Mike and Liz, who had been sitting in the forward-facing seats of the taxi had got away without serious injury. But he wasn't at all sure what he could do to save Rory and Sarah. They had both hit their heads on the glass panel and a bag which had been placed on the rear shelf had hit Rory on the side of the head with such force that the corner reinforcement had made an indentation on Rory's right temple. "The worst place he could have been hit," Wellington mumbled, as he concentrated with all his powers of delivery to try to get their autonomic systems to kick in.

Someone had obviously dialled 999 as soon the area was being cordoned off, ambulances began arriving and bodies were staggering about, looking dazed and bedraggled.

"Oh my God, what's happened?" Liz was coming round having been flung out of the door of the now crumpled taxi. "Are you OK, Mike?"

She couldn't see the children – where were they?

"Don't worry about me, I'm fine, I'm more concerned about Rory and Sarah."

At that point the emergency services took over and before they knew it Mike and Liz were being treated for superficial wounds whilst Rory and Sarah were being carefully lifted out of the taxi and put onto ambulance trolleys. The paramedics did what they could at the scene to stabilise them but soon Rory and Sarah were being wheeled into the back of an ambulance, tubes and wires coming out everywhere.

Wellington knew he should let the paramedics take the children to King's College Hospital, the London hospital with the best neurosurgery department. He could see they had serious head injuries, and hadn't responded to the first aid given by the paramedics, but he couldn't let them go that far. It had been his fault the car had shunted their taxi in the back and caused one of the worst traffic accidents he'd witnessed on this corner for years. It was his duty, therefore, to strengthen the parents and deliver the children back to them in full health, using his powers. The only way he could do that was to ensure that they were in easy reach and that meant the Evelina Children's Hospital (or ECH) at St Thomas' Hospital, just down the road. Never mind that King's College Hospital had grown out of King's College – an institution which he himself had been instrumental in establishing back in 1829, when he was Prime Minster and George IV was on the throne. No – past loyalties will just have to take second place in this case.

With as much guiding power as he could muster he persuaded the paramedics that Rory and Sarah had to get to the nearest hospital if they were to have any chance of survival.

Wellington looked on as he saw the ambulance make its way back down Grosvenor Place, blue light flashing and siren wailing, with the children's parents and all their luggage following on in a police car, whilst the driver of the offending vehicle was in handcuffs, being questioned by a traffic cop. The carnage that had been caused just a few minutes ago was being cleared away and people were continuing on their way.

Still feeling slightly shocked and shaken up himself, Wellington patted Copenhagen on his neck, and walked over to try to find someone he could talk to in Hyde Park. Even Byron will do, he thought to himself. But Byron was not in his usual place, nor was his dog, Boatswain.

That's strange, thought Wellington, I wonder where he's gone, he's nearly always here. Where is he when you want him? Typical.

"Let's go back home then boy. You need a rest after all that activity and I need to speak to Victoria as soon as I can."

Chapter Seven

"RTA on its way," the senior casualty nurse shouted to the team at St Thomas' A&E. "Stand by everyone – looks like we have two minors with serious head injuries, possible coma, and their parents, both fortunately with only superficial wounds. They'll need checking out of course. The paras were getting some odd readings in the ambulance from the kids so we need to be on our toes for the unexpected."

Dr Arnold was the on-call Paediatric Intensive Care Unit (or PICU for short) consultant and was there to meet the casualties.

"What's the matter with them, why don't they wake up?" Liz was desperate. All she could think was why had she balanced that bag on the back shelf when she could easily have put it in the front with the driver. Oh, it was all her fault. Their big trip and now it's all going to end in disaster. She clung on to Mike with tears streaming down her face, any thoughts of luxuriating in the Ritz completely banished from her mind.

Dr Arnold was puzzled. He hadn't seen these responses in coma patients before. The bangs on the head and the obvious visual traumas led the doctors to believe that the children were indeed in a comatose state but still the tests weren't 100% conclusive. Something wasn't quite right.

"We're just going to do a few more tests and then we'll have a better idea. Once they are stable we can transfer them to PICU in the Evelina Children's Hospital," Dr Arnold said, reassuringly. He was trying to be as positive as possible but it wasn't easy. The state these children are in, they'll be lucky if they pull through, he thought to himself.

Sarah and Rory had suffered massive head traumas but as they lay on their hospital beds in A&E they began to see shafts of light at their peripheral vision. Suddenly their whole field of vision erupted as if a million fireworks were going off simultaneously accompanied by an orchestra of bangs and shrieks. Then they were falling along a long, winding tunnel of light rays, flashing like laser beams of blue and red, and were being bounced around along the tunnel from side to side. It felt like a rickety roller coaster ride, almost as if they were in a washing machine of light. They were being tossed first one way and then the next, up and down, heads being thrown from side to side.

"Stop!" yelled Sarah. "I'm going to die..."

"Sarah – give me your hand!" Rory yelled at her as they began to slow down and the tunnel of light receded into the distance.

Then everything came to a complete standstill.

"Look, Sarah, we're home!"

Sarah looked around her and all she could see was a big brass sign in a swirling mist. As the clouds slowly parted she could make out the letters one by one and couldn't quite believe what she was seeing. The word WELLINGTON, in big bold brass letters, was staring straight at her.

Then two figures came into view on either side. No – this isn't home. I've never seen a sign like that, she thought, not convinced by Rory's claim. She looked around her. "Hey Rory, look! Isn't that the arch you saw and those columns? I recognise those – they're the New Zealand memorial aren't they? Where are we?" she wailed.

Rory was taking in the scenes as they revealed themselves before him, rubbing the side of his head.

"Come on, we must have missed the turning Mum and Dad told us to take."

But looking around him Rory was thoroughly confused. The last thing he remembered was hearing an enormous bang as they were making their way up Piccadilly to the Ritz. Then it was all a blank. He was trying to be brave and strong for Sarah's sake but he had a massive headache and felt sick. A wave of nausea suddenly swept over him and he knelt down. He was feeling dizzy and he could still see pinpricks of light dancing around in his vision. As he came to, he felt someone helping him to stand up. It wasn't Sarah – she was standing right in front of him and this was someone behind him. Rory turned around and to his amazement he found himself staring at the face of Arthur Wellesley, the Duke of Wellington.

"Wh... wh... what are you doing here? I thought you were dead?" Rory recognised Wellington from his old history books – he would never forget that nose.

"Now don't panic, boy," Wellington replied, reassuringly. "I am dead but you aren't, at least not yet, and neither is your sister. You've just got a bit muddled up as a result of that accident you were in and your persona has traversed the plasma divide and entered the wrong space coordinates so that your ectobeing has been transported along the medians of visual energy and entered the wrong dimension. Simple really." Blimey, Wellington had even surprised himself with his technical knowledge, he wasn't usually so au fait with these sorts of things.

"Look – just give it to me straight. We're dead aren't we and we're in heaven right? This isn't quite how I imagined it but we're here now so we'll just have to make the best of it."

"No. Hang on. Not quite. I'll just say you are in a temporary dimension owing to a slight mistake on my part. As a result you can regard me as your guardian angel and I'm going to do everything I can to get you back safe and sound to your Mum and Dad. OK?"

"Well, if you insist. I don't suppose we have any choice do we?"

"No, you don't." Wellington replied. "You will just have to trust me. Can you do that?"

Sarah butted in, "Yes, of course. We'll do anything – just get us back to our parents as fast as you can please!"

Both Rory and Sarah were shivering now, caused mainly by the shock of what they had just been through. They were happy to do whatever Wellington told them to as long as it meant they could get back to their own world.

"Come on then. What you both need is a good rest and a nice hot drink."

And with that Wellington took them both through his portal and into his cosy home. His statue had pride of place on the corner of Hyde Park and on each corner of the plinth a soldier from each country of the United Kingdom stood guard, all of whom had fought with him at the Battle of Waterloo, as well as many other campaigns. The 1st Grenadier Guards was represented by Bob, the 42nd Royal Highlanders, commonly known as the Black Watch, by the grumpy Scot, Jock. A little Welshman, Owen, who couldn't stop singing represented the 23rd Royal Welch Fusiliers, whilst a jolly Irishman called Padraig (Paddy) was the rep for the 6th Inniskilling Dragoons. In spite of their cultural differences the four men got along rather well, each one bringing a different set of skills which seemed to complement each other. Because they had been brought up in the Forces they were used to the rigorous routines which Wellington put them through and they all had a bit of a soft spot for the old general. At the end of the day they were all indebted to their master for getting them through the bloody battles they had all fought for King and Country.

***

Immediately after the road accident Byron had taken Boatswain for a walk around Hyde Park. He too had witnessed the terrible accident but had been too preoccupied dreaming of his next conquest to be bothered to go and help. After his customary constitutional, Byron was sitting back down on his seat, dreamily rubbing Boatswain under his ears when he was startled by the sudden flash of lightning across the road.

"What's he up to now?" he moaned. Of course he was referring to Wellington, that old adversary of his. "Can't he stop showing off?"

Over the years that Byron had returned to the material world as a Malachi and had been installed here at the bottom of Park Lane, overlooking Hyde Park Corner and Wellington's patch, he'd witnessed many of Wellington's antics. Normally he ignored them but the old rivalry between them still rankled even after all these years. And he was still annoyed that people couldn't get to his statue that easily.

He tried to suppress these feelings of jealousy, and reassured himself by thinking, you are and always will be the greatest romantic poet this country has ever produced; you are still read and talked about, in fact people probably know more about you than Wellington.

He looked up again. Something was going on over there and his curiosity got the better of him. He wandered over, dodging the traffic. It was now rush hour and the traffic was hurtling around the corners. He didn't want to alarm anyone and so he kept his distance. All he could see were two rather bedraggled-looking children talking to Wellington. Strange, he thought. I wonder what's going on? This could be the opportunity he was looking for. He thought back to his conversation with Napier the other day. Yes, I need to keep my eye on Wellington.

***

Sarah was a bit cheesed off to say the least that they would now miss their stay in the Ritz. She had been so looking forward to it. She had it all planned from arriving in the taxi, making her grand entrance into the lobby, gliding up the grand staircase on the plush red carpet (no lifts for her) and then sitting at the Rivoli bar sipping a cocktail (non-alcoholic, naturally). This place had better be as good, if not better.

"Wow!" exclaimed Sarah as they took in their surroundings. The inside of Wellington's monument was simply out of this world. It was a bit like the Tardis from *Doctor Who*, she thought, still not quite believing where they were. It hadn't seemed that big from the outside but inside it was one huge open plan space with separate areas around the edges for working, eating and sleeping. "I thought you lived in the eighteenth century but this is so modern. How come?"

"Oh well, when I agreed to become a Malachi one of the conditions was that I could have all the mod cons and so here they are. I was fed up with living in the Dark Ages." He swept his arm around the place indicating the state-of-the-art communications centre, plush leather sofas and modern stainless steel kitchen. The one exception to this was the camp bed in the corner. Wellington had spent so many nights on the march and in battle that he had never quite got used to sleeping in a proper bed and so preferred this makeshift item of furniture. The pièce de résistance, however, was the most lavish wine cellar you have ever seen. Not that it was a cellar in the traditional sense of the word as it was on ground level, but with transparent walls and temperature controlled sections for both red and white wine, it was a real icon of modern interior design.

Introducing Sarah and Rory to his four devoted soldiers, Wellington said, "I'll get my men to fix you something to eat and then what you both need is a good rest – you are going to need all your strength in the next few days if you want to get back to your world safe and sound.

Wellington ordered his four infantrymen, who usually stood guard at each corner of his monument, to take care of Rory and Sarah.

"Now, lads, these are my charges but I expect you to make them perfectly comfortable. Sort out the spare sleeping areas for them and make sure they have a decent meal and clean clothing, and anything else they might need."

The four soldiers were glad they had a job to do at long last. Their life was pretty dull when all they were expected to do was stand up and look smart around the plinth of Wellington's statue. They did sneak off to the pub now and then but only when they were sure Wellington was well out of the way.

Rory and Sarah were still rather frightened and confused but decidedly happier that they had a roof over their heads.

"What do you make of all this?" Sarah whispered to Rory. "It's all a bit weird isn't it? Do you really believe where we are? I thought this sort of thing happened only in fairy tales."

"I don't like it one bit. I don't see why we have to do what he says – I mean he's just some weird old man."

"Oh Rory, please don't go off and do anything stupid, like you normally would. You don't know anything about their world. I think we should just trust him, ok?"

Rory wasn't happy at the thought of being trapped in this stone mausoleum but for the sake of his sister he decided to go along with the situation. Besides he was also feeling incredibly weak and if he was honest with himself he didn't have the physical energy to go exploring on his own. Soon they were tucking into a plateful of bacon and eggs and then they settled themselves down to recover from their frightening ordeal.

At the first opportunity, Wellington got hold of Victoria. He activated his quadrisensor screen and accessed her virtual comms sector. The twentieth century had seen a massive explosion of technological inventions and breakthroughs and the Malachis were now beginning to take full advantage of them. Victoria came on-stream almost immediately.

"We need to talk," he said. "Something's come up, can we meet?"

"Yes, of course, Arthur, come over now if you want."

"No. It must be in private. Can we go to the shelter in Grosvenor Gardens? No-one will overhear us there."

Victoria sighed; a session with Arthur wasn't quite what she had in mind the evening before the contest started. She was rather surprised he felt like going out himself with what lay ahead of them over the next few days. It must be important. He sounded rather desperate. Victoria had been and would forever be a most dutiful royal. Some people thought she still took her duties rather too seriously but she had always said if a job is worth doing it's worth doing well.

She put away her books and gave a cursory glance to her appearance in the hall mirror. Not that she was vain, it was just that she knew Wellington of old and didn't want to be at a disadvantage, however slight; he was quite critical of people's appearances, and not just women's.

The shelter he'd suggested was at least convenient. She went the back way, through the Palace gardens, where she noticed her great-great-granddaughter, Elizabeth, out dead-heading roses. I wonder if she will out-reign me? she thought. Good luck to her. I bet she'll do it as well, she's pretty fit for her age. With that thought she slipped out of the side gate at the corner of Grosvenor Place and crossed the road into Upper Grosvenor Square.

As she sped past the statue of the lioness chasing the antelope she reached out her arm to stroke the wild cat. She couldn't help thinking that she was glad that these statues weren't Malachis. She didn't relish the thought of the antelope finally being caught and ripped to shreds by the lioness. Not a pleasant sight in the middle of the capital. Just think of the mess. The City of Westminster street cleaners would soon strike over having to clean that lot up, she guessed. She was certainly glad that some animal statues were blessed with Malachi-like powers though. She remembered the wonderful sight of the dolphin rescuing the boy who had fallen off Westminster Pier into the Thames and swimming back with the poor lad on his back, to his distraught parents. Oh, and then there was the time when Edoc, the beautiful Coadestone lion, had prevented a demonstration turning nasty just by the old council offices by helping to disperse the agitated crowd.

She approached the door of the shelter just as Wellington reached out and grabbed her arm – "Quick, in here."

"Heavens, not so fast Arthur. Whatever is the problem?"

"We've got an accidental cross-over category 4, with two minors from New Zealand."

Oh no, Victoria groaned inwardly. Not a category 4 – a category 3 she could cope with but anything higher at this time of year was bad news, with the contest about to start as well.

Calmly Victoria asked Arthur to explain, "Just give me the facts, Arthur, I just want the facts as they are please."

Arthur explained as best he could: the fact that he hadn't actually witnessed the accident, only the aftermath, what the injuries were and what he had done to mitigate the circumstances.

"You and that wretched horse," berated Victoria. "I'm sure he doesn't need that much grooming. I mean you hardly ride him these days do you?"

"I'll have you know I was out with the boys only the other day having a lovely canter around Regent's Park – it's so invigorating at 6 o'clock in the morning."

"Look, never mind all that. Let's get back to the point of this meeting, shall we?" Victoria was getting rather annoyed now. In her experience with cross-overs, time was of the essence. Malachis had to be on the case pretty quickly and ensure the humans were given every opportunity to travel back to their own world with no dire consequences.

"So – you've got them in your home and the bodies are in the Evelina Children's Hospital at St Thomas'. Well that's a good start. At least there the medics will have all the latest instruments and machines so that they can be monitored almost down to their last hair follicle. You do realise they are now your full responsibility don't you?"

"Yes," sighed Wellington. "I am fully aware of that thank you. My main concern is the transport arrangements and what we do about the contest. Any ideas?"

Victoria sat down and thought. This was a tough situation but something similar had happened last year and so she thought they could apply a similar solution but just tweaked a bit here and there. However, there had been a near disastrous moment right at the end when Cook had miskeyed the coordinates and the humans had almost gone into the wrong bodies on their earthly re-entry. Should she try something else instead? The what-ifs and all the possible problems and risks were going round and round in her head. Come on, Albert, help me here... She pleaded for her darling husband to counsel her and keep her mind on the right track. Eventually, she decided she could only follow her instincts.

"Very well – this is what we do. As you must realise, it's not going to be that simple. You and you alone have to look after the children, you must care for them and then make sure they are ready for relaunch when the time comes. You must provide them with the information they need to find their transport. You must also be in dialogue with the medical team so that you can monitor their progress. You will only have a matter of days to return the children to their human bodies. Any longer than that and there will be no return for them and their spirits will roam the Earth for ever after. So – you will have to get them moving pretty quickly. Now, transport will be via Fleet 2, considering the riverside location. This is the most appropriate; I'll sort out the rest."

"Got that. I can see to all that – no problem. What about the contest though? Shall we go ahead?"

Victoria had already considered this. "We'll carry on – at least to start with, but we're going to have to take it day by day. And we don't want to alarm any of the others so mum's the word – is that quite clear?"

"Right you are, Victoria. I knew I could rely on you."

***

Wellington and Victoria left the shelter each deep in thought. They parted on the corner of Grosvenor Place, with Victoria hoping this mess wouldn't interfere with the Malachi contest after all the preparations she'd made, whilst Wellington strode back up to Hyde Park Corner desperately thinking of a way he could explain the plans to Rory and Sarah.

He let himself into his home as quietly as he could. The hinges on his portal were really stiff and as he closed it they gave out a loud squeak. There's another job to add to the list. Wellington didn't really enjoy all this single living. When he lived in Apsley House, just over the road from his present abode, he had a houseful of staff who did all those little jobs, and of course a lot more besides. He loved that old place. He'd been so lucky to have been forced to buy it off his bankrupt brother – served him right, he thought, but at least we always invited him and his family back for Christmas. And now, although part of it was a museum, at least his descendents were able still to occupy the family apartments. Now that he was a Malachi he was expected to do all the DIY himself. He could call on others to help him but that was frowned on by the Malachi board.

Rory and Sarah were still sleeping and so Wellington got started getting everything in place. He thought about the transport they would need to get back to the hospital and the clues he would need to give to the children to access this. Victoria had allocated Fleet 2 to be at their disposal. It could be worse, he thought, one time they had to use a horse and cart and finding one of those in the capital in this day and age had been almost impossible.

He understood why they had to do things this way and why the children had to solve the clues to find their own transport in order for them to return to the human world from their Malachi domain. The children could not just walk over Westminster Bridge and into ECH. Their bodies had to go through a complex set of procedures so that they could be sure of re-entering their dimension fully intact.

He spent the rest of the evening deep in concentration. He logged onto the comms centre on HQS Wellington – this was the ship moored on Temple Pier and known as the Welly – which had the latest central communications systems and linked every comms pathway together in a massive conglomeration of equipment. He directed a pathway into Level 2 Forest at ECH where the children's bodies were being looked after. In this way he would have a complete image of the intensive care monitors and machines.

However, he wasn't sure of the wisdom in not informing the other Malachis that they had a cross-over situation. Victoria had her reasons he supposed, but he thought that he would need assistance from some of the others in any case – not the least, to check out the transport and commission it – so they may as well know straight away. It was also a big risk carrying on with the contest with all this going on at the same time. Not your problem, he told himself firmly. You just have to focus on Sarah and Rory from now on. Get the clues right and it will be plain sailing.

Chapter Eight

The new day dawned bright and sunny. All was quiet in Wellington's home with Rory and Sarah being carefully monitored by the soldiers as they spent the day recuperating and regaining their strength.

Rory was still not happy at having to rely on the old soldier and his side-kicks for help. He'd have much preferred to be able to be out and about in the streets of London finding his own way back to their proper dimension but he realised this was impossible. So, reluctantly, he thought the best course of action was to try to enjoy his enforced rest in the company of some rather wacky characters.

On Level 2 Forest in the Evelina Children's Hospital doctors were keeping a watchful eye over the children as they lay in their intensive care beds, machines beeping and flashing at reassuringly regular intervals. Having shown a slight surge in brain activity the previous evening both Rory and Sarah were firmly in a comatose state. Their brains were at a low level of activity, just enough to keep their own vital systems working. The doctors were rightly concerned and the only thing they and their parents could do was to wait and pray.

For the Malachis, however, it was the start of the contest. The nerves could be felt across the capital as the air shimmered in the light summer breeze and the birds were singing more loudly than normal. As for the pigeons – they were showing their nerves in a more visual, and messy manner.

Each Malachi was anticipating the day ahead and wondering if they would be up to the mark, which strengths they would be called on to use and whether they would be good enough to do justice to their zone. They were proud to be involved – it wasn't every Malachi that was given this honour. Honours had to be earned and maintained to the highest standards. They each had an understanding of what their chiefs expected of them and were determined not to let them down. They had done all the training, had had the briefing and now it was a matter of putting all their skills into practice. Easy.

The strategy for the first day of the contest was to protect the families assigned to each zone and so all the Malachis had to be on full alert to pick up their families as they arrived in central London, track their movements and use their strengths to protect them or deliver them from any dangers and pitfalls they might encounter throughout the day.

The tension was palpable in the Boudicca household. Camorra and Tasca were far too nervous to eat but promised their mother they would take cereal bars with them to maintain their energy levels.

"I'm just worried that the people will suspect something," Tasca said, as she brushed her long hair in the hall mirror. "I'm not sure I've got the hang of this silent skill deployment business yet."

"That's part of the point of it all," her mother explained. "Just watch your sister and me and you'll soon get the hang of it. The main problem you'll have is getting the messages across clearly. Remember the other day with the knees, poor old Jack was in a right muddle, wasn't he?"

That broke the tension and soon the girls were giggling away as they remembered how Tasca had Jack wheezing and then started grabbing leaves. Absurd really.

"Right then. Ready? Let's go and don't forget we're not doing this on our own. The others from the zone are working too."

***

Meanwhile, in the Taylor household the twins were getting really excited. They were going sightseeing in London and their parents, Jack and Alison, were hoping everything would go according to plan. Jack hadn't had a day off work for ages; he had spent so little time with his sons as he'd been busy with a Paris fashion show for the last month so he was really looking forward to today. Alison was meticulous. She'd worked everything out to the last detail and had even got Jack to buy the tickets for the London Eye on-line so that all he had to do was use the machine once they got there.

Jack and Ali had met at art college where Jack specialised in fashion design whilst Ali was more into art itself. Now she was a successful children's book illustrator and was fortunate in being able to work from home for the most part, a particularly handy situation now that they had the twins. They lived in a quiet street just off Jamaica Road in Bermondsey and close enough to the Tube to make it really convenient for Jack's daily commute.

Ali did a final check and off they went. The short trip on the Tube from Bermondsey to Westminster passed by in no time and soon they were clambering up the steps onto the Embankment. Dan, the eldest of the twins by 6 minutes and 12 seconds, a fact he delighted in telling everyone he met, looked up at the statue of Boudicca as they walked past.

"Hey!" he exclaimed to his brother, James. "Did you see that – I'm sure she winked at me?"

"Don't be ridiculous. It's a statue! They can't do things like that. Come on or we'll miss our slot," Ali ordered them to speed up as they hurried over Westminster Bridge.

Boudicca and the girls were just on their way, ready to get started, when Winston Churchill came striding down Bridge Street, swinging his stick in a wide arc and narrowly missing passers-by in the process.

"Good morning my fine ladies and how are you all feeling today?" Winston greeted the trio warmly. "I spotted our lot as they came up past you and so thought I'd give them a hand."

"That's great Winston. They are going to the Eye first and then I think they are planning to go to Covent Garden to look at all the street theatre and have lunch there."

And so the four Malachis followed Jack and his family at a safe distance behind as they all made their way to the Eye. Along the way Camorra diverted a runner from banging into Ali, whilst Tasca just about managed to keep the twins close to their parents and made sure they didn't run off in their excitement.

After a short walk along the riverside the family arrived at the London Eye.

"Wow!" exclaimed James. "I can't wait till we're up there. It looks amazing."

"Well, just be patient whilst Dad sorts out the tickets and it'll soon be our turn."

Jack went off to collect the tickets which he'd ordered on the

57

Internet a few days before.

"Oh no – I don't believe it. I haven't brought the correct credit card. Ali will kill me!" Jack could not believe that he had left the most important thing behind. He needed the card he had used to buy the tickets in order to collect them from the machine. "I'll just have to speak to a ticket seller."

He went up to a ticket desk and explained to the morose-looking woman standing behind the counter what he had done.

"Sorry love – no can do – you'll have to buy new tickets." And with that she turned away, took a sip of her cup of tea and resumed her chat with her colleague about what she had done the previous evening.

Jack was astounded. What service! I'm not having this he thought. "Er – excuse me? What does that mean?"

Winston was soon on the case, however, unbeknownst to Jack.

Now come on lady, he thought, as he channelled his mind on to the back of the ticket seller's head. We didn't win the war so that you could be a surly madam. This country is better than that. Now I want you to apologise to Jack, and organise replacement tickets straight away.

The woman wasn't quite sure what had hit her but suddenly her guilty conscious was surging over her and she made a sharp about turn and with a sympathetic smile on her face she was saying sorry to Jack and asking him how many tickets he needed.

Jack was gracious in his victory and took the replacement tickets with a warm smile.

The other ticket seller was amused. "Crikey, Lyn, what's come over you? How come you're Mrs Forgiving all of a sudden?"

Lyn was usually very efficient at her job but, just occasionally, like this morning, she could be rather tactless and short with the customers.

"I don't know. I suddenly felt really sorry for the chap. But you know what? It's made me feel better too! And you know something else? From now on I may actually change from being 'Mrs Grumpy' to 'Mrs Haveanicedayandimeanit' kind of person!" And with that she turned to the next person in the ticket queue, gave him a beaming smile and said politely, "Now, how can I help you today, sir?"

Winston thought to himself, job done and it might actually have a lasting effect.

"Good one, Winston," Boudicca remarked and with the problem solved the Malachis leant against the wall and looked up as the Taylor family enjoyed the whole experience of circling over the Thames in a glass pod looking at the sights over miles and miles of the London skyline.

"It's amazing what people have done since the war, don't you think, Winston?" Boudicca remarked, as she marvelled at the engineering involved.

The Taylors had a fairly trouble-free journey to their next port of call – Covent Garden. The Meridion Malachis were on standby just in case their help was needed. They had all received the communication from Boudicca about where the family was heading but it was Mozart whose strengths came in handy next.

He had just been to a rehearsal in the Opera House. He had such fond memories of this place but of course the building was very different then. Mozart still enjoyed having an influence in the music world and even though he couldn't compose any more he was in the habit of helping out struggling musicians. This time he had been to the aid of the young second violinist in the London Symphony Orchestra who was having trouble getting the timing of her entry right in the start of the third movement of Mozart's Symphony No 1. He himself had used phrases from well known German nursery rhymes to get the right rhythm and syncopation of this piece when he was composing it. It helped him if he could put words to a rhythm and then all he needed to do was remember which word he had to come in on. He remembered that for this piece he used a line from *Hoppe hoppe Reiter* and he'd managed to get this across to the young girl so that by the end of the rehearsal she was being used as an example to the other violinists.

I'm so glad I had those sessions with Victoria. I can now start to fulfil my purpose of coming back as a Malachi. Being able to help people is a fantastic thing, he thought, as he strode back to Covent Garden. And I can also keep up with the latest musical styles.

"Hang on a mo!" He stopped suddenly, hardly believing his eyes. All along the street were statues of Charlie Chaplin, Pierrot and other characters. "What are they all doing here?" He was confused. Charlie didn't look right somehow and the others were giving off an aura that was far too human. "That coffee I had must have gone to my head."

Suddenly Pierrot broke into a dance for thirty seconds and then stopped as abruptly as he had started. James Cook came up behind Mozart and whispered, "Gave you a fright did he?"

"Oh my God, what's going on?" Mozart asked.

"Just a bit of good old English street theatre," explained Cook. "Nothing to be afraid of, only don't confuse them with us real Malachis!"

"Hey, Mum, can we watch this?" Dan had stopped as Pierrot started his routine again. "Cor – that's brilliant!" Dan loved the theatre and even at his young age had ambitions of becoming an actor.

The Taylors joined the crowd which was amassing around the artist, with the group of Malachis hovering in the background looking on. Ali had just checked her phone. Her publisher had said he would call today and she didn't want to miss him. As she put her phone back in her bag she failed to notice that she had been spotted by a couple of youths who had been scanning the crowd. Nor did she notice that they were closing in on her in a pincer movement and were ready to pounce. However, the youths hadn't spotted Mozart in the background. Not that they should have done as when Malachis are on the go they are invisible to humans. After recovering his senses, Mozart was, as ever, in tune to the rhythms and motion of crowds and had sensed that something was out of sync with the rest of the captivated audience. He saw his opportunity immediately.

"Gotcha," he said to himself as, quick as a flash, he rushed over to Ali and gave one of the youths a mighty shove as he was about to grab her protruding phone from her bag.

"Oi – watch it mate," the youth was harangued by an elderly gentleman as he seemed to trip over his own feet and went tumbling to the ground just behind Ali.

"Are you all right, darling?" Jack asked, as he saw the disturbance going on behind his wife.

"Fine thanks. But I'm not sure what those two are up to," she said, as she looked around at the ensuing argument behind her.

"Well, never mind them. Just make sure you look after your bag. It's a pickpocket's paradise here."

"Oh – I'm all right. I know how to look after myself, thanks."

Camorra and Tasca looked at each other and smiled. "Yeah, right," they said to each other, knowingly.

"There you are Mozart, well done." Boudicca praised him. He had done a first class job and thoroughly deserved praising.

"Thanks. I'm glad I haven't lost the speed in my fingers and arms after all these years of not playing; glad I could put it to some use."

"Come on, boys. Who's hungry?" Jack knew this was a rhetorical question. Boys are always hungry – and off they went to TGI Friday's. After a five minute wait for a table the family sat down and ordered their favourite dishes. It was a bit of a squash for the Malachis so Boudicca suggested that only Columbus and Emmeline Pankhurst watch over them inside.

Apart from the Malachis arguing between themselves over who should have the most influence: Emily when she was defending Ali's choice to have a glass of wine, or Columbus insisting Jack show off his language skills as he tried to chat up the young Italian waitress, the meal passed without any major incident. The Taylors all agreed it had been a terrific day apart from the odd hiccup and were already planning their next family day out.

Chapter Nine

Up along Kingsway, Dezi and his sister Shaz, owners of a trendy sandwich bar, had had an interesting day.

They were a brother and sister combo who had been allocated to the Oriental Zone for the purpose of this contest. They were third generation Brits after their grandparents had emigrated to England from Jamaica after the war, along with thousands of others. Their grandfather had wanted to be able to give his family opportunities he had only read about and so had risked everything to start again in the East End of London. With sheer guts and determination he had done it and now two of his grandchildren were starting out in business together. A year ago, with the aid of a grant from The Prince's Trust, they had kitted out their first premises and started selling snacks and sandwiches, with a Caribbean twist, naturally, to the famished commuters in and around Holborn.

And so a year on they had a steady core of regulars and were just starting to make a profit. The menu was down to Dezi. He had the flair for combining traditional Jamaican flavours with the new trendy tastes of the twenty-first century. Whilst Shaz had an astute business head which made it a nightmare for anyone to negotiate with her. She had an instinct for what was negotiable and what wasn't and soon she had a pretty fearsome reputation amongst their wholesale suppliers.

This morning started badly for the pair. It was getting on for seven o'clock, the kitchen was primed and the tables and floor were pristine. But there was one thing missing. Their daily delivery van was usually here by now. Where was he? Dezi was desperate to get things going as he wanted to try out a new sandwich filler.

Just a few miles away, Mick, the van driver, was on his way to the café with the essentials – bread, milk, an assortment of cold meats and salad ingredients. He was taking his usual short cut down Brick Lane when ahead of him the traffic came to a complete standstill.

"Oh that's blimmin' marvellous!" he exclaimed. "'Ow I am supposed to get to Dezi's by 7 o'clock now?"

All around him cars, vans and taxis were hooting their horns and nobody could move.

John Wesley had been on his early morning patrol when he spotted the commotion and realised straightway the predicament Mick was in. Hang on in there, he thought, and I'll try to get you on your way as quickly as possible.

Now – if the car ahead could just move forward about two feet that will give Mick enough room to take the little side street on the left. It's unmarked and most people assume it just leads to the back of the shops but in fact it's a godsend at times like this. Not only does it connect to Commercial Street, it's also traffic free. Wesley focused on the driver in front – a young lady who was taking the opportunity of the enforced stop to re-do her makeup. She was concentrating so hard on getting her eyeliner just so that it took Wesley almost all his strength to break through into her subconscious. Aware that she hadn't been focused on the traffic the girl was reminded where she was by a sudden hooting from the car behind. Automatically she engaged gear and the car moved forward the requisite amount.

At that moment Mick felt as though the van was being driven on autopilot. A quick left turn followed by a sharp right with a succession of snappy manoeuvres and, lo and behold, he was clear of the hold-ups and on his way. Ten terrifying minutes of near misses, hoots from angry motorists and sudden stops and starts and Mick found himself careering up the road to his destination.

"Crikey – I'm not sure what happened there but I'll have to remember that little short cut!"

"Hey ma man! Where have you been?" Dezi greeted Mick impatiently, as the van screeched to a halt on the pavement outside the café. "And don't use your usual excuse of traffic, man."

"Dunno mate. All I remember is that one minute I was stuck down Brick Lane in a massive jam, the next thing I'm driving like Lewis Hamilton up and down these side streets and then I end up here."

"Oh well, never mind, man. Let's get the gear unloaded."

And so, with just a minor delay, the café was soon a hive of activity with Dezi experimenting with a new version of his infamous ackee dip and Shaz getting ready for the breakfast rush.

A steady stream of customers, some with their regular orders, others throwing spanners in the works as they asked for something different, with the associated friendly banter, was what made the café such a special place. Commuters began to look forward to their daily visit almost as soon as they left their front doors and they would spend a salivating journey thinking about which delight they would choose that morning.

Wesley smiled as he left the van. He hadn't enjoyed himself so much in ages and was looking forward to reliving the experience with Francis Bacon who was just sauntering up the road towards the café.

Being stuck as he was in South Square, in Gray's Inn, Francis hardly saw anyone other than, in his opinion, rich, bumptious lawyers who drove to work in their fancy cars with their personalised number plates. If I were them I wouldn't want people recognising my car wherever I went but I suppose that's part of the celebrity culture of this day and age. Francis was just a little bit jealous of the material extravagances to which lawyers and bankers had access. He had had the same wants in his day but sadly with no means of achieving them, and when he did try to cheat the system he was stupid enough to get caught. He did enjoy seeing what was happening to his other passion in this modern day – cooking or culinary preparation as he stuffily liked to refer to this activity. Frozen food was now part of every family's essential diet and whole industries were based on this simple means of preserving food. He had thought there was something in it when he tried preserving a chicken in snow but somehow he wasn't all that clued up on bacteria and the importance of cleanliness when it came to food and he fell foul of cooking the bird too quickly after taking it out of the ice. Never mind all that now, I can still indulge in this passion by giving Dezi and Shaz a helping hand, even if they don't always serve up traditional British dishes, he thought.

"Hello there Francis," John said, as he held out his hand to shake his colleague's. "Good start so far," and he described in minute detail the hair-raising journey he had taken Mick on. "It beats riding around the country on my horse in my day."

"Well, I hope things are a bit more sedate from now on," Francis replied, as the two of them positioned themselves in the corner of the café ready to step in when they could see an opportunity.

64

It was all systems go now as the commuters were pouring in. The new coffee machine was being pushed to its limit when the inevitable happened. Shaz tried everything to get the steam nozzle unblocked but to no avail. A loud hiss, a breathy belch of steam and then nothing.

"I don't believe this," Shaz muttered to herself. "A whole line of customers and no blimmin' machine."

Francis stepped in to her rescue. Now, Shaz – think logically, observe what has happened and then you might be able to deduce the remedy, and above all don't panic! He aimed this thought directly at her and all at once she stopped flicking all the knobs up and down and thought about the problem for a minute or two.

"Got it! It's when I was cleaning it up last night. I tucked the steam hose into that gap at the back to keep it all tidy. That's what must have got blocked." She reached behind the machine and gave the hose a slight tug. Out it came and along with it a sudden stream of steam. That had done the trick but in the process she had burnt the back of her hand.

"Damn it! That'll have to wait until I've got a chance to stop."

Francis looked over at Wesley who was leaning against the window. "Nice one, my good fellow," Wesley remarked. "That will get us a few points."

After that little incident it went smoothly with no need for the Malachis to come to their rescue until the morning lull at 11 o'clock.

"Right, I'm off, you OK with the specials?" Shaz peeled off her apron and grabbed her bag.

"Where are you going?"

"I told you, bro – there's that reception on tonight and I need something to wear."

"OK – but don't be long." Dezi despaired. How many dresses and outfits did she have in her wardrobe? So many that she was taking over his share of the cupboards. Typical!

He started gathering the ingredients he needed for his new special dish which he was keen to try out. They'd had it at home and both agreed it had something a little bit different by using chickpeas. He just hoped the beef was still OK from the day before.

By this time Gandhi had joined the other Malachis at the café. He was always a late starter as he had his ritual of meditation and exercise to get through before he could do anything.

"I think you've arrived just in time," Wesley said. "There's going to be a big expletive about some beef or other and then he'll calm down. Three, two, one..."

"Oh no man! This cannot be," Dezi had pulled out the tray of beef and just stared at it. It was no good, at least not up to Dezi's standards. "I can't serve that, especially not with this new recipe. Now what?" he exclaimed as he threw the tray into the bin in disgust.

Gandhi thought for a minute and came up with a possible answer. "Why don't you try a version of Pindi Chana but use lime and coconut instead of the usual Indian spices? It could work really well."

And with that thought flying into Dezi's mind out of nowhere he had a brilliant new recipe ready to go.

Shaz came back eventually after a tiring trip to Selfridges. She relayed her experiences to Dezi as he made her sample his new dish. It had been hopeless to start with. Nothing would fit, nothing was right and she was beginning to think she'd have to wear her LBN again. Eventually, after rummaging through the last of the sale items there it was – the perfect outfit. Bright red and curvy but at the same time really stylish. How has this little number remained unsold she thought? Little did she know that Edith Cavell had been one step ahead of her and had taken a few liberties. She could see that Shaz wasn't having much luck in her search and just did a little 'rearranging' as she called it. She knew she wasn't supposed to do anything 'illegal' according to the Malachi code but in her book moving a tag from one outfit to another was hardly wrong, was it?

And, anyway, the dress was simply perfect for Shaz. Edith knew that by the end of the reception she would have her diary filled with business appointments for at least the next two months. With shoes and matching bag quickly sourced, Shaz had jumped on a bus back to Holborn.

Mercifully, the lunchtime session went without a hitch and the new dish was gone in next to no time. Dezi was full of it – he wasn't used to receiving so many compliments.

"Now don't start thinking you can go on *Master Chef*. You've still got a long way to go, bro." Shaz was quick to bring him down to earth and with that they started clearing up. Shaz checked the till roll and added up the takings. Something didn't add up – they couldn't be £20 out, surely?

Wesley nudged the till to one side and there it was – an envelope with the words '£20 – laundry' which Dezi had put there earlier to pay for the laundry. Shaz could have throttled him. How many times had she told him he couldn't just take money out of the till without telling her first and in any case why was it under the till?

"Sorry, Sis. Promise I won't do it again," Dezi pleaded, with his eyelashes fluttering.

"I dunno, where would we be without me keeping an eye on the money?"

As she went through to the back, Dezi turned to the door to change the sign to 'Closed' when two lads with baseball caps on back to front came bursting through.

"Hey! Give us a can, man," they demanded.

Shaz peered through the crack in the door hinges.

No! she thought with disbelief. That one sounds and looks just like the chav who tried to steal my necklace the other day. I'm sorry, bro – but I'm going to stay out of their sight right now.

"This is going to take both of us, Wesley," Bacon decided. "You deal with the short one and I'll handle the fat one outside."

Using his Malachi skills, Wesley gave Dezi a sudden burst of energy, just enough to force the door shut in the unsavoury customers' faces. At the same time Bacon tempted a pedestrian to drop her banana skin on the pavement just in front of the fat one.

"Whoa!"

Wesley and Bacon burst out laughing as the inevitable happened and the horizontally challenged ended up sprawled on the floor in a most undignified mess.

"That'll do for us, I think, Wesley – now back to our positions."

And with that the Malachis returned to their plinths feeling that a good day's work had been accomplished in the quest for the zonal championship.

Chapter Ten

The Occidentals had an altogether different day keeping Tina on the straight and narrow. Tina and Peter lived in Hampstead overlooking the Heath. They had lost David, beloved husband and doting father, a year ago when he had succumbed to a virulent form of skin cancer which left him dead five weeks after diagnosis. It was a devastating experience and Tina had been completely numb and then angry for months afterwards. Fortunately, her support system of friends and neighbours had kicked in and helped her through somehow, and now Tina felt it was the right time to get herself back on her feet and into work. She was an interpreter/translator in several European languages and for now all she was looking for was a few hours work a week somewhere in central London. She knew it was a niche market and was prepared to wait for the right thing to come along but the first thing she had to do was register with some employment agencies.

She had been anticipating this day for the last fortnight – an interview with an agency on Marylebone High Street. She had brought her CV up to date, aired one of her many work suits from the wardrobe and practised walking in high heels around the house. She'd been at home for so long looking after Peter that she hadn't worn a 'proper' pair of shoes for ages. Finally, she'd also arranged a practice interview with a friend so that she wasn't going into the whole process completely cold.

The Malachis were ready for her and were already staked out along her proposed route into central London. First stop though was to leave Peter with a neighbour who was going to take him to the park with her little girl. Freud was on hand in case Peter needed any gentle persuasion at the prospect of being left for the morning and also, of course, in case Tina herself had second thoughts about re-entering the job market and all that that would entail – childcare, not being her own boss any more, having commitments besides Peter and herself, etc. etc. Just over the last few days Freud had used his counselling skills to bring Tina's confidence up to the mark. She'd had to be told that yes, she could still do the job, could still hold her head up in the job market and was worth every penny the job was paying. As it happened Freud had some empathy with Tina on a personal level as he himself had died from cancer, in a similar manner to Tina's husband; this really helped Freud to connect with Tina.

She knocked on her neighbour's door, Peter's hand grasped tightly in hers.

"Hi, you two, in you come," cried out Debbie, as she opened the door with a broad welcoming smile on her face.

"Hi Debbie. Here we go. I hope it's all going to be OK today."

"It'll be fine, don't worry. Just concentrate on what you need to do and leave Peter to me."

"Yes, but, don't forget he likes a snack at 10 and then he has an early lunch..." said Tina, anxiously.

"Don't worry, I said," Debbie insisted.

As Tina looked down to give Peter a reassuring hug and a kiss she realised he was nowhere to be seen. She looked through, down the hall, and there he was already ensconced in a game with Debbie's own children, without a care in the world.

Freud was hovering around on the pavement outside Debbie's house. "There – all sorted."

"Oh well, it looks like he's going to be fine." Tina was slightly put out that Peter had run off so easily and hadn't missed her or even said goodbye to her but she couldn't have it both ways. A final run through the timetable with Debbie, and Tina was off striding down the street to the Tube.

I'd better just ring Mum and Dad and make sure they're OK, she thought.

Her parents were in their seventies and although they looked after themselves reasonably well she did worry about them. She tried to call every other day to keep in touch.

"Hi Dad," she said. "How are things?"

"Who's this? What do you mean 'rings' – who is this?" her Dad answered, obviously in a rather confused state.

"It's me, Dad, Tina, your daughter. Remember?"

"Sorry, darling. It's this new hearing aid I've had fitted. It's still not quite right. If you want your mother she's on the golf course – gone off and left me on my own again."

"I only rang to see how you are. I'm on my way to a job interview so wish me luck?"

"What do you mean you're stuck? I hope you're OK and what about Peter?"

Oh dear, Tina knew she shouldn't have called before the interview. This was so infuriating. Her father was slightly deaf and quite frail but her mother on the other hand was as fit as a fiddle and took any opportunity she could to go and hit a tiny ball around a park with a long, thin stick.

"Look, we're both OK. I'll call back later, perhaps when Mum's back," Tina said slowly and distinctly, hoping her father would hear clearly this time.

"Oh – all right then, 'bye."

That was a bad idea, Tina said to herself as she made her way down the escalator of the Tube station. Right now I could do without worrying about Mum and Dad. She ran through the list of questions and answers she had prepared, in her mind, and slowly began to feel more confident.

After a smooth journey on the Underground she was almost there at the agency when Quintin Hogg, who was staked out on her route, spotted a potential hazard on the pavement. A large deposit made by a canine and Tina was heading straight for it. She was so preoccupied with the prospect of the interview that Quintin knew she would step right in it and that wouldn't do at all. Quintin had two choices. Either he could move the object in question or he could make Tina move to avoid it. He had no intention of getting anywhere near the disgusting pile himself and so he had to act quickly. As quick as a flash he had commanded a pigeon to swoop down across the pavement right in front of Tina. That brought her round to her senses and looking down she could see disaster looming. She did a quick one, two and adjusted her stride so that almost without faltering she stepped over the poo and continued on her way.

"Phew," said Quintin, "that was close!"

Tina finally arrived at the recruitment agency's office and stepped inside, feeling quite confident now. She was shown through into an office and the interview started.

"Now, Christina, what particular qualities do you think you have for the role of office administrator?"

Tina couldn't believe it! Didn't this woman have a copy of her CV? She was an experienced interpreter looking for similar language work. Tina did her best to remain composed whilst she tried politely to correct the recruitment consultant without appearing rude. It continued in this vein for the next ten minutes and Tina was getting exasperated. By this time Joshua Reynolds had joined Quintin in the office and decided they needed to act. The interviewer had obviously got Tina muddled up with another candidate. Joshua leaned over the desk and had a quick look at the pile of papers on the tray in the corner of the desk and, lo and behold, there was Tina's file.

"Right, Quintin, you distract Miss Muddle and I'll put Tina's file in front of her."

"OK." And with that Quintin Hogg pushed a book off the bookcase so that it fell to the floor with an enormous bang.

"Goodness me! What was that?" the consultant cried.

Quick as a flash and Tina's file was sitting in its rightful place open at her CV. After an embarrassing few moments, with the interviewer trying to decide if she was slightly mad or just plain stupid, the interview resumed and Tina was sailing through the process and feeling really confident. Just then the phone rang. It was a publishing company looking for a part-time French proof-reader – and the agency had just the person for the job.

Well – that couldn't have been better in the end, after a dodgy start, thought Tina as she made her way back to fetch Peter. Roll on Monday. I'll phone Mum and Dad once I've come back to earth, otherwise they won't understand what I'm on about.

Chapter Eleven

All day Liz and Mike had sat by the children's bedsides holding their hands, talking to them in hushed voices, playing their favourite music but to no avail. There was no change in their condition. They both remained in a deep coma and the machines beeped and flashed with relentless monotony.

At regular intervals nurses came in to check the monitors, take readings and record them on their charts and make slight adjustments to their drips. Nothing seemed to have any effect.

"Oh, can't you do something?" pleaded Liz, as the consultant came round to check them.

"At this stage, it's just a waiting game I'm afraid," he explained, as sympathetically as he could. "We've seen worse cases than this make a full recovery, so we need to keep calm and carry on."

Being calm was the last thing Liz was feeling. Guilty, yes, for coming out of the crash herself with only a few scratches. Completely helpless, certainly – whenever there was a family crisis she was the one to sort it out. And exhausted, totally – she hadn't slept a wink all night.

"Look, why don't you go back to the hotel and have a rest and something to eat, maybe even have a stroll. There's nothing you can do here and it will do you both good. You must look after yourselves and leave us to take care of Rory and Sarah." The intensive care nurse had seen this scenario a million times and if they weren't careful the parents wouldn't be in any fit state themselves.

Reluctantly, Liz and Mike walked back to their hotel circling the grounds to Lambeth Palace as they went. They had taken their cases there the night before, Liz's hopes of an evening of sheer luxury in the Ritz completely forgotten now. The most important thing for the pair of them was to make sure Rory and Sarah made a complete recovery. A future without her two babies did not bear thinking about. Oh, she knew they gave her the run-around and were so demanding but they were part of her and if anything happened to them her own life would end as well. She had been in control of their lives up until yesterday and now she had to get used to the fact that she had to rely on the medics and nurses to bring them back to her. Her head was pounding, she had been given some pills by the hospital to treat the shock she was in but they made her feel so sick she had discarded them. She desperately needed some sleep but whenever she closed her eyes all she could see was the ward with two inert bodies lying there like aliens, with various tubes coming out of them connected to a bank of machinery, and with the noise of the accident reverberating and getting louder and louder.

"Why can't all this just stop and let us go back to normal?" she wailed.

"We just have to let nature and medicine take their course," Mike reassured her as best he could. "You know our kids – at the end of the day they're tough little cookies – they'll pull through, I'm sure of it."

***

The wind got up slightly as the Malachi chiefs and their deputies from the three zones made their way over to the Wellington Arch for the Day 1 summing-up.

The counters had done their job and Havelock, Charles I and Napier had ridden round the capital to all the half-Malachis collecting the points that had been awarded throughout the day. For Napier it was a chance to escape from the clutches of Byron. Napier still felt slightly uneasy about Byron but he was fed up with having to listen to the poet all the time and go along with what George wanted and not doing something for himself. He was actually enjoying being a counter for the contest and hoped that he would do a good job. It was also a chance to learn some riding skills and fly around the streets of London at full pelt.

Not all the incidents had been observed by the half-Malachis and so the counters used reports by the Malachis themselves; not a totally foolproof system but it was the best they could do. The details had been entered on to Wellington's spreadsheet as instructed and he was clutching a copy of it as he strolled across the grass to the Arch.

"So how has it gone then?" Queen Anne asked Gladstone.

73

"From what I have heard, not too badly on the whole. Of course, it's early days yet and the team needs to get into full swing but I know they saved Dezi and Shaz from some very awkward moments."

Queen Anne was glad the café and its bright, young owners had been allocated to the Oriental Zone. Being much more into the healthy lifestyle she admired the way food could be both enjoyable to look at, tasty to eat and not at all fattening. Dezi was a real whiz at conjuring up imaginative recipes that weren't full of calories or had a high fat content. Gladstone was a bit more ambivalent about the brother and sister combination, but actually secretly admired their entrepreneurial spirit and wished more young people would stand on their own two feet instead of relying on their parents or the State. Honestly – he despaired sometimes at the modern way of living.

They settled themselves down on the comfy sofa in the Wellington Arch whilst they waited for the others to arrive.

Soon Ike and Nelson came running up the stairs, panting and puffing as they rushed in through the double doors.

"There – told you I could beat you up the stairs," Nelson boasted to Ike. "All that training around Grosvenor Square is no match for running up and down the stairs in my column!"

"OK – you win," Ike conceded. "But that means you buy the beers later."

Nelson thought this was a fair deal. Not wanting to be outdone by Ike, Nelson had actually started trying to improve his own fitness by running up and down his stairs instead of using the lift. Now they were just waiting for Victoria, Boudicca and Wellington.

Victoria and Wellington had met up on the approach to the Arch. "How are our casualties?" Victoria enquired anxiously of Wellington.

Wellington had just left the pair still sleeping in the care of his loyal soldiers. They had had a small bowl of soup for nourishment during the day but were still in a really groggy state.

"As best as can be expected at this stage. No change which actually is a good thing. At least they haven't deteriorated and nor have they made too rapid a recovery which can be just as damaging. Their bodies are taking their time to heal internally first before using precious energy resources to reactivate the frontal brain areas."

"Good. So do you think they'll be fit enough to take on their first challenge and solve the first clue?"

"Oh yes – they should be by tomorrow. I'm going to explain the situation to them this evening and if I think they're OK I'll give them the first clue then."

Byron was skulking about in the background, on the pretext of walking Boatswain, and couldn't help overhearing snippets of this conversation.

Hmm, what's going on, he wondered. Casualties…, recovery…, challenge? What is that Wellington up to? And it slowly dawned on him that Wellington was involved somehow with the strange sequence of events which had taken place yesterday afternoon – the car crash, the strange lights and now this. All most peculiar. I'm going to have to keep tabs on Arthur – this could be my chance and his undoing.

At that point Boudicca and her two daughters arrived.

"Oh, hi Byron – what are you doing here? Not your usual hunting ground is it?" Camorra was teasing Byron; she knew he liked to keep clear of Wellington's patch.

"I'll show you my usual stalking ground if you like," Byron replied huffily and at that he stormed off as the girls burst into a giggling fit.

"Leave him alone you two. Now off you go and have a wander around Harrods, suss out the latest fashions if you like whilst I join the Day 1 summation."

Boudicca, Victoria and Wellington took the lift to the conference room in the Arch and the meeting began.

"Right – let's get this started. I've something important to mention at the end so I don't want to waste too much time. Wellington, can you give us a summary of the count as far as you're concerned?"

"Well – each zone did very well, on the whole meeting their objectives. I would put them in the following order: in first place are the Meridions – the Taylor family had a really good day up in London which could have ended in disaster from the word go and

I was particularly impressed with the way in which the Malachi action reformed the ticket seller in a really positive way. So - well done.

"As for the Oriental Zone – again some good deeds there, saving Dezi and Shaz from quite a few setbacks. My only concern here is the possible damage to one of the lads who tried to muscle their way into the café at the close of day. We aren't here to cause harm, remember, but I must say I did have a bit of a giggle when I heard about the banana, so I'll let you off that one."

Gladstone coughed under his breath and whispered to Anne, "I should think so too; those lads deserve everything they get."

"I agree, but rules is rules, as they say," Anne replied, placatingly.

Wellington continued, "Now, the Occidentals didn't have much to go on which was rather unfortunate but what they did went well, especially the 'canine deposit' incident! Nelson – you'll have to pull out a few stops tomorrow to make up as I have you in third position with the Meridions as contest leaders so far."

"Thanks Arthur. Any questions? Personally I think that's a very fair view overall," Victoria concluded.

The zone chiefs couldn't really argue with that and, in any case, they were anxious to hear what Victoria wanted to tell them that was so important, so they all kept their counsel and waited patiently for Victoria to resume.

Victoria explained all that had happened yesterday afternoon with the Wheelers and outlined the state of the two poor children. The Malachis were shocked and felt every sympathy for Wellington who now had the onerous task of leading the children back to their world. They offered any help that they could give but it would be tricky if they couldn't have direct influence on the humans. They were also rather surprised that Victoria wanted the contest to continue – they felt it should be put on hold but understood Victoria's wish that everyone should carry on as normal. If there was too much interruption along the seismic inter-orbital arenas this could prove to be more upsetting to the children's recovery process. It all had to be calm and peaceful or things could really get out of kilter and that could jeopardise the children's normal return to their world.

"Now, as you know, it's a delicate procedure to return human spirits to their correct dimension. So, Wellington is going to direct them, in a roundabout fashion, to Fleet 2 and we will need the usual suspects to bring the transporters out of dock and into fully commissioned modes of transport. I'm expecting Brunel and his team to see to that. James Cook will need to check the GPS systems, and Queen Alexandra can sort out supplies."

They all murmured their agreement and the meeting dispersed.

Whilst all this was going on Byron had dashed over to Trafalgar Square. He wanted to share his thoughts with Napier and make sure Charles was still on his side. He knew Wellington was involved with something fishy. He just needed to know that he wasn't going to be in this thing on his own. He would hang around Wellington's statue tomorrow morning to see if could glean anything useful.

"Charles – are you in there?" Byron banged on the side of the plinth and after a few minutes the portal opened and Charles let his friend inside.

"Cor – you've done rather nicely for yourself in here, haven't you?" Byron looked around Napier's abode and couldn't help but admire the opulence of it all. "I suppose you brought a lot of this stuff back from India did you? People nowadays are giving it all back. You must have heard about the Elgin Marbles? I wrote about them in a poem, you know! I called it Childe Harold's Pilgrimage. Look it up if you want to. If you ask me – I really think you should return this stuff. It's just not right."

"Oh yes – well I'll have you know I fought long and hard for these things. They were gained fair and square and I've no intention of giving them up just like that. Besides, how would I do that?" In spite of this outburst Napier was somewhat relieved that Byron hadn't come to have a go at him for accepting the counter position.

"Oh – I'd find a way, rest assured. But of course, if you want me to keep quiet about these magnificent artefacts all you have to do is do something for me. You scratch my back, I'll scratch yours! Get it?"

Charles realised he had no choice but to go along with Byron and whatever it was he wanted him to do. He was trapped and they both knew it. Basically, if Charles didn't join forces with Byron then Byron would have no difficulty in letting it be known just what treasures he had misappropriated from the far-flung parts of the Empire and he would surely lose everything.

"Damn you Byron!"

***

Once the Malachis had dispersed, Wellington returned to his home.

"How are our young charges?" he asked as soon as he got through his portal.

Sergeant Bob Walker gave Wellington a debriefing of Rory's and Sarah's condition. They had gained some strength and were actually sitting up and chatting to the other soldiers, hearing all their wartime stories, and about their tours around the Empire. In return Rory and Sarah explained what their life was like in New Zealand, how Rory was an ace centre for his U15's rugby team and how Sarah loved diving.

"Nothing too taxing then."

"No, sir, and their appetite has been increasing steadily all day." These soldiers knew all about nursing the wounded, they'd had plenty of experience when they'd had real battles to fight.

"Look – get them up and ask them to come into my study. I need to have a serious word with them and I need you lot to be on standby in case they have a turn at what I am about to tell them."

Bob turned and rounded up the children who were now playing a game of Cluedo with Paddy and Owen, whilst Jock was preparing a light supper for them all.

"Now then you two, how are you feeling?" Wellington enquired, once they had settled themselves in Wellington's study.

"Yeah – not too bad I suppose, considering all we've been through. Your men have looked after us really well today," replied Rory.

"Especially Paddy," swooned Sarah.

"Oh, don't go falling for his Irish charms. He does this to all the pretty girls. Right – now I have something really important to say but I want to stress that you mustn't worry about a thing. We're here to look after you and to make sure that you get back to your own dimension. You do understand that don't you?"

"Oh yes, of course," they both replied.

"Well – here goes then. Now, as I mentioned when you first arrived here, your earthly bodies are recovering from the accident. You do remember that don't you?"

"Vaguely," Rory admitted. "I do remember being in a taxi and then there was an almighty bang and then I remember the tunnels of lights and then we saw you."

"Good," Wellington said, reassuringly. "Now, what actually happened is this: you both had really bad bangs to the head and your bodies are in a coma in hospital."

"Oh my God." Sarah couldn't quite get her head around this. "Do you mean we aren't really here then?"

"There was a slight hiccup in the transportation channels and your spirits didn't travel along the same coordinates as your bodies meaning that you are in this limbo world with me. But your bodies are being taken good care of in hospital. Actually – you're in the Evelina Children's Hospital at St Thomas' just over the river."

"Wh... wh... what about Mum and Dad?" Rory asked hesitantly, not wanting to hear the worst.

"Oh – they're fine. Just a little shaken up. You two bore the brunt of the accident. Basically, you both bumped the backs of your head on the glass partition and the impact was so severe you ended up in a coma. But don't worry, the doctors are looking after you and so am I."

"Oh, so that explains why I've been feeling sick and have a massive headache, also I've got this huge lump on the side of my head."

"Yes – and in your case Rory, a bag hit you on your temple during the accident. It was thrown forward from the back shelf. Anyway – that explains what happened; now I want to explain how we are going to get you back. But first of all let me tell you a little about myself. But even before that let me ask you a question. Do you believe in angels?"

"Well, I'm not sure really?" replied Sarah.

"Nor me," said Rory.

"OK – it doesn't matter whether you do believe in them or not. I'm telling you they do exist because they are us, or rather we are them, if you get my meaning. I am a Malachi and that is, in your world, an angel. We are heavenly spirits of the past who have returned to occupy our statues and our mission is to do good. We each have a number of different strengths which we can use to make good things happen. You can only see me and my boys because I am the one who has to deliver you back to your world, but we are not alone – we have many friends and acquaintances who are going to help me do just that."

Rory and Sarah were totally stunned by all this but there was nothing for it but to go along with what Wellington was telling them and to trust him implicitly.

"OK – so how are you going to help us then?" they asked.

"Right. First you have to find your transport, which we will then equip and fit out so that it can take you back. There is only one snag."

Rory groaned. He knew there had to be a catch.

"I can't actually tell you where to find your transport. You have to solve clues to locate the vessels, which are all in central London."

"What do you mean 'vessels', and 'all'? How many do we have to find?" Sarah asked, rather disbelievingly.

"You will need one each and it is only by solving the clues that I will give you that you will find out what the vessels are."

"Oh – I get it – it's a bit like a cryptic crossword puzzle where the answer is in the clue."

"You've got it," Wellington said. "So – the first clue is this: Shows the wind where you can buy your freedom."

"Crikey – that sounds like complete gibberish to me! How on Earth are we supposed to get this?" Rory despaired.

"Just take it one step at a time and it will become clear, believe me. Now, I think you should settle down for the night. Just let your minds wander over the words of this clue and start to think of different words for each part of the sentence."

Rory and Sarah went off to bed puzzling the clue and fell asleep dreaming of an assortment of cars, boats, trains and planes. Wellington, however, was very jittery about everything. His mind was a whirlwind of worries spinning round and round. What if the children couldn't decipher the code? What if it took them too long? What if they didn't make it back? What was going to happen to the Malachi contest? His soldiers were ensconced in a game of cards so, to try to calm his nerves, Wellington poured out a glass of his favourite claret and settled down to try to read a biography of Margaret Thatcher, the first woman Prime Minister of Britain. He was amused that her nickname was 'The Iron Lady' and felt a kind of kinship with her as he had been known as 'The Iron Duke'. He was soon immersed in the text and engrossed in her battles with the unions and the Iraqis and all his anxieties about tomorrow firmly placed in the back of his mind.

***

In the hospital Mike and Liz had returned to the PICU ward and were becoming attuned to the beeps and whirrs of the pumps and monitors which surrounded the children. Suddenly Rory's heart rate monitor began to go up and the alarm sounded.

"Quick, nurse, something's happening to Rory!"

Sister Bridge hurried over and took a look at the monitor. Rory's heart rate had indeed just jumped up but thankfully was now returning to normal.

"He's OK – he may have just had a slight surge in brain activity. It's quite normal and it means his brain is responding to the treatment. We are administering some drugs to try to help reduce the swelling in his brain, rather than just leave it to nature. So we would expect something like this to happen."

Unbeknownst to the doctors and nurses in PICU this surge in Rory's heart rate coincided exactly with his conversation with Wellington and once Rory had fallen asleep, so his own body returned to a stable state.

"It's normal for someone in a coma to fluctuate like this. Remember the consultant said it can take 3 to 4 days for the brain swelling to return to normal and until then we really can't say what the prognosis will be. It's in the hands of the gods, so to speak," Sister Bridge said reassuringly, reflecting all her years of expertise in looking after very sick children.

But little did she realise that their recovery was also in the hands of some very strange angels.

Chapter Twelve

The next morning Rory and Sarah woke feeling much more rested. Rory's headache had subsided and he wasn't feeling sick any more. Jock had made porridge for them which they guzzled down and so, with that and a cup of tea inside them, they were ready for the challenge ahead. The two of them were excited at the thought of the quest. Sarah, in particular, was glad to be doing something positive to get them back to their real world. Where they were was fascinating but she missed her parents.

They went outside with Wellington who pointed them in the right direction. But they didn't see Byron who was skulking behind the trees nearby. He'd left Boatswain behind, as he didn't want any barking to give away his position, and tried desperately to overhear the conversation going on between them.

"You've remembered the clue, I presume?" Wellington double checked they hadn't forgotten this vital piece of information.

Sarah recited, "Shows the wind where you can buy your freedom."

"Exactly, and now all I'll say is that you need to head in a north-easterly direction from here for just over 1 mile, which is just under 2 kilometres to you. You've got the map and so all you have to do is think logically and you'll be fine. My chaps will give you a start."

Sarah got the map open in front of her. Bob had a ruler at the ready and they quickly drew an arc of radius two kilometres from Hyde Park Corner, in an approximate north-easterly direction. This resulted in the area around Oxford Street and Tottenham Court Road being marked out as the most likely spot.

"Looks as though you might get your shopping spree in after all," Rory said, as he peered over Sarah's shoulder at the map. "I would say the simplest route is to go along Piccadilly as far as Piccadilly Circus and then we just head up Regent Street. Are you feeling OK? We'll take it nice and gently, there's no hurry and this way we can do some of the sightseeing we had planned to do." Rory was feeling quite positive about the challenge ahead – he always liked crosswords.

Sarah nodded her head. "But we've still got to decipher the words. Let's just think for a moment."

"I'll be exercising my horse but if you have any problems whatsoever, just call me on this angelicaphone and I'll be right by your side. Let's just test it first."Wellington handed Rory what looked like a mobile phone but without the keypad. "Now – all you have to do is press the call button and that will connect straight to my sensory cortex. Your exact coordinates will be transmitted and I will be able to reach you in a flash."

Wellington then left them to it as he went to saddle up Copenhagen for his morning ride.

Once the gizmo had been tested and the children knew which way they were going, off they went, map in hand and muttering to themselves as they tried to decipher the cryptic clue which would give them their first means of transport.

Byron had caught some of the conversation between the small group and was intrigued. I'll stick close by them and see what they get up to. I'll need to take any chance I can get.

Rory was getting excited about their mission. Here they were in the middle of London on their own walking along one of the busiest streets in the capital.

"You know what, Sarah? Mum and Dad would never have let us loose in London on our own with only a map and a rather odd phone. Can you imagine their faces if they could see us now?"

Sarah had been trying hard not to think of her parents for the last twenty-four hours or so. She could only imagine the anguish they must be in as they kept a vigil for them in the hospital. Oh, how she wished she could get a message to them to let them know they were safe, in an odd sort of way. She knew it was impossible though and the only thing for it was to think really hard about the clue and make sure that she and Rory got back across the divide and into the real world as soon as they could.

"Let's not if you don't mind. Now, I really think we should be trying to solve the clue, don't you? But I really don't understand why we can't just go straight to the hospital ourselves. I mean, why do we have to solve these ridiculous clues?" said Sarah petulantly.

"Don't ask me. Look, we're in a really strange world here with Wellington and as far as I'm concerned I'm happy to go along with whatever he says," Rory replied.

"OK, OK – sorry I spoke! Hey – look! I've heard about this place!" Sarah exclaimed as they walked past the Hard Rock Café. "Isn't that where all the stars go and eat? I wonder if there are any there now."

Rory dragged Sarah away as they strode along Piccadilly leaving Green Park on their right. They both marvelled at the grand buildings lining the street. Never had they seen so many grandiose mansions with so many floors. As they looked up at the rooftops their heads went further and further back. And there was such a mix of new and old which seemed to blend so well together. It was very different from their home country where the oldest buildings were no more than 200 years old. Soon they arrived at the Ritz – the place where they were supposed to have started their stay in London.

"Oh, Rory – look! This is where we should have been. Let's have a quick peek inside shall we? We'll be really quick and no-one will see us."

They both crept inside and were amazed at the sheer flamboyance and luxury of it all.

"Oh my word," gasped Sarah. "It's ten times better in real life than I imagined it would be. Look! Isn't that Russell Crowe checking in? I wonder what he's doing in London."

Sure enough it was the famous actor, with his head held down as he signed the hotel registration documentation.

"At least you can't embarrass me by asking him for his autograph!" joked Rory. "I'll never forget the time you accosted Jonah Lomu back home. So embarrassing."

"All right. Now, have you thought about the clue? Do you know where we should start once we get to Oxford Circus?" Sarah demanded, changing the subject as quickly as she could.

"Let's have a think. I reckon the words 'where you can buy' could mean a shop? Oxford Street is full of them after all – it's the main attraction of this part of London."

"Yes, that's what I was thinking. Let's get ourselves there and then we can start to think about the rest of the clue," said Sarah, being as practical as ever.

Byron was still following them, keeping a safe distance behind. He knew they couldn't see him, as they could only see Wellington and his boys, but he still didn't want to take any chances. They might be able to sense him and they would activate the angelicaphone straightaway and then he would be spotted by Wellington. He could bide his time, after all he'd been waiting for years already.

The children continued along Piccadilly but soon Sarah made Rory stop again. She was standing outside the most famous food store in London, a place where her father had promised he would take her when they had been sent one of their famous hampers one Christmas. The clock on the wall outside was chiming 10 o'clock and Sarah just stared in wonder at the beautiful sight that she beheld. The turquoise colour of the shop front was far more vivid in reality and the ladies going in and out were definitely of the category 'the beautiful people', the window displays were stunning and Sarah just knew she had to go inside and marvel at the fantastic displays of food, chocolates and other mouth watering goodies. She was definitely coming back here.

Rory had given up – he hated shopping at the best of times but this was even worse as he knew they couldn't buy anything or try anything on and so it was all for nothing in his opinion.

"Just let me know when you want to move on," he said wearily, as he leant on the railings outside and looked up and down the street.

Eventually Sarah came out in a bit of a state. "Oh, you should have seen these gorgeous bags, and the perfume, I've never smelt anything like it. Oh, and the honey – did you know they have their own hives on the roof? So cool!"

"OK, OK, calm down – look, we aren't here for the window-shopping. We have a mission to do. A clue to solve and, if you don't mind, I would quite like to get on with it. I want to get back to reality, even if you don't"

And with that Rory marched on, oblivious to the hustle and bustle of the tourists and shoppers as they milled around Piccadilly Circus, the buses and taxis careering around corners and stopping every few yards, the music blaring out of the record shops and the newspaper sellers shouting at the tops of their voices to be heard above everything else. He rounded the corner and strode up Regent Street, following the map, which he had by now commandeered. Sarah ran after her brother, trying desperately not to lose sight of him in the crowds. Byron was finding it even harder to keep up with them both, being of a slightly more delicate nature and decidedly less fit than the two youngsters.

Eventually Rory stopped, right opposite Hamleys.

"Oh, so you want to go in there now do you?" Sarah said, pointedly.

"Come on, just for a few minutes. We'll stick to the ground floor."

They all crossed over the road and stepped inside the world-famous toy store where they were immediately accosted by a whole menagerie of characters demonstrating all sorts of new toys.

Byron decided it was time to have a bit of fun. Just a little, it won't harm anyone. And with that he took control of the remote-controlled aeroplane that a clown with a silly grin on his face was flying. Soon it was performing loop the loops and flying in and out of people's legs, almost brushing their noses and coming seriously close to getting tangled up in an Afro haircut. Unfortunately, Byron didn't know when to stop and very soon the whole fleet of aeroplanes was performing an aeronautical display to rival the Red Arrows.

"Oh my goodness! Get the manager, they've all gone mad here!" screamed the young girl on the till.

"Quick! Let's get out of here. I'm not sure what was going on there but I think we'd better make a quick exit." And Rory and Sarah dashed out of the shop and continued on their way.

Meanwhile Byron was chuckling to himself. I bet their sales go up now, he thought, as he too left and hurried to catch up with the children.

Rory and Sarah were now at Oxford Street and having a good look around them, noticing all the stores and shop fronts. They sat down and started to think about the clue.

"Shows the wind where you can buy your freedom," Sarah

muttered the clue over and over to herself.

"Hmm? Now what does 'shows the wind' mean? It could mean one of those things they have at airports, you know, we saw them as we flew into Heathrow – those sock things on poles that show the wind direction. A windsock – that's the right word. I suppose it could mean 'sock'. Maybe we should be looking for a sock shop?" Rory proposed.

"Yeah – maybe. Let's have a look around here then for a shop that might sell things like that."

"Of course, it may mean wind as in to wind up a spring, so perhaps we should be looking for clocks or watches or something?" Rory proposed another theory.

"No, I don't think so. The phrase doesn't make sense if it is the verb as opposed to the noun," Sarah replied, as she showed off her literacy knowledge. "Why don't we both go and have a look around the area and meet back here in 10 minutes."

And with that the two of them went off to scour the shops for something that would fit the clue. Every shoe shop which Sarah went past had to be inspected to see if it also sold socks, and she couldn't help but also look longingly at the beautiful shoes and sandals on display.

Byron had also been musing over the clue and thought he had cracked it. He'd started with the last phrase and, of course, with his literary knowledge soon had the name of the shop sussed out. He was still puzzling over the first part though. He couldn't quite get what was meant by 'shows the wind'.

Soon the two children were back at their starting point looking very despondent. Nothing had even come close to being the answer to the clue. What had started out as an exciting mission was slowly becoming really frustrating. They were beginning to get tired after all the walking around and they were both thinking of the comfort of Wellington's statue and the company of his soldiers. They could do with a big bowl of something tasty cooked up by Bob.

"Let's have one more look around these streets – I'm pretty sure it must be near here, we'll give it 5 more minutes," said Rory decisively, trying to keep Sarah's hopes up.

So off Rory went, west along Oxford Street this time, whilst

Sarah wanted to explore some of the little streets at the back of Oxford Street. Sarah was walking down Argyll Street when it hit her. There she was staring at the one word which meant freedom. Of course – Liberty – that's the answer to 'freedom'! And it's a shop so that fits the middle part of the clue. I must find Rory and tell him.

She dashed back to their meeting spot but of course Rory was nowhere to be seen. In fact he was striding along the busy shopping street while Byron was interfering with his thought processes and trying to convince him that he should try looking for a shop called Sock Shop. Soon he came upon it and bingo! He had a eureka moment and thought he had solved two-thirds of the clue. "Just the part about freedom to sort out and we're done, he said to himself, excitedly. "I must get back to Sarah and tell her I've solved it."

Byron was looking smug. This will be interesting, he thought to himself. They'll never solve this clue if they're looking for a vessel around this part of London.

"Oh Rory – there you are!" yelled Sarah.

"I've got it, Sarah!" Rory exclaimed. "Come on, follow me!"

"What do you mean? No – I've solved it – this way!"

And they were each intent on dragging the other to the shop they were adamant was the answer. Rory explained his thinking to Sarah but couldn't account for 'your freedom' whilst Sarah thought it was obviously the famous store Liberty and she would solve the first part by looking round the store itself.

The two of them stood their ground trying to convince the other of the validity of their answer whilst Byron looked on amused. In the end it was Rory who gave in. He did agree that Liberty was a good explanation for 'your freedom' and so he conceded by giving Sarah ten minutes to scout around the store to solve the first part of the clue.

"You're going to have to be quick otherwise we'll go with my idea," Rory laid down the challenge to his sister and reluctantly went along with her to be another pair of eyes to search for the meaning 'shows the wind'. "You go inside and check out the floors, especially the hosiery department, and I'll just hang around outside, see if anything obvious springs to mind."

Rory let Sarah dash down the road and watched her disappear inside the revolving doors of the main entrance. He glanced up at the building he was passing. It was a theatre but in the style of a Greek Corinthian palace. He loved the great display at the front of the building over the main entrance and as he glanced up even more he noticed the beautiful statues on the roof. I wonder if they're like Wellington, he thought. It is a strange world isn't it? He stood rooted to the spot as he slowly moved his head around to his right, scanning the skyline. And there it was. The most beautiful thing he had ever seen and all in perfect proportion.

He couldn't believe his eyes. That had to be it but how were they expected to travel back in that thing? But it all fitted the clue. No doubt about that. What will Sarah think? But, hang on. Wellington had said they were to trust him so he supposed they should, about everything.

Rory grabbed Sarah as she came out of the store looking really despondent. She hadn't found anything remotely close which would fit the clue.

"Look – that's it! Can you see it?" Rory shouted excitedly, as he made her look up above the main entrance to the roof of the building.

"You're kidding me!" she exclaimed. "How can that be the answer?"

"It's a weathervane and weathervanes show the direction of the wind, don't they. And it's a vessel so it must be our transport. Goodness knows how. That's down to our friend Wellington. Remember Peter Pan and Captain Hook, maybe it's something like that?"

Rory and Sarah were staring at the most beautiful weathervane they had ever seen (not that they had seen that many, of course). It was gilded and shimmering in the sunlight and looked the exact replica of an old Tudor vessel, and it was right on top of the Liberty shop building.

And then the next thing Rory knew was Sarah fainting and collapsing on the pavement.

"Quick – I must get Wellington over here." He tried to activate the angelicaphone but he was all fingers and thumbs and he couldn't find the call button (little did he realise that Byron had witnessed their find and had made Rory a bit befuddled in the head).

"Oh, what's the matter with me?"

He kept stabbing at the phone and eventually he made contact, and he sat down on the pavement trying to cradle Sarah in his arms as he waited for his knight in shining armour to appear.

***

Wellington came as soon as he was summoned, riding Copenhagen. He wasn't at all surprised by the sight which met him. Rory and Sarah were both slumped on the pavement looking completely worn out. They had had a long, arduous morning, albeit a successful one and they were now paying the price.

"It's OK, Rory, Sarah will be OK," he said, as he started to revive her. "You've done jolly well to solve the clue. I'm very proud of you even though you did have a few false starts."

"Yes, but I just don't understand how we can use the boat weathervane to get back to our real world." Rory was completely bewildered by the logistics of it all still.

"Look, I said you must trust me and so you must believe me when I say that it will all work out. I must get you both back to my place and you must have plenty of rest. It's been quite an exhausting day for you. You've walked a fair distance and you've been exercising your grey matter which, after your accident, is still in a very tender state. I'll get the boys to make you something to eat and then you must both rest."

By now Sarah was coming round but feeling very groggy; she was relieved to see Wellington there. Things would be OK with him in charge, she thought.

Wellington helped both of the children up onto Copenhagen whilst he remained on foot leading his horse by the reins. It was when he turned round to go back towards Regent Street that he spotted Byron.

"Oh, hello, George. Doing a spot of window-shopping are you?"

"What's going on with those two then?" Byron said accusingly to Wellington.

"Never you mind. Let's just say they need a helping hand."

Byron was even more convinced something strange was going on. Why wouldn't Wellington tell him? Did he think he couldn't be trusted? We'll soon see about that, he thought defiantly, and off he went in the opposite direction as Wellington took a long, slow route back to Hyde Park, avoiding all the main roads and keeping to the back streets of Mayfair.

Chapter Thirteen

Earlier that morning the Malachis were gearing up for the second day of the contest. This time it was more of a free-for-all, where they didn't have to target specific families. Instead, they could help anyone who looked as though they needed it. They were all feeling slightly more confident after the first day, even though not all the team members had been used; they were all getting into the swing of it. The Malachis who had demonstrated their skills yesterday had recounted their deeds with bravado, and a certain amount of hilarity in some cases, to their colleagues and everyone seemed raring to go. The teams for the zones were predetermined for this second day and each had a day-leader who was to direct the others.

First to go was the Oriental Zone. Edith Cavell and Isambard Brunel, the zone's senior Malachis, had had a tactical session the evening before and had agreed that they would use Isaac Newton and Robbie Burns today. They were lying in second place after the first day and really wanted to improve their scores. Neither of these Malachis had known each other in their real lives and it was only since they had returned in their present status that friendships had blossomed. Brunel was always so grateful to Newton for his work on forces, and calculus in particular, which had developed his own interest in engineering. In fact, now the two of them had fascinating conversations about the developments they had both witnessed and Newton in particular felt particularly pleased that he could see the results of his ideas in the flesh. He had had no idea that so much would have come from what to him seemed statements of the obvious. He was amazed and at the same time relieved that his ideas on calculus had proved to be so accurate and were an invaluable tool with which most of modern living had been built. It did amuse him though when he heard the Great and the Good discuss the relative merits of his versions of calculus compared with his arch rival Leibniz's. Newton's opinion was that at the end of the day they were both right and both lucky to have so much theory based on a simple approximation. Still, that's life he supposed; compared to God, man is an approximation.

With his statue positioned outside the British Library, Newton spent a lot of time sitting and thinking. If he was really alive today the world would be an incredible place, he thought. He would really have got all this nanotechnology sussed by now and the challenges regarding renewable energy would be fascinating to solve, especially with electromagnets. Of course, Einstein had caused a bit of an upset when he first got involved with particles and waves, but Newton could see the merit in Einstein's thinking. However, at the end of the day Newton was secretly pleased that whenever there was a popular vote he was always considered to have had the most impact on humankind compared with the German genius.

Today, though, Newton was glad he was able to get out and about around the capital. He liked his home but felt rather annoyed at the position he had been cast in, a pose he regarded as rather undignified but he understood the reasons behind it. The sculpture had been inspired by the artist William Blake who thought Newton could only think along singular, sterile lines. Well – so much for that. When what Newton had determined were, in fact, the fundamental laws of motion and force upon which everything else could be determined. Anyway, he would have to put up with it now. At least as a Malachi he didn't have to stay in that position as inside his statue he had his cosy home which was full of the latest gadgets. He couldn't help collecting useless knick-knacks for the kitchen, just so that he could see how they were made and which of his laws were being exploited.

Newton's thoughts came back to the matter in hand: the contest. He quite liked the young Scotsman, Robbie Burns, he'd been paired up with. He'd actually read some of his poetry and found that it was quite readable, up to a point. He did struggle with the language though, but he could generally get the gist of things. And he recognised that the poet did have a sense of humour which, for a Scot, he thought was quite an achievement. They had been allocated the Strand and they had an hour in which to perform various Malachi actions. They could then use the three highest scoring ones recorded by the half-Malachis who were stationed around the area.

Robbie's statue was positioned in the serene Victoria

Embankment Gardens just south of the Strand. This morning Newton strolled over to Euston Station and took the Northern Line Tube to Charing Cross. He loved travelling on the Tube (apart from the nasal challenges involved); he had so much admiration for the engineers and designers of this intricate transport system. In fact, if he was alive today he would love to be a train driver hurtling along the dark tunnels, one minute going deeper and deeper into the Earth's depths and then the next emerging all of a sudden into bright daylight. But for now he was satisfied with travelling on it whenever he could.

Robbie was still at home when Newton arrived in the gardens. Daydreaming as usual, Newton thought, as he banged on the log which formed the portal to Burns' statue. Robbie appeared looking dishevelled and hardly ready to face the day's contest.

"Whatever is the matter with you?" Newton asked.

"Oh, it's Byron, as usual. He's been causing trouble again trying to get the half-Malachis to say that they prefer his poetry to mine. I mean – I really don't care about that any more. It's not as if we are both still writing and, in any case, it's up to the general public."

"You really must ignore him. He's been acting very strangely recently and no-one knows why. Apart from the fact that he didn't make the grade this time for the contest. Come on – let's focus on today's objectives."

And with Newton being as practical as ever he and Burns set off for the Strand. They were chatting about which strengths they might be called upon to use when Robbie stretched out his arm to stop Newton from taking another step.

"Watch out!" Robbie shouted. "Just look at that lunatic on the bicycle. Honestly, they think they are kings of the road these days."

A cyclist, all kitted out in helmet, goggles and extra padding, came careering round the corner and almost knocked them over. Although Robbie's quick reactions had saved the two Malachis they could see that the group of students huddled around the window of Topshop weren't going to be so lucky if they didn't act immediately to prevent a major accident.

"Quick! You try to distract the students whilst I try to apply some additional forces to the lunatic's brakes," Newton instructed.

And with that Newton forced his power of thoughts to make a

discarded fast food wrapper, one of the many which litter the streets of the capital, fly up and get wedged between the cyclist's rear tyre and the mudguard causing a sharp and very sudden decrease in the flying tornado's speed. At the same time Robbie ran over to the store's window display and started moving the mannequins' limbs about as if they were dancing to music.

"Oh my goodness! Just look! How cool is that?" One of the students exclaimed, as she dragged her friends over to the other window where this extraordinary display was taking place.

Hardly five seconds after the group had moved to the safety of the second window the cyclist had lost all momentum and balance and came to an abrupt stop falling off onto the pavement at the same time. Other passers-by looked on with some amazement as they realised that a major accident had been avoided but they couldn't quite work out how.

"Did you see that?"

"Well – I'm not really sure what I saw but I know that the cyclist got what he deserved."

"Those kids moved away in the nick of time."

"They don't know how lucky they are."

And so on and so on.

The cyclist was getting up feeling rather dazed, but unhurt thanks to all his extra body padding, and extracted the cause of his fall from the rear wheel. The girls had by this time gone into the store to find out how the window display worked.

"I dunno wot you're talkin' about," the sales girl said. "Those dummies don't move. That's why they're called dummies. Know wot I mean?" And she walked off thinking to herself that girls these days really don't seem to know which planet they're on.

"Now that's what I call an equal and opposite reaction to an action," chuckled Newton, as they gave each other a high-five and walked on along the street.

They soon bumped into Gladstone who was wandering up the Strand to the Law Courts.

"There are a couple of interesting cases being heard today so I thought I'd have a look. How is it going for you two? I hope you are keeping to our game-plan?"

"Fine, so far, I think. One major accident averted with not much aftermath so I think we should score a few points there," Newton said.

"There's a load of paparazzi here already so a case must just have finished. Let's hang around and see who it is," Robbie said, always on the lookout for a famous face.

"Over 'ere love," one of the cameramen shouted out to the forlorn-looking, waif-like figure coming down the steps of the Law Courts, surrounded by her bodyguards.

"What did you get then? How many hours of community service for hitting your postman?"

The Malachis recognised the young girl as the up-and-coming actress who seemed to have her picture everywhere. On celluloid, paper, computer screens, any flat surface and there she was staring out at you with her huge, soulful eyes. They had seen her in her latest production and agreed she had a certain je ne sais quoi about her but couldn't quite understand why she also had a fearsome temper whenever anyone disagreed with her. The case that had been heard this morning involved a poor delivery man who happened to ring her doorbell at 8 o'clock in the morning when she was performing her regular morning meditation exercises; she hated being interrupted in the middle of them. Instead of a signature on his delivery sheet the poor man got a rather large impression on his nose as her arm was the first thing which had appeared out of the door, flying towards his face at thirty miles per hour. Needless to say, his GP had no hesitation in signing the poor man off for several days and his union had taken the matter to court.

"None of your bloody business!" was her retort, which should have been enough but she felt the old anger welling up inside her and Robbie had a sudden sense that things were going to get nasty. He tuned into the sensory section in her brain and desperately tried to get some comforting words inside her to settle her down. He tried, "O, my love is like a red, red rose", but could see that wasn't having much of an effect. And so tried a couple of lines from his poem to a young friend, "May prudence, fortitude, and truth, Erect your brow undaunting!" which made some impression but it wasn't until he fired the flattering words from Young Peggy Blooms, "Young

Peggy blooms our boniest lass, Her blush is like the morning, The rosy dawn, the springing grass, With early gems adorning," that he could see her temper begin to subside and the threat of another assault seemed to diminish.

"Get a grip on yourself, Anya," her lawyer instructed, "or you'll be back inside and this time it may be for some time."

Anya suddenly felt all light-headed and a bit queasy. Where had those thoughts come from, she wondered. She recognised the first line and thought it might have been written by that funny Scottish poet she was made to learn at school. I must write those lines down and look them up. They might be just what I need to keep me on the straight and narrow.

"Well done, Robbie," Gladstone remarked, as they continued on their way. "The half-Malachis will have clocked that one." He looked up and noticed several of them high up on the walls of the law court making notes in their score sheets ready to pass on to Charles I, the Oriental Zone counter.

The two Malachis left their leader, Gladstone, at his home on the Strand and they met up with Brunel on the Embankment near the Temple. Along the way they dealt with one or two minor incidents following the two main scoring ones but it was the argument between the elderly couple which was going to prove the decisive one.

Newton and Burns were debating the relative merits of various forces in nature – physical ones deemed by Newton to be the only ones which counted as these you could measure as opposed to emotional forces of the heart which Burns considered far more important for human happiness which he conceded had no way of being measured, but at least you could see the effects. They often had arguments of this nature, but there was one thing they both agreed on – that being a Malachi and returning to the human world to have another bite at the cherry was a real privilege, especially as it meant having these encounters with people you weren't necessarily alive with.

An elderly couple were resting on a bench overlooking the Thames, just beyond Temple station.

"It's my turn to choose dinner tonight; you had your choice last night with the meat pies."

"Well, I say we try that new Chinese takeaway which has just opened on the High Street."

"Oh, do we have to? I'd prefer a fish pie."

And so it went on, back and forth, until Newton and Burns were so familiar with the contents of the couple's fridge and their culinary likes and dislikes that they felt they could appear on Ready, Steady Cook and cook a meal which both would find equally appealing.

"Oh, for goodness sake! Just listen to them both. Why aren't they just glad they can have a choice over what they eat? And they should be happy that they still have each other," Newton said, never having married himself. He was descended from a family of farmers which had given him a real appreciation for the value of food.

"You'll have to sort them out, Newton," Robbie said, handing over the mantle of responsibility to his friend.

"OK, let's see what we can do." Newton thought for a few minutes. He liked these challenges where he had time to think and plan, as opposed to reacting to events on the spur of the moment as they had had to do for the first two challenges of the day.

As he stared out over the Thames he let his mind wander. The wind was particularly blustery just then and as it swirled around he got a whiff of the salty sea air from the water. A fishing boat was chugging its way upstream, probably to unload its cargo at some fancy restaurant in Chelsea.

"That's it!" he shouted. "Fish and chips. They can't go wrong with that. One of the traditional dishes of this country and of this capital city."

He channelled his thoughts into the minds of both of the septuagenarians sitting on the bench and simultaneously they said "It'll have to be fish and chips then!"

"Hey – that's what I said!"

"It's funny how we both thought and then said the same thing, isn't it dear? It must be because we know each other inside out – we've been married for so long."

Newton and Burns looked at each other and smiled. "What rotters we are to hoodwink these people," Newton remarked.

"Now what's next on the agenda?"

Chapter Fourteen

The Occidental Zone had a job to do. Lying in third place was not good and Florence Nightingale and William Shakespeare, the zone's senior Malachis, had had a meeting with Nelson and Eisenhower to discuss tactics. Basically Florence and Wills had been given an ultimatum by their chiefs – either come up with the goods and get them back in contention for the championship or they could rethink their value as Malachis. It was a bit harsh but they appreciated the pressures that Malachis were under. There were quite a few spirits who would happily take their place back on Earth as new statues were being erected. The late Queen Mother for one was in training at this very moment. If she passed the test and kept off the gin then no doubt she would make an excellent Malachi. It wasn't just a case of resting on your laurels; oh no – if you wanted to stay as a Malachi you had to keep on proving your worth.

Florence and Wills had selected de Gaulle and Charlie Chaplin as team players for today's contest. Unlike the participants for the Oriental Zone, these Malachis had lived through the same decades but had never actually met. Strangely, though, they had both sought out anti-ageing treatments at the same Swiss clinic but at different times; Florence had always thought it odd that two people from seemingly very different backgrounds could both be so vain. However, de Gaulle had also enjoyed relaxing in front of the silent movies of Charlie Chaplin – they provided him with much needed relaxation after a hard day of politicking. The two of them seemed to get on really well.

The six of them had met in the shelter on Hanover Square first thing in the morning. Nelson and Ike had given the first pep talk and then had left it to Florence Nightingale and Shakespeare to spell out the nitty-gritty to the two chosen to perform for the zone for this day's contest. Nelson and Ike were the good cop/bad cop combo with Ike trying to relax the others with his chummy banter whilst Nelson followed it up with all sorts of ultimatums. Florence and Will's job was to pick up the pieces and convince de Gaulle and

Chaplin that they did have the necessary skills to do well. They needed to score lots of points to edge up the leader board. At the end of the session de Gaulle and Chaplin were 90% certain they could do it, the other 10% would remain to be seen.

Leicester Square was filling up with tourists whilst de Gaulle and Chaplin were on patrol looking for any opportunities to act. Chaplin's statue had faded, as it should as he was officially not 'in residence', and his bamboo cane looked decidedly floppy. Shakespeare was doing his best to attract attention away from his friend's diminutive statue, but as usual people could never quite work out who he was as he had no name on the plinth; and even though the likeness wasn't bad some folk even thought he was Roald Dahl.

As usual there were hordes of foreign students hanging around in groups, each spilling over from the pavements onto the roads and causing a real nuisance for the regulars who just wanted to get from A to B as quickly as possible. With their backpacks protruding behind and cameras in their hands they had no regard for Joe Public and were completely oblivious to the mayhem going on around them as passers-by had to step out into busy roads to get past, hoping that one of them did not decide to step back to take a better photo. De Gaulle and Chaplin were used to these scenes and usually kept well out of the way of these insensitive groups.

It looked like business as usual in one of London's busiest squares. But de Gaulle had spotted something which didn't look quite right. Two of the aforementioned individuals appeared to have become separated from their pack and were desperately looking left and right to try to distinguish their own group from the many dotted around the square. Fortunately for them they were American, as were approximately half the groups of tourists in the locale, as at least it meant they could speak a form of English.

"They said they were going to stay where we left them," moaned one of the boys.

"Yeah – well – I guess they didn't figure it would take you 30 minutes to decide which flavour ice cream you wanted," retorted the other.

"Nor that you would want to get some more gum."

And so it went on. The two of them having a go at each other whilst not solving their predicament of trying to find their own group.

"We are supposed to be going to Ripleys next and I don't want to miss that."

De Gaulle realised they had lost their group and if he didn't reunite them with it in the next five minutes there could be a diplomatic incident.

De Gaulle took charge of the situation and instructed Chaplin to do some light entertainment, "You keep them amused whilst I try to locate their group. But remember, they can't see you so you'll have to do it by thought transference."

OK here goes, thought Charlie. All he could think of was things he'd said in his past life and so he fired a few of these thoughts into the brains of the two young lost Americans.

"Life is a tragedy when seen in close-up, but a comedy in long-shot."

"A day without laughter is a day wasted."

"In the end, everything is a gag."

"Laughter is the tonic, the relief, the surcease for pain."

And he kept on and on sending these same four sentences into the boys' subconsciousness until they were both completely helpless with mirth, doubled up and laughing their heads off.

"Oh, that is soooo funny," they were both saying. "Now just stop making me laugh so much!" And so on and so on until half of the people in Leicester Square were standing there staring at them.

"Oops," muttered Chaplin, in alarm, "I think I've overdone it slightly."

Meanwhile de Gaulle had done some detective work and had located the boys' group just as they were about to leave the square and head off along Coventry Street towards Piccadilly Circus. In the end though he didn't have to do much more as the booming sound of the lost boys' laughter soon made its way over to their side of the square.

"Oh my," declared the leader, "I'll have some of what they are on! Come on you two. You'll have to share the joke with us!"

The pair of stragglers had no idea what had made them laugh so much but all they could think was that they were happy to have reconnected with their own group at last. They vaguely remembered thinking about a small figure dressed like a tramp and holding a walking stick but as they tried to think about him again they didn't find him funny any more. It was all rather baffling.

"I bet it was the e-numbers in those ice creams you had made you both a bit hyper," their leader said as they joined the group. "You just can't trust English food. Stick to American fast food if I were you! Come on let's see who we can find in Ripleys."

"Well, you certainly excelled yourself there, Charlie," de Gaulle said, feeling rather relieved that in the end he hadn't had much to do to resolve the predicament of the lost boys.

"Let's see what other good deeds we can do!" Charlie said as they continued on their patrol around the square, which by now thankfully had returned to normal with everyone continuing on their busy way.

De Gaulle and Chaplin were heading towards Haymarket when their services appeared to be called for again. All they could see was a young girl running, bags flying off each shoulder, and a No. 38 bus disappearing into the distance.

"I'm going to be late, I'm going to be late." The young girl was distraught, and she was in danger of losing one of her dangerously high heeled shoes as she sprinted down Haymarket after the bus.

"Here we go again," Charlie said excitedly to de Gaulle. "This time I'll sort out the bus and you deal with the girl."

Chaplin drew his stick up to eye level, parallel with the ground and pulled back his arm. He had perfected this audacious javelin move in training and although he hadn't quite got it to be 100% effective he was pretty good with it for basic manoeuvres. Here, though, he was dealing with a moving object which was also crammed with people so the hazard was considerably higher than he'd practised on. But what the heck, he thought, I can't really do too much harm. I mean, bamboo isn't that dangerous.

He took aim and fired. He was aiming for the wing mirror. He was hoping that it would get jammed in the arm and cause a minor distraction to the driver so that it would make him brake and slow down, just enough, hopefully, to let the girl catch up with the bus at the next stop. However, as luck would have it, just at the moment he let go of his precarious projectile a pigeon decided it wanted to take a closer look at the speeding cane and swooped down trying to peck at the handle. Of course, this was not good for keeping the cane on the course Chaplin had intended for it. Instead of making a rather neat arching parabola in the air towards the bus it ended up making a bumpy wave-like motion which then caught the attention of the rest of the winged population in the local vicinity. A whole flock of birds began to attack the cane as it headed towards the No. 38. Suddenly the sky went black and the noise of the pigeons was deafening. Not only did this have the effect Chaplin was intending, but everything came to a complete standstill. No-one could see anything anyway as the sky was filled with a black, amorphous mass of wings and feathers.

"Keep going, girl." De Gaulle made the young girl continue on her exhausting run to the next bus stop as the area was in gridlock. "You'll make it."

The young girl hardly knew where she was going as she kept on pounding the streets. The other pedestrians seemed to just melt out of her way as she ran and ran unimpeded.

"There, I've made it," she breathed heavily as she arrived at the next stop, her bags falling heavily to the ground.

And then it was as though the lights had been switched on again. The sky cleared, the sun shone and the noise of the screaming pigeons faded away to nothing and there was the bus, arriving ready to pick up its next load of passengers.

"Next time you do that move, please warn me so that I can duck. Look at my coat, completely covered in bird droppings!" De Gaulle was furious with Chaplin. His beautifully tailored black overcoat now looked more like a Dalmatian dog.

"Oh, that'll clean." Chaplin responded, dismissively. "Don't worry about that. I thought the manoeuvre worked well in the end."

"Up to a point. You should have thought about these darned birds. The Mayor of London really must do something about them, they're ruining our reputation!"

"Yes – well it was a bit risky, I'll admit that. I'll buy you a coffee to make it up to you."

And so the two Malachis wandered over to a coffee shop for a well deserved elevenses.

Once they had had their fill of caffeine they were ready to do more Malachi deeds. This time they decided to go their separate ways for a while on the proviso that they could summon each other straight away if they needed to.

They were making their way back along Shaftesbury Avenue and then up Charing Cross Road. Chaplin was looking at all the theatres and cinemas and seeing what productions were on. Sometimes he sneaked into the auditoriums to take a look at the modern films and plays. It would be easy for him to say, "They don't make them like they used to," but he did admire the modern film directors and producers, especially the way in which they had revived the film industry. Twenty years ago people hardly went to see a film; they could just so easily rent a video and watch it in the comfort of their own home. However, the way films were made nowadays with the surround sound and imaginative cinematography, not to mention 3D effects, made people need to see films on the big screen surrounded by other people.

De Gaulle, meanwhile, was taking the opportunity of glancing in the windows of the second-hand book shops that were so abundant in this part of London. He liked to scour the shelves looking for his own works on the military and World War I; he also loved reading about the campaigns of the Second World War and often wondered if he could have done more.

The two Malachis were oblivious to each other as they walked on opposite sides of the road, but both had suddenly noticed the same predicament. The traffic lights had jammed on green on all streets of the busy junction of Oxford Street with Tottenham Court Road and the cars and buses went mad. Horns beeping, lights flashing as cars and taxis nearly collided - it was a scene of pure mayhem. White van man duly stepped out of his vehicle and tried to sort out the situation with a few choice words, whilst the taxi drivers looked on resignedly as their meters continued to rack up the fares.

As quick as a flash de Gaulle and Chaplin were there, one on each side of the junction, both of them ready to react. The lights flipped to red, and then back to green and then to red and so on and so on. The place erupted with vehicles starting to move off and then screeching to a halt to avoid certain collisions.

"You stupid fool, Charlie, let me handle this!" de Gaulle bellowed across the road at his fellow Malachi. Unfortunately, Chaplin could only see the funny side and made things worse by switching the lights to amber as well so that all that could be seen was a colourful display of changing lights. The pedestrians all thought the situation totally hilarious too; it made a change to see the traffic being held up on the streets of London.

Eventually one of the sets of traffic lights fused and stopped working altogether at which point de Gaulle lost his cool completely and started gesticulating wildly like some mad windmill as his arms went round and round over his head. By this time the streets were in gridlock, all vehicles were in state of paralysis.

Oh this is fun, thought Charlie, but oh so not allowed! Chaplin had decided to take it upon himself to break the Malachi code of honour – do not do unto other Malachis what we do unto humans, and had made de Gaulle lose control so that he looked like a whirling dervish, although, of course, he was invisible to the humans looking on in complete bewilderment around him.

The traffic had backed up so much in central London that it had even reached Florence Nightingale further down on the Charing Cross Road. She stormed up to see what all the fuss was about and as soon as she realised what was happening screamed at Charlie to stop immediately.

"What the bloody hell do you think you are doing? Stop that immediately! You fool!"

"So you finally admit it now, do you?" Chaplin laughed as Florence stood there horrified at the sight before her, more bothered about the state of the traffic than the state of de Gaulle, it had to be said.

"Just get the traffic moving again. As quickly as you can, and then you can sort out de Gaulle!" barked Nightingale.

"OK, OK – just calm down will you," replied Chaplin as he

readjusted the lights and slowly the traffic began to clear as calm and order was once again restored to the streets of London.

He then turned his attention to de Gaulle who was getting redder and redder in the face and looked as though he was about to take off into the upper stratosphere.

Arrêtez-vous, cesser vos bras! Chaplin tried to get through to de Gaulle's subconscious but his naff French wasn't helping.

"It's no good, Florence. He's not letting me get through to him in his native language and if I try English he may go completely bananas."

"Ok – let me try. I'll try Italian – he may respond to that. Stop, stop il braccio!" Florence gave the command and miraculously de Gaulle's arms started to slow down, his colour lost its beetroot hue and his breathing returned to normal.

"Dimentica tutto!" Florence added. "You owe me one, Chaplin," she whispered to the diminutive figure standing next to her looking rather sheepish.

De Gaulle looked slightly embarrassed as his arms flopped to his side. He looked around and coughed into his handkerchief trying not to look conspicuous. He couldn't remember anything of the past ten minutes and looked surprised to see Florence Nightingale standing there with Chaplin.

"Oh – what are you doing here? We've been getting on really well this morning haven't we Charlie?" de Gaulle was beginning to get his composure back and didn't want Nightingale to think they hadn't performed.

They had certainly performed this morning, that wasn't the issue. But a few liberties had been taken, she explained as she walked with them back to the cottage in Soho Square to debrief the pair of them.

Chapter Fifteen

The last zone to go on Day 2 was the Meridion Zone, leaders after Day 1 but still with much to prove. Emily Pankhurst and Christopher Columbus, the senior Malachis, had decided to play devil's advocate and be the performing Malachis for their zone themselves. They had discussed this with both Queen Victoria and Boudicca who gave their backing to this plan. Whilst it was not usual for the senior Malachis of a zone to compete on the second day, this usually being saved for the finale, for this year's contest all four of them felt that this would give the zone a real boost and hopefully put them way out of sight of the other two zones. It was a risky tactic but if the strategy didn't work out as planned they still had some excellent Malachis in the squad to fall back on.

Chris made his way over to Emily's statue, stopping along the way in the cabmen's shelter by Grosvenor Gardens for a quick cuppa. Emily's home was a prime example of the classic art deco style of the 1920s. Whilst Emily had been so preoccupied with politics during her natural life she had had no time for the niceties of homemaking and consequently once she returned as a Malachi she went completely over the top, designing the inside of her statue to be a perfect replica of the 1920s style. Her plain polished parquet floors were covered in large geometrically patterned rugs. The centrepiece of her sitting room was an enormous circular one with the motto of the political group she founded, the Women's Social and Political Union, Deeds, not Words embroidered across the middle in the three colours of the Union: purple, white and green. Purple representing dignity, white purity and green hope for the future. She never wanted to forget what she and her sisters had achieved for womankind. Emily still liked wearing purple and green clothes today and even her walls were covered with wallpaper of mostly purple and green hues, but she cleverly contrasted this colour scheme with white furniture and accessories. Most Sundays were spent with her daughter scouring the tables at the car boot sale in Battersea where she often found pieces of china by Clarice Cliff and glassware by René Lalique.

In contrast, Columbus's home was a perfect replica of his flagship the Santa Maria in which he made his first crossing of the Atlantic. He had such fondness for this beautiful ship that he had made his present home almost entirely out of pine and oak in tribute to her. He always did a double take when he came to Emily's home, it was such a contrast to his own simple tastes.

Fortunately, Emily was watching out for him and as he approached she made a swift exit from her portal to meet him on Milbank. Together they strolled up to Parliament Square, the scene for their activity today.

"So what's your plan and strategy for today Emily?" Chris asked, knowing that Emily liked to take charge of things.

"Well – as you know, we really need to be on the ball and look for any opportunities we can. Boudicca wants us to get as many points as we can today so we are way ahead of the other zones by the close of play this afternoon."

"Righto. But can I just say one thing to you?" Chris hesitated. He had something of a rather delicate nature to say to Emily and he wasn't quite sure how to put this to her, and he hoped she wouldn't overreact.

"If you must," she replied, cautiously.

"Please be a little careful when assessing certain situations between couples. I know that you fought for women's emancipation and all that, but things are a little different now in the 21st century, especially the language and everything. What you may take to be an insult, may be quite acceptable today." Phew – he had said it and got it off his chest at long last. He didn't want Emily to be rampaging over every little slight to every woman on the street just because in her eyes it was ever so slightly disrespectful to women. After all these years women did have a far more equal place in society compared with her days, it just might not be so obvious.

"Yes, I know. Both Queen Victoria and Boudicca gave me a little pep talk about this very subject only yesterday. Why don't we rely on your judgement to decide when there are opportunities?"

"That's fine with me." Chris was immensely relieved at her attitude.

Chris and Emily were walking behind two ladies, Gabby and Tessa, who were planning their day's shopping together, when suddenly a young man collapsed in front of them.

"Oh, look out!" shouted Gabby.

"Now what?" Tessa said, as she looked around and realised that apart from themselves there was no-one else on that part of the square.

"Looks like our shopping just got delayed. I did a first aid course some time ago but my mind's gone blank, I just don't know where to start," Gabby replied, feeling completely helpless.

Without waiting for Chris, Emily took the initiative.

"Chris – make Tessa call for an ambulance will you? I'll go and help Gabby – remind her of her emergency first aid routine. I'll get her to check the chap's responses and then to get started on CPR."

Chris did as he was instructed whilst Emily saw to Gabby. Suddenly Gabby felt as though she was on autopilot. She was going through the motions of what she had learned on the course with hardly a thought about what she should be performing. How odd, she thought, it's all come back to me. Something the instructor said would happen when a real emergency happens, something to do with being in an 'unconscious competent state' I think he said. Anyway – who cares? "Tessa – have you called the ambulance? Tell them the patient can't breathe normally, will you, and tell me when it's going to be here."

"Already in hand, Gabby," replied Tessa.

"Good girl," Chris said to himself. And soon an ambulance had arrived and the paramedics had taken over performing CPR from Gabby.

"Let's leave them to it now. It's all under control." And Emily and Chris continued their patrol around Parliament Square.

Gabby and Tessa felt that they deserved a reward for all their efforts and made their way to the nearest bar where they started their day's shopping with a glass of fizzy stuff.

Soon the Malachis' services were called on again as they noticed a £10 note flutter out of the pocket of an old man with a walking stick who had stopped at a kiosk to buy a newspaper. A couple of schoolboys, on their way to school, had also noticed. As quick as a flash one of them had bent down, seemingly to do up a loose shoelace, and surreptitiously stuffed the note into his school bag.

"Oh no you don't!" Chris boomed over his inter-brain superhighway, landing with an enormous echo in the boy's subconsciousness.

"Wh... who said that?" he said as he looked around, terrified that he had been spotted.

"What are you on about?" questioned his friend.

"Nothing – it's just that I found this on the ground and I reckoned we could do something useful with it," and he showed his friend the booty he had snaffled.

"Cor – yeah. I know what we can do with that," as his friend rubbed his hands with glee.

"But then I heard this voice yelling at me... and here it is again..."

"Just give that money back to that poor old gentleman at the kiosk – it's his you know and he needs it far more than you – and in any case it's stealing what you have just done," Chris boomed over the airwaves again.

"No way – I found it fair and square."

"Who are you talking to? Are you going mad?" his friend said in disbelief. "Come on we'll be late for lessons."

"Hold it right there, sonny," Chris made the boy's shoes stick to the ground preventing him from moving off with his friend.

"What's the matter, now?" said his friend, as he realised that his schoolmate wasn't walking next to him. He went back and gave him a tug.

"What's the matter with your shoes? They're stuck to the ground. You'll have to step out of them."

But Chris had already thought of that and had made the boy's socks stick to the insides of his shoes so that now the boys were going through some sort of hilarious dance as the free one pulled and tugged at his friend's arms whilst Chris just made the stuck boy spring back into position after every tug.

"Look – if you want to go free you know what you have to do." Chris said to the boy after about ten minutes of this ridiculous pas de deux.

"OK, OK," he said. "If you just let me go I'll give the money back to the old chap."

"That's a good boy," Chris said, releasing the boy to do the honourable thing.

The boy went up to the old man who was shuffling along the pavement by now. "Excuse me, sir – I think you dropped this."

"Oh gosh, did I? Well thank you my good fellow – I'm enormously grateful to you. Here, you take it as a reward for your honesty."

How were they to know he was a quiet millionaire? And with honour restored and faces saved, everyone was happy and the boys ran laughing all the way to their lessons.

Emily remarked, "We never know precisely what effect our actions will have, do we? Thankfully this had a most unusual and serendipitous ending."

"No – that's what I like about being a Malachi," Chris replied, agreeing with her.

And so on they went. Nothing much needed their attention as the morning progressed. There was a slight kerfuffle on the taxi rank when a politician arriving at the House claimed not to have enough change for the poor cab driver, but he was soon sorted out when Emily made him check his back pocket and, lo and behold, there was an extra fiver. Honestly – these politicians – not really very honourable when it comes to money, she thought. But – 'twas ever thus, as she reminisced to her days.

The last thing she heard as she walked on was, "Give me a receipt then!"

They had almost done a complete circuit of the square when a group of schoolchildren was standing around looking at the statue of Oliver Cromwell. Well, at least, that was what they should have been looking at, as their teacher, Miss Dickenson, remarked as she kept checking her map. The group had come into central London for a history project on the English Civil War and were desperate to see the monument to the man who had been so central to the civil war in Britain in the 17th century. But where was he? His lion was there, sleeping happily in the sunshine, but Cromwell himself seemed to have disappeared.

Miss Dickenson couldn't understand it. "Follow me, children,

I need to find someone to ask – maybe they've taken him off to get him cleaned up." She led the group down the street towards the public entrance into the House of Commons where lots of people in fluorescent jackets were looking important. They are bound to know, she thought to herself.

"Oh crikey - look Ollie's gone on a walkabout and not shut his portal properly. He has been told so many times about this but he still forgets. Oh, he is so careless that man," Chris said to Emily.

If a portal isn't fully closed then, to protect the Malachi and enable them to return to their statue, the statue fades to an almost translucent state, and becomes so pale that it doesn't register on the visual cortex of humans at all. In other words it appears to disappear. And this is precisely what had happened to Cromwell's statue.

Clarence, the lion, must know where Cromwell is, thought Chris. We'll have to find him and get him back, otherwise that teacher is going to start blabbing and all hell will break loose. They'll blame it on the protesters opposite. And with that Chris instructed Emily to use her feminine charm on the lion to get the information they needed.

"He's in the House. There's a debate going on and he wanted to sit in," Clarence growled. "Now let me go back to sleep please!"

"Quick – you go and find him. You know your way around the Houses of Parliament. It hasn't changed that much since your day and I'll try to distract the group. I'll try to keep Miss Dickenson's mind on other things," said Chris.

Emily raced inside. This time no-one barred her way and she was free to go wherever she liked. She made for the House of Commons, ran to the visitors' gallery and looked around. There was only a law student there busy taking notes. Come on, Ollie, show yourself please! She looked down into the Chamber. "Well – I don't believe it! There he is sitting on the backbench along with a few Liberal Democrat MPs."

Emily shouted down at him, confident that only he would hear her.

"Ollie – what do you think you're doing? You left your portal open and all hell's about to break loose. There's a party of school children looking for you."

"Oh damn it. I thought I heard it click but it must have been the wind, or Clarence. I must have a word with him, he's been getting a bit too free and easy with things just recently. Coming!" He couldn't believe he had been that careless. He would have to leave the Chamber now just as the debate was getting to the really interesting stage.

The two of them raced back to the outer courtyard and soon Ollie was climbing up onto his plinth ready to go back in through the portal.

"It won't open. Now what do I do?"

And sure enough the portal had jammed itself shut.

"Just give it a tug, here I'll help," Chris shouted as he ran over to help. He'd managed to persuade the group to go and look at Richard the Lionheart's statue over in the car park, as they had studied the Crusades last term.

And so the two of them, with Emily also helping out so as not to feel outdone just because of her sex, made a very comical sight to other Malachis in the square, as they stood in a line each holding on to the one in front as they pulled and tugged and pulled and tugged at the portal.

Suddenly the door gave and the three of them fell back off the plinth and on to the grass below.

"Right," ordered Chris, "just get in there, turn on the lights and act normally."

As the group of bewildered schoolchildren and their equally bewildered teacher wandered back along Abingdon Street, they saw Cromwell's statue in its full glory.

"There we are children – I said it was only a matter of time, didn't I?"

"Yes, Miss," they all answered.

"But it wasn't here five minutes ago, I'm sure of that," retorted one of them.

"That'll do, sonny. Just get on with your drawings now," admonished the teacher sternly.

The children sat on the grass around the plinth and sketched away, little realising that they were being helped by Chris and Emily as their pencils and crayons made the most lifelike of drawings of both Cromwell and the lion.

"They've had a day they'll never forget, haven't they?" Emily said to Chris.

"Yes – and let's hope Cromwell never forgets either!"

"Let's go and report back to Victoria and Boudicca. They asked us to call in at Boudicca's for lunch," Emily replied and off they went down Bridge Street to fill them all in on their morning's work.

Chapter Sixteen

By the end of the second day of the contest the Malachis were feeling the effects of their efforts and were all exhausted. Normally they would perform the odd minor Malachi action each day, but sometimes nothing would be required of them for days. And so to be performing at such an intense level for the contest took it out of them and left them reeling with the effort of it all.

All apart from one of them that is – Byron. He'd seen enough of the two lost children to know that Wellington was in the middle of something fishy and he was determined to use this information to his advantage to get back at the whole sorry lot of them for excluding him from the contest. There – he'd said it and it felt good to finally admit to himself what he was so angry about. All he needed to do was to keep close to Wellington and bide his time. With Napier roped in to help him he would soon have his revenge.

He made his way through Green Park and over to Trafalgar Square where Napier had just returned from the count with Wellington and banged on his plinth demanding to be let in.

"Right – I've got a job for you, Napier," he said, as he barged his way in.

"Oh, and how are you too? Don't you have any manners, man, or have you lost all sensibilities?" Napier was furious with him and with himself for letting himself become a pawn in Byron's game.

"Just remember our agreement, if you will," Byron retorted. "Oh, but first do tell me what happened at the count. Who's leading at this point?"

Napier gave an account of the session with Wellington. They'd all gone to Regent's Park this time for a change of scene. They had tethered their horses near the lake and had wandered off into the centre of the inner circle where they could get some privacy. Wellington preferred this park for more private meetings as all the paths were edged with hedges and so, along with the trees and abundant shrubs, they could always find a really secluded spot.

116

Not that they could be seen of course, but he always liked to make doubly sure.

Each of the counters had relayed the scores along with the counts from the half-Malachis. Even though Wellington had suggested they all use the on-line web-entry forms for the counts there was such a lot of debate about each of the actions performed by the Malachis that they had needed a face to face meeting after all.

"And how was Wellington?" Byron asked.

"What do you mean?"

"Well – was he acting normally or would you say he had other things on his mind?"

Napier thought hard back to earlier that afternoon. "Well – now you come to mention it, he did seem rather distracted. I mean he hardly questioned our judgements when it came to the points we had awarded and usually he's so blimming pernickety and has to know every last detail. I think he only convened us all there to take his mind off something else."

"Yes, and that doesn't surprise me one jot," said Byron, with a knowing smile on his face. "When you hear what I know then you'll understand why he was so jumpy with you lot. But first – get me a drink will you? A large one with lots of ice and lemon. "

Napier disappeared into his kitchen and Byron took the opportunity to admire the booty Napier had brought back with him from India. This stuff's not half bad, he thought, I'd quite like it in my abode.

Napier returned with a drink in each hand and the two of them sat down on opposite sides of the fireplace.

"So – come on then, you old devil, what have you got to tell me?" Napier demanded.

"Not so fast! First you have to promise me, and I mean a proper 'blood-is-thicker-than-water' promise, that you and me are in this together, otherwise you know what the consequences will be."

"I don't seem to have any choice, do I? You made that perfectly clear before!"

"Just checking," Byron said, making his friend suffer. "Come on – I want you to say it."

Napier whispered, "Promise," and he shuffled uncomfortably from one cheek of his buttocks to the other.

"Sorry, what was that?" Byron persisted, leaning forward with his hand cupped behind his right ear.

"Promise!" Napier shouted. "There – are you satisfied?"

"Thank you. That's all I wanted to hear. Anyway – who's in the lead? How's our zone doing? And what about the Oriental Zone with that mad Scottish poet?"

Napier answered, "You know that Emily and Chris went solo for the Meridions hoping to get a really good lead but things didn't go too well. Cromwell went awol and upset the apple cart. Charlie Chaplin had a narrow escape with de Gaulle and needed Florence to get him out of trouble and actually the only zone that did OK was the Oriental zone. So the leader board looks like this: Orientals in the lead with Meridions and us tying in second."

"So – looks like it'll be a thrilling final day tomorrow," Byron said sarcastically.

"Look – you can't still be upset about your assessment can you? It was the same for me but look at me now. Wellington can't have any objections about my counting role in the contest. I'm performing it really well, my riding has improved and, actually, I'm quite enjoying it too for that matter. You just have to put it all behind you and move on."

"Easy for you to say that isn't it, Charles?" Byron said dismissively, as he took a long slurp of his drink.

"Now – come on man. Tell me what's really going on?" Napier insisted.

And Byron did – telling him about the two lost souls and how Wellington had to get them back to their own timeplace, and how he, Byron that is, with Napier's help was going to make things a little difficult for the old warrior.

Napier didn't like it one little bit but realising his hands were tied agreed to go along with Byron for the time being. Knowing his old ally and how hasty he could be he thought he would be able to find an opportunity to get out of his clutches sooner or later. At least that was what he hoped.

"And – there we have it Charles, and I know I can rely on you for a helping hand. How about another one of your fancy cocktails? This time with a little less ice, if you don't mind."

"First – you'd better spell out what it is you want me to do. What is this 'job' you have for me?"

And so Byron explained as best he could, given that he himself wasn't sure precisely what stunts Wellington would pull off regarding the kids. "We'll have to play it by ear after that," Byron said and stared hard at his friend as if daring Charles to contradict him.

***

Back at his home Wellington checked to see how the children were doing. They'd had tea and were watching TV so Wellington took the opportunity to have a quiet word with Victoria and update her on their day solving their first clue.

First, though, he needed to check on the actual bodily conditions of Rory and Sarah in ECH. His route through to the intensive care monitors via the comms centre on HQS Wellington told him all he needed to know. The children were as well as could be expected – their brain swelling was going down slowly and all other vital signs were normal for a coma. He also did a quick check on the parents just to see if they were coping and weren't suffering from any symptoms of shock. All fine on that score too. He logged off that system, reactivated the quadrisensor and soon Victoria's face filled the screen.

He updated Victoria on the children's progress and how well they had done in solving the first clue. He explained that although they had solved it, it had taken them quite a bit longer than he had anticipated; it was almost as if they were being misdirected, but maybe that was just the effects of the crash. He assured her that the next clue would be easier for them as they knew now what they were looking for.

"I'm relying on you, Arthur. You can't afford to slip up on this one."

"I know. It's all going to be fine, trust me."

Victoria ended the call and Wellington went over to Rory and Sarah.

"How are you both feeling? Better after your little outing today, I hope. You did well though – you've solved the first clue and so only one more and you'll be on your way home."

"I quite like it here," Sarah said. She was enjoying being the centre of attention and being waited on hand and foot.

"You mustn't get too comfortable," warned Wellington. "You really do want to get back to your dimension, even if you don't think you do at the moment. It's the effects of the coma. Your electrical activities have got a bit scrambled because of the swelling in your brains. Some of the nerves have got compressed and are interfering with each other, but once the swelling starts to subside then you'll feel more like your normal selves. The doctors in ECH are looking after you really well and monitoring you. They are the experts and have seen many, many cases like yours. And your parents are still keeping vigil. I think they've been playing your favourite music from your mp3 players."

"Well – I hope they've got them the right way round," Rory said in a huff. "I can't stand Sarah's 'pop' music. If I hear that that's going to be a right turn off."

"I'm sure they know whose is whose," Wellington said, reassuringly.

At the other end of Constitution Hill at Buckingham Palace, Victoria had some thinking to do. Should she carry on with the contest or defer it until the children were sorted out? She had to consider what was more important and really the answer was very simple. Of course the children were her top priority and it really didn't matter if the contest was delayed slightly. After all, the timetable for that was determined by her and her alone anyway. But then, if all her resources were focused on Rory and Sarah that would put a lot of pressure on them and it could tip them over the edge. Wellington was handling them really well in his expert fashion. He was used to dealing with delicate situations. He wasn't one to rush in and dominate things. He liked to let other people have a say too. Well, at least that was how she remembered him from his soldiering days, or so she had read.

"Albert, my darling – what would you do?" she pleaded with her true love and reached for her box of keepsakes, as she often did when faced with a dilemma. It helped take her mind off the details she was battling with and for some reason made her see the big picture. As she took out some old letters, photographs, even a curl of hair in an old locket, she let her mind wander to the glorious days she had shared with him. No-one could have ever loved someone as much as they had cherished each other, could they? They knew instinctively what the other was thinking even when they were miles away and they never really minded being apart for that long as they knew they would always be there for each other. As long as they were both walking on the same planet was enough for them. To know that the other was constantly thinking about them was almost as good as being together in the flesh. Maybe she already had some Malachi blood in her when she was alive. And maybe that's why Albert still couldn't decide about becoming one himself – maybe he felt he already was one, only not here on this Earth.

She got up and looked out of the window along The Mall. She could see James Cook up on his ship-shaped plinth. If it hadn't been for one of his earliest discoveries then perhaps New Zealand would be a very different place compared with what it is today. No – she could see it so clearly now. The answer she had been waiting for had come to her. She owed it to Cook and to the Wheeler family to defer the contest. She would direct as many resources as it would take into helping those two poor children recover and get back to their normal dimension. She felt an enormous sense of relief at having made this difficult decision and knew that it was the right one. She could now go to bed at peace with herself as she realised where her priorities lay.

***

During the night all was not well in PICU at the Evelina. Mike and Liz had reluctantly gone back to their hotel under strict instructions from the hospital staff that they should get as much rest as possible and have a decent night's sleep and so fortunately were spared the emergency situation which occurred at 1 o'clock in the morning. It was Rory again. The swelling caused by the bang to his temple was not receding as much as the doctors had hoped the previous day and now his monitor was sounding the alarm.

Sister Bridge rushed over. "OK let's see what the problem is shall we, little man? Right – your oxygen supply looks as though it is being impeded."

She was an experienced practitioner having worked in PICU for most of her long career. She paged the on-call emergency paediatrician.

"Doctor, I think we should do an emergency CT scan on Rory. See if we can do an intervention procedure to help things along the way."

"Of course, Sister. Be right with you."

And so Rory was wheeled into the operating theatre where he was examined and a drain was put in his brain. After the delicate procedure he was back in his cubicle out of the immediate danger for now but still in a fairly critical condition. Sister Bridge would have to be extra diligent with him for the next 12 hours.

This was all communicated back to Wellington in his morning status report from HQS Wellington. And it was as he had feared as he had been disturbed in the middle of the night by a horrific bang. He'd woken up to find Rory stumbling around his abode, clearly sleepwalking but fumbling about all over the place and knocking things off shelves as he went. Wellington carefully guided the poor boy back to bed thankful that Rory hadn't actually hurt himself but concerned nonetheless.

"Right, this calls for serious action now. We must call an emergency meeting," he said, as he called up Victoria. "The contest must be stopped – we can't waste a moment in helping Rory and Sarah back to their own dimension."

"Yes, I'd already made that decision, Arthur, and we're all meeting at the Arch in one hour. See you then. Just make sure the clue is clear and not too taxing for them, will you?"

"Of course."

This gave Wellington time to have a serious word with the children and give them the second clue.

"A sweet airline from east of Greece. Now children, you know the sort of thing you are looking for, don't you – some sort of vessel and it may be another weathervane. I have an important meeting to go to but I'll be back soon and then I'll get you on your way."

He dashed over to the Arch where all the other chiefs, deputies and senior Malachis were already assembled, Victoria having brought them up to speed with the latest news. Immediately he was bombarded with a hundred questions from them all, each wanting to know precise details of when, where and how the accident had happened and how were the little mites doing now, and wanting to help in whichever way they could.

"Hang on a moment," Wellington said, holding up his hands. "Not so fast. You know we can't just go in with all guns blazing and hope to get them out of this mess. That'll only make things worse. No, the way forward is to tread lightly and carefully. They are both in a very critical condition and the last thing they need is you lot using all your powers and overloading the networks with your positive energy. We need a steady balance of neutral neural thought transferences in order that their brains recover from the comas. Their neural pathways must be retained and restored as normally as they were before the crash.

"Some of you can help with the parents and I want Edith on guard at the hospital. Oh, and it would be a good idea if Florence can help out there too. Brunel and the team can start the process of retrieving and recommissioning the boat weathervane that the children found. You need to bring the boat to my comms ship at Temple. You can moor her up along the Embankment there."

The Malachis murmured their agreement with all of Wellington's plans.

"The children now have to solve the second clue 'A sweet airline from east of Greece' and this time I want Camorra and Tasca helping them please. They are going to be more on their wavelength considering the ages of the children. Is that OK with you Boudicca?"

"Yes, of course, Arthur. The girls will be really honoured that you've asked them," Boudicca replied, feeling very proud.

And so the meeting continued with the Malachis discussing amongst themselves how they could be of help and how important it was to put the contest on hold until the children recovered. They would need to use their most sensitive powers if they were to make a difference and get Rory and Sarah back into their rightful dimension.

123

Florence and Edith prepared themselves to go to ECH to keep an eye on the children and the nursing care, whilst Queen Anne volunteered to comfort the parents along with Gandhi. Brunel and Columbus went off to get hold of Cook.

Chapter Seventeen

Wellington came back from his emergency meeting to find the children and his men discussing what the second clue could mean.

"You need to have a starting point again," Wellington said, hastily. "And I'm going to give you another clue for this – A common place where you can buy dried grass. You can start by looking at the A-Z but it's not that far from here; due north-east for approximately 1.8 kilometres, and in a similar direction to where you were yesterday. Now, you need to take it easy so I'm going to take you to Piccadilly Circus myself and I will have some extra helpers on hand."

Earlier that morning Byron had summoned Napier to the corner of Hyde Park and the two of them were skulking behind the railings of Apsley House ready for whenever Wellington and the children came outside.

"Now, Charles, all I want you to do is to follow the two children who are staying with Wellington. They have been tasked with solving a clue and if you sense they are thinking something across your sensory wavelengths all you have to do is think the opposite. It's quite simple really. I'm sure you played a game like that when you were a little boy," Byron said, smirking. "Just make sure none of our fellow Malachis spot you. The children can't see you but they may be able to sense something. They are in this peculiar transitory world and no-one is really sure which receptors are active. Also, remember they've had pretty severe brain injuries so again, it's all a bit muddled inside."

"What will you be doing whilst I'm doing this then?" Napier demanded.

"Just taking care of a few other details. Nothing for you to worry about, but I won't be far away, you can be sure of that."

Suddenly Wellington's portal opened and the old warrior with the two children came outside. Wellington's men had already saddled up his horse and they then helped Rory and Sarah up onto Copenhagen, Sarah in front with Rory behind holding on with his arms wrapped tightly round his sister's waist.

"I'm going to walk you up to your starting point so that you conserve as much energy as you can and keep it all for solving the clue," Wellington explained to them. "Rory – you've remembered to bring the angelicaphone with you, haven't you? Same procedure with that as before and there will be one or two of my colleagues around. Although you can't see them you may be able to sense them but you have nothing to worry about. They are there under my instructions to help you. Is that clear? And a little less of the sightseeing today. I fear that was partly your undoing yesterday. You spent far too much time and energy in and out of shops!"

The two children were feeling a little subdued after the exuberance of the start of their adventure yesterday. It had all seemed so new and fresh and they had set off at an extraordinary pace. They hadn't realised that even in this dimension their bodies were still incredibly fragile. They would have to leave all thoughts of sightseeing behind until they were back in their own domain and fully fit. At least, if everything worked out as Wellington had promised it would. One good thing was that they weren't going to be alone today. Wellington had mentioned that some of his fellow Malachis would be around, but not visible to them. They just had to trust him as always.

And so they set off up Piccadilly with Napier following on at a safe distance behind. It was Copenhagen who sensed Camorra and Tasca first. He could smell the horses from Boudicca's chariot on them and, as they all converged on Piccadilly Circus, he gave a bright whinny as the two girls approached with some naughty treats for him.

"Who's a beautiful boy, then?" Tasca said, as she rubbed Copenhagen between the ears and offered out her flat hand with some slices of apples and carrots.

"Morning, girls," Wellington said. "As you can see, here are Rory and Sarah. All I want you to do is give them a helping hand if they appear to be going off the mark. The clues are: 'A common place where you can buy dried grass,' and 'A sweet airline from east of Greece.' You can probably guess the answers already."

Camorra and Tasca looked at the poor children, who were gazing around the Circus oblivious to the two Iceni girls.

"And we're looking for part of Fleet 2, is that right?" Camorra asked.

"Yes – this vessel and the one they found yesterday should be enough to get them back to their own dimension, once they've been recommissioned of course. Now, what I have asked you two to do is a very delicate job. I've had good reports from your mother as to how you've performed in the contest so far and I have every confidence you will do a good job for me today."

Camorra and Tasca beamed with pride and gave Wellington some time to speak to Rory and Sarah in private and set them on their way.

"The first part's pretty easy, don't you think Tasca? The street where they need to start looking. It's just over here."

Rory and Sarah had dismounted and were scouring the *A- Z* trying to find the answer to the first part of the clue.

"Dried grass can only mean either straw or hay, don't you think Rory?"

Napier had already realised what the answer was and was desperate for the children's thought to be filled with the word 'straw'. He conjured up a myriad of images which he tried to project into their subconsciousness - milkshakes with a hundred straws coming out of the glasses; a mile-long length of straws all interlinked into one another; a whole bar of colourful cocktails crammed to the brims with parasols and straws; a party table full of toddlers' drinks with straws winding around the outside of the gaudy plastic beakers; even scarecrows with straw hair.

Camorra and Tasca had thought the children would get the first part pretty easily and couldn't understand why it was taking them so long.

"Just get them to look up at the street sign, Tasca, and then I'm sure they'll realise. They seem to be focusing in on the word straw at the moment. Try and break through," Camorra instructed.

Tasca did everything she could to do just that but it was no good.

"Let's try them on the first part then," Camorra suggested. "Maybe their thought processes are still a bit disjointed after their accident; Wellington did warn us."

"OK then – A common place where you can buy has got to be

market hasn't it. So come on – think of stock market, indoor market, market place, market stall."

The sudden switch to the first part of the clue had caught Napier completely off his guard and he could sense that he had lost Rory. Instead of continuing to think about straws and strawberry milkshakes, Rory was coming round to the girls' way of thinking. "I get it, it's coming to me slowly now. Something to do with marks, no hang on there's more coming to me. Market – that's it! Now, let me see that A-Z again. I'm sure that name rings a bell."

"It's a pretty common enough name isn't it Rory? I mean, it could be anywhere."

"No, but listen, Wellington brought us here specifically and so it must be near here."

Napier tried one last attempt to get onto his wavelength but Rory's thoughts were racing too fast away from Napier. "Damn it, I've lost him," he said in desperation. It was this lack of concentration which had led to him not being selected for the annual contest in the first place so it was hardly surprising he hadn't succeeded with Rory.

"Of course – it's obvious. Haymarket!" Rory exclaimed. "I had all these weird images of different drinks with straws stuck in them. I don't know what made me think of that!"

"OK," said Sarah. "So, we go this way then." And she led the way round the far side of Piccadilly Circus to the HMV shop and looked across at the wall above the Aberdeen Steak House and there it was - Haymarket.

"How did they take so long to work that out?" Camorra asked Tasca. "That really shouldn't have taken that amount of time. I think Wellington may have overestimated their recovery."

"Let's hope they don't dither about with the second clue - A sweet airline from east of Greece," replied Tasca.

They made a very odd procession as they all started walking down Haymarket. Rory and Sarah in the lead muttering, "Sweet, planes, Cyprus" under their breath as Camorra and Tasca followed a few feet behind, trying desperately to get them to think of 'Turkey' 'baklava' and other such delicacies.

Bringing up the rear was Napier, who was determined to

make them think of greasy spoon cafés, greasy hair, and other such revolting things. As much as he felt uneasy doing this he realised he had no choice as far as Byron was concerned. Besides, Byron could turn up at any minute and he didn't want to risk upsetting him, as he thought of all the things he could lose if he did.

It had to be said the children's geography was not up to much, not when it came to European countries. They tended to focus on their own continent in their school geography lessons. So they knew a lot about the islands around New Zealand and Australia and also a fair bit about Tonga, Samoa and so on. They had heard of Greece, but tended to associate that particular country with Cyprus, something to do with the Forces base there, as they remembered their great-grandfather reminiscing so much about his war days.

Soon Rory and Sarah passed another Corinthian palace, another theatre, this time with fabulous gold figure work on the top of each of the six supporting columns at the frontispiece of the building.

"I get so confused about this city, Rory," said Sarah. "I mean, this building should really be in Greece shouldn't it?"

"I guess that's what our parents wanted us to appreciate when we were here. They kept going on about how fantastic this city is. I'm only now beginning to realise what they meant."

Their conversation was interrupted by the ever-increasing noise of fifty automatic machine guns going off all at once.

"Crikey, Rory. What the heck is that?" Sarah shouted across to her brother, trying to raise her voice above the sudden intrusion of noise that was overhead and threatening to overwhelm them completely.

Rory looked up and laughed. "Look – that's all it is! A helicopter – and it's coming to get you!" he shouted back, teasing her as he stretched an arm out to tickle her.

"Stop it, will you. That really scared me! Cor – the noise really echoes around these buildings doesn't it? And they can't see us anyway so why would they be coming for us?"

"Oh – just keeping you on your toes!"

Camorra and Tasca could see where this was heading. If you can just keep your heads and eyes up for a few more seconds you will soon see the weathervane you need to find, Camorra thought hard to get this through to them. All they needed to do was to carry on looking up and it would come into their full vision.

Meanwhile, Byron had joined Napier, having sorted out his other business. He saw the perfect spoiling opportunity. A lonely black flag on the pole on the building adjacent to the one in question was flapping about with gay abandon and the buffeting of the rotary blades was too much for the stitching on the rope which was the only thing keeping it in its place. With a little help from Byron it had broken free and was fluttering up into the sky.

Tasca had seen the same thing.

"Oh no you don't," she said, as she battled with the wind to try to get the flag to stop being carried upwards. She just knew it was going to get lodged over the pinnacle on top of the building which housed the Turkish Airlines, and so hide the answer to the second clue.

"Rory and Sarah will miss it if it gets as high as that," she reasoned. "They've got to spot it, surely."

But Byron wasn't going to give up either. He sent his strongest waves up to energise the flag. He wasn't concerned about its flight path, just so long as it prevented Rory and Sarah from seeing the vessel on the roof. The flag, with its added energy, was now making a masterly display as if being guided by a prize kite runner as it dipped and soared over the rooftops. Byron looked across at Tasca and smiled. "Let's see who has the strongest guiding power now then, shall we?" he said to himself.

The flag's flapping furore grew so intense that it suddenly roared off into the sky like a Harrier jet. The noise made Rory and Sarah look up and they both noticed the name on the building. Turkish Airlines it said in large, gold capitals above the windows.

Rory then realised the meaning of the clue. Just as Wellington had suggested, another boat weathervane.

"Look Sarah. There it is on top of the Turkish Airlines building. I suppose we have our two ships now."

"That was lucky," Camorra said to Tasca. "Did you feel the force on that flag? Not quite natural if you ask me." She was slightly suspicious of what she had just witnessed but didn't want to alarm her sister unnecessarily; she was just relieved that the children had succeeded in their second mission.

Camorra and Tasca left the jubilant pair, Rory and Sarah, to call up Wellington and make their way back to Hyde Park Corner. They wanted to go and look in on Queen Elizabeth the Queen Mother, just to check how she was shaping up. She was in training as a new Malachi and the girls had promised their mother they would find out how her morning session with Queen Alexandra had gone.

The two sisters were sauntering along The Mall, feeling relieved that the second vessel had been found, when they came across Byron and Napier deep in conversation. "You two again, you are like a couple of bad pennies." Camorra couldn't believe it as they bumped into that pair of reprobates, Byron and his sidekick Napier.

"We've just come to pay our respects to our grand Duke of York, if you must know. There's no crime against it is there?" Byron retorted, but feeling quite smug as at least he hadn't made it easy for the second clue to be solved and also the girls had no idea of his involvement in the kite flying episode either.

"Just keep out of our way in future please," Camorra said as the two girls strode off, heads held high.

"There's no need to be quite so off with them – is there?" her sister asked.

"You don't know what blokes like than can be like. Just take my advice and keep clear of them. Come on, let's go and check on Liz."

Chapter Eighteen

Whilst Rory and Sarah were busy solving their second clue, other Malachis were recommissioning the first vessel. First it had to be retrieved and regenerated, always a tricky task. The Malachis had a number of fleets at their disposal for their different transportation needs. Fleet 2 was an assortment of sailing vessels which were moored in miniature away from human intervention high up on buildings, and were disguised as weathervanes. This way the ships retained their original sense of purpose as they sailed around in the wind but they were kept safe and sound by being tethered to the rooftops of London buildings. Brunel's able assistants, James Cook and Christopher Columbus, were looking forward to their tasks ahead. As Malachis, their sailing skills were rarely called upon and so it was with a great amount of excitement that the team assembled at Brunel's statue.

"Oh good, you're both here," Brunel said, as he answered their knock and let them in. His statue was one of the grandest in London housing several engineering laboratories inside, each fully equipped with the latest research equipment. Brunel hadn't given up his yearning to design the first safe, motorised flying automobile and spent his days trying to perfect his prototypes. Michael Faraday often came across and the two of them spent hours discussing their ideas; occasionally even Newton would join them and provide some valuable objective criticism. The roads were getting far too congested for the simple commuter and Brunel's idea was to create a small commuter-vehicle capable of travelling short distances of about 60 miles a day, all on renewable electricity of course, but able to fly at a distance of approximately 50 metres above ground level and travel at a maximum speed of 25 knots. This way he could have airways dedicated to the private air-commuter pod, with no lorries or other commercial vehicles blocking them up, and so leave the ground level roads to these other users. It would certainly help with rush hour and parking was already taken care of on the flat roof spaces of the office buildings in and around the capital. It made so much sense he was surprised that humans hadn't designed such a vehicle already. His idea was to harness the electro-magnetic energy that was so abundant in a large city, being given off from the wireless electrical waves that enabled Wi-Fi Internet access. This power source would both provide the momentum for the vehicles themselves as well as the guiding power needed to provide fixed transportation channels up in the airways.

It all made perfect sense to Brunel if only he could develop the channels for varying the power. His latest prototype travelled at constant speeds and so that was OK for a Malachi – they could cope with massive accelerations and decelerations – but it would be a complete non-starter for humans. What would be alarming, though, is if these pods just ended up looking (and sounding) like giant flies – perhaps they wouldn't sell that well if they did. It was based partly on this new technology that he had converted Quadriga, the horse-drawn chariot situated on top of the Wellington Arch, into a usable retrieval vehicle for the purpose of transporting the Malachis' fleets around the capital but, of course, this chariot had her original horsepower.

"Right, this is what I want you both to do," he said, as he outlined his plans to his loyal assistants. "You need to get the Liberty first, using Quadriga, and bring her back to me at the Temple Pier. Once I have word from Wellington on the second vessel you will retrieve that too. I'm not sure which one Wellington has allocated yet. The children are solving the clue as we speak. As soon as they do that I will get word to you. Now, with the Liberty you will have to be extremely careful. We haven't used her for a number of years and her mooring could be a bit fragile, and you can't land Quadriga on the roof. You'll have to hover so have plenty of fuel feed with you. Once she's back in the water she'll take a while to re-size and then the others – Captain Scott, Michael Faraday and Ernest Shackleton – will be here to check her out and recommission her. Is that OK?"

"No problem," Cook assured Brunel.

"Here's the key, then. Good luck." Brunel handed over the key to Quadriga and James and Chris set off to the Wellington Arch to start up their flying transporter.

Within ten minutes the men were climbing out of the trapdoor on top of the Arch. The horses were being fed by Herman, the stable lad, who was happy to see the two Malachis.

"Morning Herman, how are you today?" asked James.

"Not bad, sir," Herman replied. "It's just that one of the horses, Gabilan, is slightly lame. I took them out yesterday and she caught a hoof on a cable. It's nothing serious but she's a bit delicate, shall we say. The others are fine – Fador, Ezona and Harod – all in great condition."

"Oh well, I hope that's not going to be a problem. We have a job for you all today, a matter of life and death, and we've all got to be on our top form. You've probably noticed quite a lot of activity going on around here over the last few days? Well we've got a situation and we need to use Quadriga to retrieve two of our vessels. Can you get Quadriga ready for us to go in about five minutes?"

"Leave it with me, sir," replied Herman, more than happy to oblige and get his four beautiful horses ready. Herman always kept the chariot in tip-top condition. He thought it looked better to humans down below if he'd given it its morning polish. There are always hundreds milling around taking photos.

"Oh, and we need to be over-loaded with fuel feed as we've got to do a suspended grab manoeuvre. Better chuck in a few spare bars if you've got any charged up," Chris added.

"I'll check in the storeroom, sir."

James and Chris checked the GPS one more time. They knew the compass points off by heart but always liked to double check. Humans were always adding new roads or knocking them down and they'd been caught out before when Chelsea Harbour was being redeveloped. Roads they had used for years had suddenly gone, or been renamed.

"I'll get the toolkit, James," Chris said, as he knelt down to rummage around in the plinth under the carriage. "We don't know the state of the fixing and Brunel did warn us it could be tricky to get undone."

Soon the chariot was ready and the horses were champing at the bit. Normally, Herman would stay behind on the Arch with the Peace Angel but this time both James and Chris thought it might be useful to have an extra pair of hands, small ones too at that, just in case they needed to do any fiddling around with tiny screws in hard to get at places. With a billowing of dust and a flash of lightning the chariot took off from its mooring and swept round Hyde Park Corner high up into the sky above and was soon making its way across the rooftops of Mayfair to the Liberty store on Argyll Street. Herman was in his usual place driving the horses with the reins, whilst James and Chris were standing up holding onto the front rail of the chariot.

"Steady on there," Herman shouted to the horses. "Not so fast and watch out for the haunted houses in Berkeley Square. We don't want the ghosts sensing us."

A few bumpy minutes later and the chariot rounded a corner and drew up above Argyll Street.

"There she is," James said, as he pointed to the weathervane. "Now Chris, can you and Herman keep the chariot in the floating position? I'll take the tools and release the boat from its fixing."

"Fine. Just tell me when you want to drop down and I'll keep everything steady here. Herman, can you keep a tight hold of those reins. I don't want any of the horses startled – this is a very delicate procedure."

James prepared his harness and checked his tools for the fourth time.

"OK – now!" he gave the command and let himself down gradually as Chris kept the chariot in position above the rooftops. A gusty wind wasn't helping but Chris was doing a grand job keeping the horses and the chariot still. James belayed to the roof and undid the clip from his harness. So far, so good. Now – I've just got to reach over to the top of that gable and unscrew the retaining pole. He was concentrating so hard that he didn't notice the wrench slip out of his pocket and fall to the ground, narrowly missing Jack Taylor as he went into Liberty for a meeting with their Head of Fashion. James stretched his arm out as far as it would go and felt for the nut. Scrambling around he located it at the back of the pole and with his free arm fumbled around in his pocket for the wrench.

"That's odd, I thought I'd brought it with me. What's happened to that now?" James wondered.

Herman had noticed James's predicament and shouted out to

him, "Look – it's down there! It must have fallen out of your pocket. Now what are you going to do?"

What indeed? James thought, grimly.

"There's only one thing for it. You'll have to pass me over another one," he shouted back to Herman. "Have you brought the spare?"

"Yes but I'm not sure how I'm going to get down there?" Herman was just a little bit scared of what was expected of him. He could feel his heart starting to flutter and his hands getting a little bit sweaty, due to the enormous waves of nerves he could feel welling up inside him.

"OK. Steady now. Just get Chris to lower you down on the rope and I'll catch you. Put the wrench in your inside zipped pocket and leave the rest to us."

The wind was really starting to swirl around now and as the rope was lowered it began to twizzle like a ribbon around a maypole.

"I don't think I can do this," Herman cried anxiously. "I never liked carousels."

"Close your eyes and just wait until you touch down," Chris said reassuringly from above, as he lowered the rope down to James.

A sudden gust of wind whipped Herman from out of reach of James's outstretched arms and he went billowing off, swinging like a pendulum way over the pedestrians below on street level.

"Heeeellllpppp meeeeee!" Herman screamed.

"Blast!" James exclaimed. "Chris, take the horses round and retract the rope as you go."

"Righto." Chris said as he yanked at the reins, and with a, "Giddy-up," and a, "Come on my beauties," he was driving the chariot up into the sky whilst he pulled Herman back into the safety of the chariot.

Eventually, calm was restored, Herman's heart rate had returned to normal and the chariot was hovering again above the roof of Liberty. A second go at lowering the young lad onto the rooftop equipped with the spare wrench went without a hitch and soon James was able to detach the vessel from its housing. Carefully the two of them lifted the weathervane into the chariot and then scrambled back inside themselves.

"That was a close run thing," Chris said, feeling most relieved that they had all escaped unscathed and, more to the point, they had retrieved the vessel safe and sound.

"You're telling me. I'll hang on to the boat whilst you drive us back," James said. "Are you OK, Herman? That was probably a bit more than you bargained for wasn't it?"

There was no reply. Herman was too shocked to speak. He just lay in the bottom of the chariot, a quivering wreck, oblivious to everything.

In next to no time they were coming in to land along Victoria Embankment and soon had the boat moored up at Temple Pier. Malachi vessels regenerate themselves once they are in their natural habitat – they just need to be given their size coordinates. Brunel was waiting for them on the pier.

"Any problems?" he asked the trio.

"One or two hiccups but nothing we couldn't handle." Chris offered, as he and James looked at each other with raised eyebrows. "I think the excitement was a bit too much for Herman though."

"What size are you going for, Brunel?" he asked.

"Seeing as the vessels are for children I'm going to go for 50%. That way they will have enough power without being too cumbersome and strong for them to handle. We can always make any slight adjustments nearer the time. Stand clear."

As he gave the command the little weathervane which looked so dainty and delicate suddenly expanded and grew before their eyes with a great flapping of sails and sheets, and a creaking of timbers as it erupted into a perfectly proportioned replica of the old Tudor sailing ship, the Mayflower.

"Right, now we just need to have her checked over and we'll soon have her shipshape. I've also had word from Wellington. Rory and Sarah have found their other ship. They are to use the Turk, on top of the Turkish Airlines building at 125 Pall Mall, so when you've had a short rest you can go and retrieve that one for me."

"Let's make sure we carry our tools safely this time, shall we?" Chris muttered under his breath to James. "Shall I retrieve this one?"

"See if you can do any better, I suppose." James retorted. And with that they went back to the chariot to see if Herman had recovered from his ordeal.

With Herman feeling a bit more human, so to speak, he was persuaded to do it all over again. This time things went much smoother. The horses made their way swiftly to Pall Mall and apart from getting the reins a bit snagged up on the wire globe on which the weathervane was supported, the two Malachis detached it with relative ease. The journey back was not so straightforward, however. James and Chris decided they would take a little detour as they had time to spare and they couldn't resist showing off to their friends. So naturally they rode a few circuits around Trafalgar Square where they tried to grab Nelson's bicorn hat from the top of his statue, much to his annoyance. Then they made for the Duke of York's column just off the Mall, where his sword was their target, and finally they dashed over to Kensington Gardens to pay their respects to Peter Pan, at Herman's request, as he loved re-reading that old favourite by J M Barrie. It was on their journey back to temple Pier that Gabilan's step started to falter.

"Oh no, I think we may have overdone things," James said, as he pulled on the reins to slow the chariot down. "Herman, can you go and check her out? She may need some treatment."

Herman, now almost fully recovered from his earlier ordeal, made his way along the carriage shaft to Gabilan's harness and reached down to feel her fetlock.

"I can feel a slight swelling here so I think we'd better walk them back," he shouted.

The journey which should have taken ten minutes ended up taking a good fifty and by the time they reached the pier Brunel was fuming.

"What the bloody hell have you been up to? What's taken you so long?" he shouted to the three of them.

"Sorry, we took a slight detour and now Gabilan's lameness has got worse. She needs a complete rest," Chris offered as some sort of explanation.

"Well – just get the boat moored up in the water and then take Quadriga back to the Arch. Let Herman take care of her and the horses."

Once he had calmed down, Brunel reconstituted the second vessel and soon there were two fine Tudor galleons of half life-size ready for the Malachis to check them out for their seaworthiness.

***

Captain Scott, Michael Faraday and Ernest Shackleton were at the pier waiting for the boats to be reconstituted. Shackleton, the natural leader, had prepared lists of jobs which he handed over to the others. Once the ships were a more lifelike size they got to work checking every last inch of the vessels. The first thing they had done was to take the ships out into the middle of the Thames and swing the compass on each vessel. Even though both vessels had GPS installed the Malachis still preferred to check the compasses in the traditional manner. They couldn't do this in the usual method of aligning the boat along two waymarkers on each of the four main points of the compass as London was so built-up now that they couldn't see the markers which they used to use. Instead they positioned the boats' own markers first along a north-south line of longitude which lined up Cleopatra's Needle on the Embankment with the end of the Waterloo Millennium Pier on the South Bank, just by the London Eye.

Shackleton made the necessary adjustments to the Liberty's compass and then repeated the exercise along the east-west meridian from Embankment Pier to Festival Pier. They had found that this method gave them a pretty accurate compass, and it would certainly be good enough for the journey the two children would be making in these ships.

Captain Scott was in charge of the exterior of the hulls, the interiors and all the sea-cocks, whilst Faraday looked after the electrics, the heads and emergency equipment leaving Shackleton to attend to the masts, rigging and sails. The masts had special retractable hinges which allowed them to be lowered parallel to the deck so that the ships could pass safely under the bridges along the Thames. Every little detail had to be checked and double checked and nothing could be left to chance. The boats were going to have to transport the children across a time divide and the Malachis needed to make sure that the boats were in their best possible condition.

Scott gave both hulls a thorough scrub and removed layers of moss and other debris which had grown on the wooden panels as they had been moored on the rooftops. The interiors of both ships were in pretty good shape and all the plumbing seemed to be in order. The pipes were allowing water to flow freely where it was supposed to but at the same time preventing it from escaping where it was not wanted. Faraday's job was slightly harder as the electrical systems had all been upgraded on the Malachi fleets a few years ago to bring them up to date with all the new satellite positioning equipment and comms systems. The training courses he'd been on recently helped him greatly and he was soon rewiring sections to make some of the controls more accessible for small hands.

There wasn't such good news, however, when Shackleton came to check out the rigging and the sails. The masts and sails for the Liberty were all intact and mostly useable – there was the odd mizzen sail which was torn but there were enough sails to get them through any waters they might encounter. It was the Turk which had the problems. Not only was the rigging warped and rusty, but the sails were all in shreds. It was as if they had been used by flocks of pigeons for their winter nest linings. As he pulled them out of their sail bags they fell apart in his hands and lay in tatters on the floor.

He called Brunel over to see what he would make of it, "Brunel, come and have a look at this will you?"

"Yes, I was worried about that. This boat hasn't been used in years. Can you use any from the Liberty?"

"I'll try but they use different sail gauges. I would be surprised if they are interchangeable."

Shackleton examined the sails from the Liberty hoping he might be able to use even one sail from this boat but he could see that his fear about the turnbuckles and pins was correct. They were the wrong size. Not only that, the stays and roller furlongs on the Turk were all frayed and frankly dangerous.

"No – it's no good, Brunel. The Turk will need a lot of work done on her to get her back to a serviceable condition and I don't think

140

we've got that much time. What are you going to tell Wellington?"

Brunel was worried. "Good question. I'm not even sure I want to tell him but I know I'll have to bring myself to. It's not as if the children can share the boats either. They need to be separated in case anything awful happens to either one of them on their way. Their parents can't lose both of them in one go."

"Oh, look – he's here. He's come along to check things out for himself," Shackleton said, as he noticed Wellington sauntering along the Embankment.

"Arthur, bad news, I'm afraid. The Turk isn't up to scratch and I can't risk either of the children making the journey they have ahead of them in it. It's just not seaworthy. If we had a couple of weeks we could get her sorted out but my understanding is that we only have one or two days left. You're going to have to sort out one of the other vessels."

"Oh no," Arthur groaned. "I'm not sure how much more the children can cope with. They certainly can't go through another clue-seeking ordeal. I'm going to have to discuss this with Victoria and see if we can make a few compromises. Still, doesn't the Liberty look splendid? She's done well after all this time, hasn't she? Can your team finish what they have to do to her and also get her fully kitted out with provisions, safety equipment – you know the drill – everything that a teenage boy would need to sail back home. Also, I suggest once we've got this present situation sorted out you organise a complete service and repair programme for the Turk before we put her in air-dock. Finally, we need to think about better protection from the elements and those other airborne rogues."

The Liberty was indeed looking resplendent. Her sails had been hoisted and she looked every inch as fantastic as she would have looked back in the 1620s when she was one of the boats which transported all those souls looking for a new future across the Atlantic. Captain Scott, Faraday and Shackleton had done a grand job on her. The Turk looked a little the worse for wear moored up next to her with her battered rigging and tattered sails but at least she was salvageable. The Malachis were rightly proud of their work. The three of them each knew that they had made enormous contributions of their own to world progress and so were more than happy to return to Earth as Malachis knowing that they didn't have to prove anything to anyone any more.

Wellington strode over to his comms ship and called Victoria up on his system. He was a bit apprehensive about telling her the situation with the boats but he knew he didn't have any choice. Better get it over with quickly, he thought.

"Do you want the good news first or the bad?" he started. And without giving Victoria a chance to answer he blurted out, "Good news is the Liberty is in fantastic shape, bad news is that the Turk isn't!" There! He'd said it and now he waited for the news to sink in and for Victoria to realise what it all meant.

"I see," she said in a measured voice. "So you're telling me you have a 50% success rate, is that it?"

"Pretty much," Wellington admitted.

"But actually, Arthur, what you are telling me is possibly better than that isn't it?" She was scarily pleasant and smiling in the manner of her response, which made Wellington feel very uneasy.

Arthur had done the maths and couldn't see what she was getting at.

"Because what this really means is that the children are going to have to find another vessel and supposing that this one is fit for purpose that will then mean that two out of three boats will be OK. I call that a 67% success rate."

Wellington was thoroughly confused. How could having to find another boat improve the success rate?

"Yes – you could say that I suppose, Victoria," he agreed, having to go along with her.

"Well – then you are a complete idiot, aren't you?" she yelled at him so loudly that it felt as if half of London could hear her. "How could you let the fleet get in such a state? Do you realise how little time these children have left? How do you propose to tell them they have to do it all over again? Just answer me that, hey?"

"S... sorry, I'm really sorry," Wellington felt like a quivering wreck and wished he could disappear.

"I'm not going to let those poor children loose in London again. I'm going to get special clearance from the Malachi Chief Council to sort this mess out. I want you to go back to Hyde Park, prepare

142

Rory and Sarah, I don't care how you do it, just make sure they have no more blips on their machines, and wait until you hear from me. Understood?"

"Of course, speak later." And with that Wellington returned to his statue desperately trying to work out what he was going to say to his young charges.

Chapter Nineteen

As he walked into his statue Wellington thought he'd come to the wrong place. There was complete mayhem inside – cushions were strewn all over the floor, cards from the monopoly game littered the table and to top it all there was some awful out of tune singing going on.

> *"It's a long way to Tipperary; it's a long way to go*
> *It's a long way to Tipperary, to the sweetest girl I know!*
> *Goodbye Piccadilly, farewell Leicester Square.*
> *It's a long, long way to Tipperary, but my heart's right there!"*

was being sung at full volume followed by:

> *"I'll take the high road, and you'll take the low road..."*

"Oh, Wellington, we've had a brilliant time. The boys have been teaching us these wonderful songs, one from each of their countries and in return we've taught them the Haka. Just watch Paddy and Jack – they're brilliant at it. They've even got the facial expressions almost perfect – just like Maori warriors," Sarah gasped, as she rushed to tell Wellington all about it. "We're so excited that we've found the boats. Rory and I just can't wait to get back now. But we'll really miss you all. You've been so kind and good to us, part of me doesn't want to go."

Wellington couldn't believe the scene before him. Sarah dissolved into laughter as she fell back on the sofa clutching a cushion, and Rory tried to rugby tackle Bob.

"Men – a word," he shouted sternly to his four soldiers.

Bob looked up and knew immediately from the look on Wellington's face that he was in deep trouble. He extricated himself from Rory's arms and, looking at his colleagues, muttered, "We're for the high jump now lads!" and they followed their commanding officer outside for a 'quiet word'.

"Right! I don't need to hear any excuses and I'm not going to ask you what you all thought was going on back there," Wellington started off his tirade quietly and then built up and up as he got more and more incensed, until he was yelling at them at the top of his voice. "Do you know you could have killed them?!!! I leave you in charge of these poor lost souls and all you can do is behave like a bunch of chimpanzees at a tea party getting high on cola and chocolate buttons!"

Wellington felt his eyes popping and his cheeks burning red-hot with the anger he was felling inside. Get a grip man, he willed himself, you can't put all the blame on them.

"So, you will now go back inside and calm those two children down. And understand only one thing, they are still in great danger!" he ordered.

Wellington left his men to go and sort Rory and Sarah out whilst he tried to compose himself by taking a stroll around the Arch. After about thirty minutes, with his blood pressure returned to normal, he felt able to go back inside and confront the present situation.

"Now listen children, I am all for you enjoying yourselves while you are here with us but you are still in a critical condition in the hospital. If anything were to happen to you on this side it can affect the state of your minds and bodies in your real world. Also..." Wellington hesitated. "Er... I know you have done really well solving the clues but I'm afraid there's some bad news."

The children were now sitting quietly on the sofa, all the disturbance cleared away and their full attention was on what Wellington had to say next.

"Yes, you did well to find the boats but when we checked them out we found that only one is seaworthy."

"We can share, can't we, Sis?" Rory said optimistically, as he looked over at his sister and took hold of her hand.

"Yes, well that's the problem. In this situation you're in I'm afraid you can't. You have to have your own transport otherwise we can't be certain we'll get you back inside your rightful bodies. I mean to say, Rory, you wouldn't want to end up in Sarah's body now would you? It would mean you'd have to listen to that awful pop music of hers."

"Oh, I see what you mean. But does that mean we have to solve another clue? I don't think I can face that again!" Rory and Sarah looked despairingly at Wellington.

"Oh no! You can't be serious" Sarah cried, when Wellington

145

didn't answer. "Please don't make us. That's just so pants! I can't stand this any more; I just want to go home!" She sobbed and sobbed as Rory put a comforting big brotherly arm around her.

"I'm working on that as we speak. I do hope not but I probably won't have an answer for you until the morning."

***

Edith Cavell and Florence Nightingale had followed their instructions from Wellington and had spent most of the day watching over Rory and Sarah as they lay in their intensive care beds. They took it in turns not only to watch over the children but also to make sure the nurses and doctors coped with the pressures, especially after the emergency surgery they had had to carry out on Rory during the night. Florence was very proud of the new Evelina Children's Hospital which had been built as an extension to St Thomas' Hospital. In fact, she had had a fair amount of influence over the design, although not many people knew that. With her 'office' as she liked to call her museum, based on the hospital site she had the perfect excuse for just 'popping across the river' from her statue to check on progress.

She had often sat in on the project meetings and had to admit to 'influencing' decisions using her Malachi skills of persuasion. Naturally, she was only doing this in the best interest of the patients. Sometimes these developers had no idea what was really needed in a modern hospital and by the same token some of the doctors and nurses had difficulties expressing their priorities in a quantifiable way to the developers. She had also seen this as a perfect opportunity to make her amends in kind to her old contemporary, Mary Seacole. Florence had totally underestimated Mary when they were both fighting to save lives in the Crimea. But Florence now saw the error of her ways and used some of Mary's good practice she had gleaned from the rest home which Mary had built out in the Crimea to influence the design of the new ECH here in London. It was fitting also that her statue was being planned and so she could be returning as a Malachi in the near future. Florence was looking forward to a possible training opportunity.

During the building project for the ECH, Florence had found that if she enabled cross-transference of ideas and language at key moments the project went along a lot smoother and there appeared to have been far fewer instances of 'misunderstanding' that so often occurred in big projects like this. Now the hospital was up and running and everyone seemed pleased with the result.

Edith was impressed too and said so to Florence.

"Thanks, Edith. That means a lot to me coming from you. I know you worked in some pretty terrible field conditions. You would just love working here. The colours of the floors are so vibrant; it just doesn't look like a hospital at all. And you know, they've named the floors in a really imaginative way. From the Ocean right up to Sky level. You would have thought they should have an extra floor, though, for us – something like Spirit level perhaps."

Edith groaned. "That's not funny, Florence!"

"Even though it's our job to keep things on an even keel?" Florence continued.

"Stop it!" cried Edith.

And so they had spent their day making sure Rory and Sarah got the best possible treatment whilst Queen Anne and Gandhi comforted Mike and Liz as they spent their tortured time at the bedsides of their beloved children.

It was all seemingly horribly boring, Sarah's condition had hardly changed since she had been admitted but that was a good thing. With her situation, no change was good news. At least it meant her systems were stable and functioning regularly. The nurses had had to make no change to her oxygen levels or her temperature, and the levels of fluid and sugars administered were also stable. It was Rory who was causing some concern, although now the medics thought he was stable again and should be making some progress with the drain in place.

Florence and Edith were just on their way out to give Wellington an up-to-date status report when the machines suddenly started going mad. It was Rory. There was a high pitched alarm coming from his bed and a red line going straight across the monitor.

"Emergency on bed 5," Sister Bridge shouted. "Get everyone

here NOW, I need a crash team! Come on Rory – don't do this to me, you've got to keep fighting, don't give up on me!"

There was mayhem around Rory's bed. Doctors and nurses appeared from every doorway and there were a thousand instructions being shouted all at once. The bed looked as though it was a free for all, a bun fight where the winner was the one who could get closest to the body.

Edith and Florence rushed back to see what they could do to help.

"I know this is a long shot, Florence, but why don't we try to get into Rory's brainwaves? I realise that his brain is a touch scrambled but if we both use all our powers of deliverance and really focus you never know. If even one tiny photon gets through to him it might be enough to bring him back from the edge."

"Good idea. Let's go for it." And so the two of them focused all their Malachi energies on Rory whilst the medics used their medical skills to resuscitate him.

Over in Wellington's statue there was a similar atmosphere of desperation.

"I don't know about you, Sarah, but I'm really fed up with this place now. I mean I just want to stop and go to sleep and wake up back home in our Wellington." Rory was really tired and had had enough of his stay in Wellington's statue.

"No Rory. Now come on, you've got to keep going." Sarah did everything she could to persuade him not to give up. "You know what Wellington said. We have got to get back into our bodies otherwise we'll never get home. We've got to find one more boat. We can do that. I can help you." She was really worried that Rory would give up.

"Oh, I dunno. I'm just sooo tired." Rory was lying flat out on his bed trying to get into a comfortable position to get to sleep. "And my head hurts so much..."

Sister Bridge repeated her command to Rory, "Come on, Rory, don't give up on me!"

"No Rory!" Sarah shouted at him. She was really worried now and started shaking him by the shoulders. "No! Don't do this to me Rory. You can't leave me, what will I do without you?" she wailed. "Think about Mum and Dad, and what about all our friends back in the real Wellington?"

Another burst from the defibrillator but still the line was flat. "Come on team, we have to try again!" Sister Bridge shouted.

"Come on Rory!" begged Sarah.

"What's all this then?" Jock said, as he poked his head around their door.

"It's Rory – he's giving up. You have to talk to him!"

"Come on, little fella," Jock said, sitting down on the edge of Rory's bed. "You can't give up now. I thought you were made of proper stuff not this weak namby-pamby 'I just can't take any more' stuff? Hey? Where's the soldier in you? You know if the four of us had given up like you we wouldn't be here now. You should have seen what we went through on the battlefields of Waterloo!"

"Yes, well it was different then," Rory mumbled.

Dr Arnold arrived to assist. Sister Bridge shouted, "Still nothing. Try increasing the output!"

"Nothing's different. If you want something in this life you have to go out and get it. And I want you and Sarah fit and well again and back where you belong. I don't want you hanging around here any more. Come on, I bet you an ice cream I can beat you at whist!"

"You're rubbish at whist. I've never seen anyone so bad, even Sarah's better than you. There's no way you can beat me." That seemed to get to the heart of Rory and it seemed to Sarah as though Rory might be coming round.

"Come on Rory," she pleaded with him, *"just give it another go, please, for my sake?"*

"Oh, OK," Rory replied wearily. "I can't let Jock think he can beat me at cards, now can I?"

"That's more like it, mate," said Jock, heaving a huge sigh of relief. "I'll get the cards, you can deal."

A beep was heard and a wavy line appeared on the output monitor.

"I think we've got some output," Sister Bridge declared. "Yes, we're getting something. Well done everybody. Right, he's back with us. I want Rory on five minute obs from now on."

Everyone on Forest had been holding their breath for the last ten minutes and it seemed they all sighed at the same time. Phew! The building itself appeared to exhale.

"That was close, Florence," Edith said. "Let's go and update Wellington now, I think Rory's stabilised."

Chapter Twenty

That night all was peaceful. In ECH all eyes were on Rory and Sarah, everyone was praying and willing them to remain stable and to make a full recovery. In Wellington's home the children slept soundly with the four soldiers taking it in turns to be on watch.

By morning Rory was feeling a lot more optimistic. He'd had a weird dream about playing rugby for the All Blacks where he was the ball and was being tossed from player to player before being kicked over the posts for a drop goal and had woken up determined that he and Sarah would make it back to their own dimension.

Victoria was also in a good mood. She'd had word from the MCC who had given the children special dispensation and they had decreed that they didn't need to solve the third clue themselves. Wellington was both delighted and relieved with this news. He could keep Rory and Sarah in his home under the watchful eyes of his men whilst Camorra and Tasca retrieved the other vessel. Then, if all went according to plan, the children could be ready to return tomorrow. At last he could see light at the end of this dark and dingy tunnel in which the children had found themselves.

There was one potential hazard though and that was that, as part of the dispensation in allowing two Malachis to retrieve the third vessel, the Marble pet had to be used. Wellington wasn't happy with this but he had no choice. He'd had a tense conversation with Boudicca as he needed to use her two young girls for this task as they were the lightest and most nimble. It would be a dangerous mission as Marble could be quite fiery when roused but Wellington had every confidence in the young Iceni girls. They had proved their mettle so far in this contest, showing determination and courage. Boudicca was naturally nervous but at the same time proud that her girls had been chosen and confident that they would succeed. She had to trust them to do the right thing, especially Camorra, and she knew she would take good care of her younger sister on the mission. Naturally the girls were thrilled to be asked and had had an early morning briefing from David Livingstone on how to deal

151

with Marble. In his day he had come across many strange, untamed beasts during his travels and explorations in Africa and was a dab hand at taming and training them.

After a healthy breakfast, Camorra and Tasca made their way along the Embankment. Their first port of call was to check out the location of the third vessel and its mooring point on the River Thames and then go and harness Marble. Wellington would meet them at the mooring when he would give them the special bridle and other equipment they would need for the ride. They were chatting away feeling slightly apprehensive but enjoying the responsibility which lay on their young shoulders.

"I still can't get over the fact that Wellington has asked us to do this. I mean it's a real honour isn't it?" Tasca asked Camorra.

"Yes and it feels as though the whole Malachi world is on our shoulders. I must admit to being a little nervous but I also think this is our big chance to prove to the others that we are up to the mark."

"I just want to do what we can to help Rory and Sarah return to their world. They do seem lovely kids and their parents must be in an awful state," Tasca added. "How are you feeling about Marble? Did you believe everything they said about him?"

Camorra was reassuring, "Just do what I say. I've been going through it all in my mind and we'll be fine."

They had reached Temple Place by now and as they went past the cabmen's shelter Camorra thought she recognised the dog tied by its lead to the railing. She stopped suddenly.

"Uh, Tasca, there's something I've just got to check out round here. Look, you go on ahead and find the right address. I'll catch you up in a sec." Camorra was not sure what it meant but thought she had better make sure before they went on, but under no circumstances did she want to alarm her younger sister.

"Oh – OK – if you're sure. Is anything the matter?" Tasca was a bit put out. What was Camorra keeping from her?

"No – honestly everything's OK. I just want to visit a statue. Mum asked if I would if we had time." Phew – had she got away with that as an excuse? It would have to do for now. She had to investigate this on her own and she didn't want Tasca's nerves being increased any more than they already were.

She could have sworn the dog was Boatswain, which meant only one thing – Byron was inside. She'd already had her suspicions aroused yesterday and now, as she thought about it, she wondered what he had been doing the other day when he was hanging around the Wellington Arch. I bet he's up to no good, she thought, and his sidekick, Napier. They are like a couple of bad pennies.

She waited until Tasca had walked on and then she crept forward to the shelter and crouched down under the open hatchway. Slowly she reached up so she could just see through into the inside. Yes! She had been right. There were the two of them tucking into plates of roast beef and Yorkshire pudding.

"Your straws were hilarious Charles! That really did hold them up and then when you got them thinking of all that revolting greasy stuff – ingenious!" Byron chuckled.

"Yes – well, I know I need the practice but at least I did what you asked of me, George."

"So that's why it took Rory and Sarah so long to get the first part of the clue," Camorra said to herself, as what the two men were saying sank in. But there was more.

"Your flag flying skills are quite remarkable. Where did you learn those?" Napier asked Byron.

So that was Byron! Camorra couldn't believe what she was hearing, but it was all making sense now. But why? What's his problem? I'll see if I can learn any more.

"Come on Sis, what's taking you so long?" Tasca was shouting from further up Temple Place.

Damn it, Camorra thought, I'd better go otherwise Tasca will begin to get suspicious. I'll have to try to find another opportunity to get to the bottom of Napier and Byron's little activities. "Coming!" and she hurried to join her sister outside 2 Temple Place.

"Look – there's the vessel. Up on that wrought iron stand. Isn't it beautiful?" They looked up in pure wonderment. What a beautiful weathervane it was, all gold and glistening in the bright sunshine.

"So this is what we need to retrieve and then we need to lower it into the water just along here," Camorra showed Tasca where the vessel had to be positioned. "Now, let's find Wellington, get the gear and then walk up here onto Fleet Street to find Marble."

"Looks straightforward so far. Let's just hope Marble hasn't had too many fried eggs for breakfast - we don't want him too fired up."

Wellington was there to meet them with an armful of equipment. "Morning girls. How are you both feeling?" he asked.

"Slightly nervous but on the whole OK," Camorra replied, reassuringly. "At least it's only a short ride on Marble. He'll hardly realise what's happened before he'll be back on his perch."

"Let's hope you're right, Camorra," Wellington said, with some trepidation in his voice. "If the worst happens I just want you to bail out – understood? I don't want lives being risked unnecessarily. The children aren't at the end of the road just yet."

"Understood," both girls replied in unison.

Camorra was about to mention something of her misgivings about Byron to Wellington but Brunel appeared and interrupted her train of thought.

"Got everything you need, you two?" he asked.

"Oh, yes thanks Brunel, we're just off" and with that the girls strode off up Essex Street to find Marble.

***

As they approached the Temple Bar, on Fleet Street, they could see that Marble was still sleepy, which was encouraging.

"Follow me Tasca and do exactly what I say," Camorra whispered to her sister, giving her a share of the equipment to carry.

They climbed up the monument to the top of Marble's perch.

"There, there," Camorra said soothingly to Marble, as she stroked his neck. "We have a little job for you today, my sweet," and she whispered the instructions into the dragon's ear making sure all the words went safely inside and none escaped, in the exact manner in which she had been instructed by Livingstone.

"Let's get the saddle and bridle on him and then we can get going," she instructed Tasca.

The two of them got to work trying to soothe Marble as much as possible and soon they were ready to go.

"Up you get, Tasca. I'll be in front with the reins and I want you to take this backpack to use to carry the vessel. Don't worry, it's not that heavy."

Camorra gave the mystical instructions to Marble and slowly Marble's wings started flapping. Tasca could feel a tremendous surge of wind as they got faster and faster and then they were off, flying high above the City, with great roars of fire being exuded from Marble's gaping jaws. It was a wonder the rooftops didn't catch fire. As Camorra led Marble round to their target building they flew over Inner Temple and the oasis of calm and tranquillity, the Inner Temple Gardens. Camorra looked down with amazement at the beautiful sanctuary laid out beneath her. But just at the same time Marble decided he wanted to land there and he started to descend lower and lower in ever decreasing circles.

"Oh no you don't!" Camorra urged. "Come on Marble – we're not landing here!" She started pulling on the reins and digging her heels into his sides to encourage him to ascend.

"I think he's seen Pegasus, down there behind the lilac tree," Tasca shouted from behind. She thought she could see the winged horse grazing in the corner of the garden.

"This was what Livingstone warned could happen. Can you remember what we have to do if he did this, Tasca?" Camorra shouted back to her sister, panicking now as she desperately tried to get Marble back on his proper flight path.

"Here, he gave us these special sugar lumps. Can you reach forward and pop one in his mouth?" Tasca pulled a handful of large, multi-coloured sugar crystals from her pocket and passed them to her sister. Camorra knotted the reins and looped them over the saddle to keep them in place. Letting go of the reins, she edged herself forward gripping Marble's neck as tightly as she could with her knees and, using his scales for grip, reached up towards his gaping mouth. He was getting quite agitated now, both at the sight of Pegasus, his old friend, and the fact that he was being prevented from going where he wanted to. He started to belch out great billows of smoke and flames from his jaws. The noise he was making was deafening and it was so hot Camorra had to retract her arm as she felt the burning vapours scorch her flesh.

"It's no good," she cried. "I can't get anywhere near his jaws. It's just too hot!"

"You've got to try one more time, Camorra," her sister urged her.

Camorra reached out again but to no avail. Marble was fuming and there was no way he would allow Camorra to get close to his mouth.

"There's one thing I could try," Camorra said. She had spotted a birdbath along one of the herbaceous borders and had an idea.

"I'm going to throw some of these sugar lumps into the water in that birdbath down there and then try to fly Marble over it. He is getting so hot that the minute he senses the water I'm hoping he'll make a beeline for it and drink what's in there without even noticing the taste. I think that's the best we can hope for," she shouted back to Tasca.

"That sounds like a great idea. Let's try it," Tasca said, feeling relieved that one of them had come up with a plan.

Marble was flying round and round, lower and lower and Camorra took aim with a couple of lumps.

"Damn it – missed. I'm going to have to try on the next time around."

They were getting worryingly close to the ground now and the flames coming from Marble's mouth were singeing the trees. Tasca was getting really nervous but was trying hard not to show it.

They flew round again and this time, bingo, the lumps flew right inside and straightaway they started to fizz and splutter dissolving in the murky water. Almost immediately Camorra felt Marble beginning to relax and she sensed he had smelt the water. "Yes, come on, just take a sip and you'll be fine," she willed him.

Marble started nodding his head and abruptly stretched out his long tongue into the birdbath. He sucked up the entire contents and straight away he started to cool down, his flames receded and he began responding to Camorra's commands.

"You had a bit of a fright there, didn't you, my lovely?" Camorra stroked his neck as they began their ascent. She eased herself back in the saddle and took up the reins again feeling mightily relieved that disaster hadn't struck.

"Cor – I really thought he'd lost his marbles then," Camorra joked.

"Not funny, Sis. I was seriously frightened back there. Can we get on with the mission now, please?" said Tasca, her nerves beginning to recede.

Camorra eased Marble back onto the correct flight path and they rode over the rooftops to 2 Temple Place where they landed on the flat roof containing the flagpoles and the weathervane housing.

"It's supposed to unclip really easily," Camorra said hopefully. After what they had just been through she didn't fancy any more hiccups on this mission.

"There we go," she said, as she quickly released the weathervane from its support and handed it over to Tasca.

"Please, whatever you do, don't drop it. Keep it safe. We only have to drop down onto the Embankment and then we're done," Camorra instructed.

Marble seemed to be his old self now and as a treat Camorra let him fly over to the Lady Henry Somerset statue just further along Temple Place so that he could have another refreshing drink of fresh water from the birdbath she was holding up. He gurgled up all the water in the bowl and seemed much more content. Soon they were touching down in front of Wellington, Brunel and Livingstone who had been anxiously waiting for them on the Temple Pier.

"Well done, girls, excellent job. We lost contact with you over Inner Temple but then saw that everything seemed to be OK and you were able to remove the vessel quite easily from its mooring. Now, once you dismount we can let Marble go. He deserves a free flight after all that he has been through and he'll be quite safe on his own over the City. He'll make his own way back to his perch at nightfall."

Camorra and Tasca almost fell out of the saddle, they were so relieved to get back to ground level and hand the vessel over to Brunel.

"Thanks. I'll take over with this little beauty now." Brunel carefully took the vessel out of the bag and carried it off to immerse it in the River Thames where he had his team of engineers ready to reconstruct it for Rory and Sarah.

***

The two girls started walking back along Temple Place where they bumped into Byron and Napier coming out of the shelter.

"Oh, hi you two", Tasca said cheerily. She was still feeling on a high at having achieved their mission and almost blurted out what they had been doing.

"You should have seen us a few minutes ago..." she started.

Camorra interrupted her trying to change the subject. "Just look at this little fella." She bent down to stroke Boatswain.

"Oh yes, so what have you two been up to then?" Byron asked, dying to know if they had anything to do with what Wellington was involved in.

"Oh nothing," Camorra said sternly, glaring at her sister. "We've just been for a stroll, haven't we Tasca?" She looked at Tasca with such severity, Tasca was completely taken aback.

What have I said now, she thought to herself. "Oh yes – that's right, Sis" she replied hesitantly, but then realised that Camorra didn't want to reveal anything of what they had been doing that morning.

"Look, ladies, we were wondering if we could talk to your mother about something. We were going to invite you all to join us for a coffee or a milkshake, what do you think?" Byron said ingratiatingly.

Tasca was just about to say what a lovely idea that was when she was interrupted again by her sister, who thought it was a rather strange invitation.

"Oh, thanks but I don't really think so."

Byron hated being turned down and this only made him more determined.

"Oh, come now, my dear, what harm is there in you, your sister and your lovely mother accompanying myself and my loyal friend, Charles here, to a light refreshment at that little café along the river? You know the one I mean? The one that's just opened. They

158

do lovely frappés and iced teas. I'm sure you would find something to delight your taste buds."

Camorra thought about it a bit more. It might not be a bad idea, after all. Perhaps she would be able to tease something out of the old weasel, like what his motives were yesterday.

"Look – I tell you what. We need to pop home for a while, and we just need to check this with Mum, of course. Let's meet there later this afternoon, shall we say around 5 o'clock?"

Byron smiled. "Excellent – we'll see you all then. Ta-ta for now."

Camorra and Tasca let the two men and the dog walk on, before continuing themselves.

"What's the matter with you?" Tasca asked, feeling rather annoyed that her sister had curtailed the conversation.

"Let's just say they're not all that they appear to be. They're up to something I'm sure of it. I just don't know what it is yet. But I need to think about a few things first. We've agreed to meet up with them later haven't we, as long as Mum can make it? I may ask some strange questions but you will just have to trust me. Just go along with me, will you?" Camorra was already thinking of various suspicious incidents with the two men that she had witnessed over the last few days. Things certainly weren't adding up as far as they were concerned and she was determined to get to the bottom of things.

"Sure thing, Sis," Tasca replied and the two girls made their way back to Westminster Bridge.

Chapter Twenty One

Wellington stayed on at the pier to oversee the recommissioning of the Temple. Once she was in the water Brunel again reconstituted her to half-size. She was a replica of Columbus's flagship the Santa Maria in which he sailed on his maiden voyage across the Atlantic and she was in beautiful condition. Her location on the rooftop of 2 Temple Place was tucked away and quite secluded and so she was hardly bothered by nimble-clawed pigeons on the lookout for good quality nest-building materials.

Brunel's team of Malachis had checked her out thoroughly and it was with a great deal of relief that he declared that she would be ready to set sail tomorrow. Queen Anne had organised hampers from Fortnum's to be delivered first thing in the morning to provide Rory and Sarah with refreshments for their journey. Several Malachis had wandered over to the Embankment to see the final preparations take place. Commissioning Fleet 2 was a rare event for them and they were all keen to witness it, especially considering it was for a category 4 cross-over – even rarer for them. Columbus looked on with tears in his eyes – he remembered so well that first voyage when he had sailed in the little carrack. He chuckled to himself at the memory of how he had thought they were sailing to the far east of the Earth and hadn't realised there was a huge land mass in the way! Nowadays, virtually every square inch of the planet is known about, recorded on digital storage and can be accessed from anywhere – quite remarkable.

At last both ships were ready and James Cook entered the coordinates of the Evelina Children's Hospital into the GPS system. The children's last task was to sail the ships from the Temple Pier to the other side of the river, upstream and land just south-west of Westminster Bridge. From there they would have to get themselves into PICU and back into their own bodies so that they could return to their own dimension. They weren't out of trouble yet. Wellington appreciated that there were still lots of hazards on the perilous journey but at least he could see light at the end of the tunnel and he sincerely hoped that by this time tomorrow the children would have done so too.

Columbus and Brunel were just giving both boats a final going over.

"I'm so thrilled that Sarah will be sailing in my little *Santa Maria*, or rather the *Temple*, as she's called nowadays. I had such a good voyage in her in my day, I know she will look after Sarah and get her safely across to the other side. Look – I've brought a little present that I want Sarah to have," Columbus confided to Brunel. "Do you think she'll appreciate it?"

Columbus opened his hand and there nestling in his palm was the most perfect little wooden model of the *Santa Maria* Brunel had ever seen.

"Gosh, that's lovely, Chris. Did you make it?"

"Well – I did most of it, but Baden-Powell helped me do the really intricate bits. I've started making these just to pass the time really, what do you think?"

"I mean it – it's beautiful. She'll love it. Why don't you leave it on the captain's chair? That way she'll be bound to see it?"

"Good idea."

"We have had a strange few days, haven't we? Let's just hope the children get back to their own dimension and are reunited with their parents. They must be so worried," Brunel pondered.

Wellington gathered everyone round him as he made a final announcement.

"I just want to say a big thank you to everyone who has helped out with Sarah and Rory. It's not been easy but I think we're almost there. The children need to get back into their own bodies which are in the Paediatric Intensive Care Unit at the Evelina Children's Hospital just over the river at St Thomas' and as long as the wind is right tomorrow they're scheduled to set sail in the morning. Now I want you all to go home, get a good night's sleep and then we'll see them off from here around 11 o'clock tomorrow morning. Does anyone have any questions?"

Byron was about to ask something but then thought better of it and decided to keep quiet.

"No? OK then – see you all tomorrow."

***

When they heard the news, Rory and Sarah were over the moon that another boat had been prepared. Wellington gave them their instructions, spelling out how they should sail the boats, where to land them and what to do once they reached the other side of the Thames. This was the last stage of their adventure and the most dangerous. Whilst they were on the water they would be on their own and Wellington's boys gave them all sorts of advice as to how to keep the sails trim, watching out for other ships and river users, and the most important thing – how to lower the masts to allow the ships to sail under the bridges. After a while it was too much to take in.

Sarah said, "Oh, I don't think I can remember anything else. I'll just have to use my initiative if I need to."

"You'll be fine," Wellington said, encouragingly.

"I wonder what state our real bodies are in?" Rory asked. "Actually, now I don't care if we're not going to make a full recovery. I really just want to get back to Mum and Dad now. It's been something of an adventure, I suppose, being here with you and the boys, Wellington, but it's not our real place is it? I'm really worried about Mum and Dad too. I don't want them worrying about us anymore. They said it would be a trip of a lifetime and they were right, weren't they Sarah?"

"Yeah, too right!" she said, nodding in agreement. "And I'm desperate for a change of clothes!" They'd been in virtually the same clothes since the accident. Owen had been good to them as he'd managed to give the garments a wash a couple of times and had lent them some old shirts and trousers, all of which swamped them of course.

"The reports from the hospital are encouraging; as long as you return tomorrow you've every chance of making a full recovery." Wellington didn't want to alarm them by adding that if they didn't make it back tomorrow then their chances would diminish quite rapidly. He would keep that particular piece of information to himself and worry about that if it came to it.

162

"Now, we'll just have a quiet last evening here as you have to have lots of rest for what's ahead of you tomorrow. So, definitely no singing!"

***

Camorra and Tasca flung the door open and called out, "Mum, we're back!"

"Oh, thank goodness for that," Boudicca replied, running to greet them with her arms out wide. She enveloped them both in an enormous hug. She hadn't had the nerve to join the other Malachis at Temple Pier and had spent the morning trying to occupy herself around the house to keep her mind off thinking of all the things that could possibly have gone wrong.

"Steady on Mum, it wasn't that bad," Tasca said, laughing.

"No. It could have been but it was fine. We had the most amazing ride on Marble. That was quite an experience, a bit hairy but we got the boat safely removed and delivered to Brunel. Have you ever seen one reconstituted? It was incredible the way it just got bigger and bigger until Brunel signalled for it to stop," Camorra explained, trying to keep the worst bits from her mother.

"Oh, and Byron wants to talk to you about something," Tasca added.

"Oh? What could he want with me?" Boudicca asked, puzzled.

"He didn't say but we've agreed to meet in that new café just along the Embankment at 5 o'clock. Hope that's OK with you. We can all go, can't we?" Camorra said.

"Well, it's not that convenient but I suppose I'd better go and see what he wants," Boudicca sighed, feeling annoyed that her evening's plans would have to be rearranged to suit the demands of a Malachi who isn't even in her zone! She had been looking forward to a quiet evening after the last few days' events. What with all the pre-contest preparations, the first two days of the contest itself, which had taken a lot of strength out of her, and then the business with the lost children, she was feeling quite exhausted. Although the contest had been put on hold the worries she had had over the last two days concerning her daughters had really stressed her out. Normally she was more than happy for the girls to get involved in Malachi business but for some reason this time it had just got a bit too much for her. Am I losing it, she thought to herself? Maybe my Malachi powers are on the wane, after all I am, in human years, quite a fair age now, the oldest of all of us. Maybe I should relinquish my position and retreat? And now, to cap it all I have to go and meet that old Casanova, Byron. Honestly, he'd better not be thinking of swapping zones, I don't think I could put up with his romantic musings. Maybe he wants to talk to me about some training, after all he didn't do so well in the pre-contest zone assessments? Boudicca became lost in her own thoughts until she was brought out of her reverie by Tasca shouting, "Hey, Mum are you ready? We should be going now?"

Boudicca laughed as she got up off the sofa, "Wow, Tas you've changed your tune. It's normally me doing the chivvying around here. What's got into you?" and she grabbed her jacket and put on her sandals, wondering why her younger daughter was so keen to get going.

"Nothing," Tasca said defensively. "I just don't think we should be late that's all."

"Oh yes?" said Camorra, suggestively. "I think I know why you're in such a hurry."

"Oh shut up, why don't you? You don't know anything!" And with that, Tasca flounced out of the door and left her mother and sister to catch up.

"What's got into her?" Boudicca asked.

"Oh, I think it's something Napier might have said, but I could be wrong."

"Napier? What's he got to do with this?"

"Oh, didn't we mention it? He's going to be there with Byron. Honestly Mum, you should see the pair of them. They're like Siamese twins. They can't go anywhere alone, they're always together."

"That's strange. Oh well – let's go and see what this is all about shall we, the sooner we get this over with the sooner we can get on with supper."

After a pleasant stroll in the late afternoon sun along the Embankment the three Iceni women found themselves walking into the new café where, as expected, Byron and Napier were already waiting for them.

"Well, good afternoon ladies!" Byron greeted them warmly.

"Hello you two, now I don't mean to be rude but I was hoping we could make this quick as I have a pile of ironing to do tonight." Boudicca groaned inwardly. Oh dear, that sounded awful – it's worse than saying I've got to wash my hair, she thought.

"Well, we won't keep you any longer than we have to, will we Charles?" Byron looked at Napier hoping for some support.

"No... of course not," he muttered.

"So, ladies, what can I get you?"

The five of them placed their orders and there followed a brief exchange of views about the contest and how disappointing it was that it had been put on hold.

"Look, can we just cut to the chase? What was it you wanted to discuss with me, George?" Boudicca demanded.

"Well – it was Charles really, he wants to talk to you about your horses and if there's any chance of riding them." And at that Byron left Napier to talk to Boudicca to see if he could have some riding lessons from her while he turned to chat to Camorra and Tasca.

Camorra saw her opportunity. "So Byron, what have you been doing whilst the contest has been going on?"

"Oh, this and that. You know me," Byron said, desperately trying to think of a good story to put her off the scent.

"You know about the two children do you?" Camorra asked abruptly.

"Yes – I was there this afternoon, at the pier when Wellington mentioned about them being in the Evelina."

"Poor things. It must be awful for them, don't you think?" Camorra said.

"I suppose so, but they've been well looked after," Byron added.

"What do you mean by that?" Camorra demanded.

Damn it, Byron thought, what have I given away now? "Oh nothing, only that I thought I saw them with Wellington the other day."

"Oh did you? What were you doing then?" Camorra insisted.

"Oh, just walking, you know, taking Boatswain for a walk." Byron tried to sound innocent but it wasn't fooling Camorra.

"You haven't been spying on them have you?"

Byron laughed awkwardly. "No, why would I be doing that?"

"It's just that we were following the children yesterday and you know what - I had the strangest feeling we weren't the only Malachis around. Do you ever get those feelings?" Camorra was determined to tease it out of Byron, but she had to lead him very carefully into her trap.

"Oh? What were you doing down Haymarket yesterday?" Byron demanded, trying to get on to the offensive.

"Who said anything about Haymarket, George?" Camorra said accusingly, knowing that he had just made a big blunder.

"You did, didn't you? Just then?" Byron stuttered, realising what he had done.

"No! I never mentioned where we were." She had him and they both knew it.

Camorra smiled. "So – are you going to admit it? It was you then, wasn't it, trying to interfere with the children's minds?"

Byron looked embarrassed and just stared at his coffee in front of him.

Tasca had remained silent throughout all this exchange, feeling thoroughly confused to start with, just as her sister had warned her she might feel when they were discussing this encounter earlier that afternoon. But now it was gradually becoming clear. What a scoundrel Byron is, she thought. He hasn't changed at all after all these years as a Malachi. He's still mad, bad and dangerous to know, as someone once said about him.

"Come on, George, you've virtually admitted it so why don't you tell us why? What have those poor children done to you?" Camorra wasn't going to let him off the hook now that she had him.

Again Byron just stared down in front of him.

"Look – if you tell us why, no-one else need know. They've got their transport sorted now and they're going to go back to their own dimension tomorrow so there's no harm done." Camorra was desperately trying to wheedle his motives out of him but it was like pulling teeth.

"Look – I can see Mum and Napier have nearly finished their conversation so do you want me to tell Mum what's going on?" This was her last attempt and she had her fingers crossed hoping it would force him to tell her.

"Oh, for heaven's sake," Byron said, despairingly. "Look, I have nothing against those children do I, how could I? No, it's that awful Wellington. I'm afraid I still can't forgive him even after all these years and I can't stand having to sit on my corner and look over to his fantastic statute. And it's not fair that I didn't get through the assessment for the contest. I should be taking part in it and it wasn't just me yesterday in Haymarket – Napier was there too," he blurted out.

"Oh is that all?" Camorra said, feeling wise well beyond her tender Earth years. "Don't you realise that all those feelings have to be left behind if you want to be a fully-fledged Malachi? That's probably what impeded you in your pre-contest training. It's all those negative feelings that are interfering with your abilities to use your strengths properly."

"Yes – well, you might be right," Byron admitted, hesitantly.

"Look, I won't mention anything to Mum, nor will Tasca," and she looked across to her sister. "But you really must stop all this and get over it, and you shouldn't have involved Napier in your troubles either."

"OK – I suppose so."

And at that moment Boudicca and Napier re-joined them, having agreed some times when Boudicca would take Napier out riding.

"You know, having had to ride in my role as counter for the last couple of days has renewed my enthusiasm for the equine sport, and now I'm looking forward to it even more," Napier said, beaming at Boudicca. He looked across at Byron hoping to get some friendly support but all he got was a scowl.

"Right, Charles – I'm off. You can stay here if you want," and Byron stood up abruptly and stormed out of the café.

"What's the matter with him?" Boudicca asked.

"Oh – we were just talking about the contest and then about those poor children," Camorra said, glaring at Napier.

Napier looked embarrassed. Had they been rumbled? But it really wasn't his fault, he thought, as he tried to justify his own actions. Byron made me do it, and that's what he would say in his defence, he decided.

"Well, I don't know about anyone else, but I'm going; busy day tomorrow. Coming girls?" Boudicca got up and, as a final farewell, said, "See you on Saturday, Charles, and we'll try some easy jumps."

As the three were all on their way out Camorra hesitated for a minute and under her breath muttered to Napier, "He's admitted trying to hinder the children in their quests so if I were you I'd keep out of his way. We'll tell Victoria if there's any more stuff going on."

Napier took the warning as she had intended and rather embarrassingly whispered back, "I understand."

Camorra was really pleased with herself that she had got Byron to admit to what he'd been doing. She wasn't entirely sure of his motives and she couldn't see what hold Byron had over Napier but they both seemed to have got her message. Hopefully this will be an end to it, and she walked home chatting with her sister and mother about the differences between lattes, frappés, espressos and Americanos and a whole host of other delicacies served up at the new café.

***

Victoria called Wellington up on the quadrisensor. She had been thinking about the safety of Rory and Sarah and, even though Wellington and his boys had done a good job over the last few days and looked after the two children really well, she felt that they were slightly vulnerable and exposed over in Hyde Park. She wanted them closer and in a place where security would be much tighter. Their safety was the most important thing to her now. They had all come this far with them and the last thing she needed was anything to go wrong at the eleventh hour. All the Malachis involved had done a tremendous job, in particular Camorra and Tasca. She had been told about their escapade on Marble and felt they deserved a special award for their bravery in retrieving the *Santa Maria*. She also couldn't face the MCC if there were to be any mishaps.

"Arthur – look, I know it's getting late but I'm not happy about the children spending their last night over in the Park. I want you to bring them to the Welly right away. I've already spoken to them on board and they have a full watch for night-time security, and being right on the pier it'll mean they won't have to travel in the morning. What do you think?"

Wellington thought about it and realised that as usual Victoria was right. The boys wouldn't like it but they would understand. They would just have to say their goodbyes now, instead of in the morning. He couldn't abandon the children at this hour.

"You're right, of course, but I'll stay with them if that's OK?"

"Oh yes – I was expecting you to say that. Bring them over on Copenhagen, I've got bunks sorted for you all already."

Wellington ended the transmission and thought about what Victoria had said. As a precaution, to increase security, he decided not to say too much to his men but to give them the evening off. He suggested they go to the pub and that they should say their goodbyes now to Rory and Sarah.

"Thanks for everything," Sarah said. "I'll never forget you all."

"Same here," Rory added. "I'm going to tell all my friends the wonderful stories you've told us. They'll never believe me though!"

After hugs all round, Wellington broke the news to Rory and Sarah that they would be staying the night on the Welly. They didn't mind, they were quite prepared now to do anything as long as it meant that they had a better chance of returning to their normal dimension.

"Are you ready to go?" Wellington asked.

"I guess so," the pair of them said, resignedly.

They crept out of the portal and climbed up on Copenhagen's back with the help of Wellington. Soon they were walking up the gangplank and into the warmth and comfort of the comms ship where the three of them would spend the night.

Chapter Twenty Two

Sitting in his statue at the bottom of Park Lane George Byron was getting really angry. He had spent the whole evening replaying the conversation he had had with Camorra in the café and felt really cross with himself. How could he have made such a simple mistake as he had done to give away his position like that? Camorra had been on to him in a flash. She hadn't missed a trick in cornering him into admitting his involvement. Oh, he was such a fool! He wasn't going to let Napier get away with it though. No. He'd made sure that she knew that he had something to do with it as well. How did she suspect anything in the first place though? Hmm… he couldn't understand that, but in any case that hardly mattered now. What did matter was that no-one else should have any idea of what had gone on yesterday. He could be certain that if word got out then that would be the end of his life as a Malachi, Wellington would see to that, for sure. And Byron didn't want to give up this special role. Even though he didn't always find it easy, it was a lot better than just staying up in heaven with nothing to do all day, every day. He'd said he promised he wouldn't do anything else, hadn't he? That should be enough for her.

Oh, and why is Wellington so popular with everyone all of a sudden? Honestly – he didn't have that many friends in his day but now they're all over him. He and Victoria seem to have a special bond at the moment. They are always getting together for their cosy little chats. He thinks I don't notice but I do. And he's so lucky to have those servants of his. I bet he doesn't do anything around his home. Well, he doesn't have to, does he, with those four at his beck and call?

And so it went on until he was so wound up he could hardly sleep.

So – he'd made his promise and he should jolly well stick to it. He should just forget about Wellington, ignore him, rise above it all, just get on with his life as a Malachi. Other Malachis don't carry their grudges into this world, so he could just as easily forget his rivalry and at least try to be civil. They had been getting along quite well recently, so why had he let it all well up again? Wellington often came over for the odd chat, so what's changed?

"Oh, to hell with it all!" he shouted. "I need to get out of here!" and with that he grabbed his coat, threw open the portal and strode out into the streets of London not giving any thought as to where he was going. He just needed to walk away from everything in the hope it might help him clear his head. Boatswain looked up and whined. Where was his master going at this time of night?

After walking for what seemed like hours, not really knowing where he was going, Byron found himself on Lambeth Bridge and he crossed the river to Lambeth Palace. Walking up along the river bank he suddenly realised his location. He had calmed down by now and was thinking like his old self. It won't do any harm if I just take a look at the children, will it, he thought, as he made his way up to Forest level in the Evelina.

***

Rory and Sarah were really excited at the prospect of spending their last night on board HQS Wellington. Rory remembered the stories of his elderly relatives of how they used to spend days watching this ship when it served with the Royal Navy and was stationed in New Zealand. They would while away the time watching the serving sailors clean the decks, paint the hull and perform drills on deck. They had dreamed that one day they too would serve the King and Commonwealth and now here was Rory exploring the very same ship. He could hardly believe it and had to keep running his hand along the smooth banisters just to reassure himself that this was real – well, real in a different dimension, but real to him and Sarah. That brought him back to reality and to thinking of the journey they had to take tomorrow. He had hardly had a chance to let it all sink in, as they had been suddenly brought here by Wellington, supposedly for their own 'safety'.

But now the thought of having to sail a ship up the Thames, moor it on the other side and find their way into the intensive care ward where his real body was lying all seemed a bit overwhelming for him. His heart was filled with dread and a deep anxiety permeated through his whole body. What if they couldn't navigate the Thames, if they ended up in the wrong place? What would happen to their bodies then? Would they stay in a coma for years? He'd heard of stories where people do just that and in the end their families decide to turn off the life support systems, and that could be after years, maybe ten or fifteen years. Oh, he couldn't bear that! And then what would happen to their bodies in this limbo dimension? Would they just float around on Earth with these strange Malachis? It was all getting a bit too much.

Wellington brought him back to reality. "Rory, you and Sarah will be in this cabin. OK? There are bunk beds which are already made up for you and you don't have to worry because I'll be in the adjoining one. If either of you need anything just call and I'll be there. First, though, there's supper prepared for us in the mess so just leave your things here and follow me."

Rory tried to focus on what Wellington was saying and gave a wan smile to Sarah.

"This is OK isn't it, Sarah? We'll be OK, won't we?" he said, looking for reassurance from his younger sister.

"It's all cool. Especially after everything that Wellington's done for us, and more especially with you looking after me," Sarah replied.

That was what was worrying him more and more, this dreadful feeling of total responsibility for both of them. He couldn't let Sarah down, now could he? It was beginning to feel like the weight of all the statues in London was bearing down on him and would bury him alive.

They were led into the Court Room where a table was laid for the three of them and on it was the most mouth-watering assortment of food you ever saw. All their favourite food was piled high on enormous gold platters and they could help themselves to bucket-loads of chips, sausages, kebabs, slices of fresh pineapple, the reddest strawberries and raspberries, pasta with Bolognese sauce, fajitas, chicken legs in barbecue sauce, chocolate brownies, crisps, jugs of exotic fruit juices… the banquet was endless.

"We thought you needed a good send off for your last meal," Wellington said. "I hope there's plenty you like here."

But there was no answer. Both Sarah and Rory were stuffing their faces, grabbing anything from every plate until their taste buds were exploding with sheer delight. Not only did it look good, it all tasted the absolute best they had ever tasted in their whole lives. Every aspect was magnified a thousand times, the colours were deeper and more vibrant, the flavours were more intense and the smells were more delicate and enticing and it all just melted in their mouths. Sheer perfection! Now this is what a meal should be, Rory thought, as he helped himself to the last burger and dipped his last chip into the ketchup.

"Wow," he said, "I'm completely stuffed after all that. Thanks Wellington, that was the best meal I've had in my whole life!"

"Good, that's the idea. Now, I think it's time you both headed for your bunks, don't you?"

Rory and Sarah made their weary way back down the ornate teak staircase, stopping every now and then to admire the model ships displayed in the glass cabinets and the old artefacts rescued from other ships. Sarah spun the wooden globe around as fast as she could as she went past and tapped on the marine bell which was a replica of the Liberty Bell.

"I'm never going to forget this place as long as I live," Sarah said, wistfully. "It's been quite an adventure, hasn't it Rory?"

"Yes, you could say that, and it's not over yet," Rory agreed with her but couldn't hide the trepidation he was feeling at the thought of what tomorrow could bring.

"Oh Rory, you mustn't worry so much. You have to keep remembering what Wellington said the very first day we met him. He said we have to trust him."

"Oh, I know, but I still can't help feeling just a bit nervous."

"Do you remember that song Mum used to sing? It was when we were tiny and she used to get really fed up with being at home. All I remember is the song was by someone called Amanda Marshall, I think she was Canadian, and the one lyric which Mum used to sing was 'trust me, baby this is love' or something like that. Well Rory, try to think back to those days. The song went something like this I think," and Sarah sang the first verse of the song.

"It does seem vaguely familiar. Maybe I'll just think it in my head; it seems a bit sissy to sing it out loud!"

Sarah chuckled. "Yes, Rory, you're right of course, especially with your voice! Come on – let's go and snuggle up in those comfy-looking bunks. You can have the top one if you like."

***

Camorra and Tasca were making their way to bed too. What a day it had been. They were both exhausted and couldn't wait to settle down on their duck down duvets. At least these hadn't changed much since their day. One of their main jobs when they were little was to collect all the down and feathers which came off the ducks and geese. Their grandmother would spend hours cleaning and combing it and then stuffing it into woven cloth bags. They would sleep on an extra thick one and have a lighter one on top. They were so warm and comfy but they didn't stay clean for that long, a couple of months at the most, and so they would have to collect the raw materials pretty much all year round. The down did seem much thicker then; maybe the ducks were hardier in those days and had to have thicker coats under their feathers. It was a relief that the bedding they had now didn't go off and start smelling. That was always the first sign that it was deteriorating and time to be replaced. After a few days it then began to clump together and then it seemed to solidify. If you left them for too long it was like sleeping on concrete. No – there were some definite advantages to being alive in the twenty-first century compared with the first.

"Mmm, my legs feel like dead weights," Tasca said to Camorra as she wrapped her covers around her.

"It's my arms that feel as though every sinew has been stretched double and then stretched again. I think it was holding on to Marble's neck that did it; he really scorched me with his breath and his scales scratched my arms too," Camorra said dreamily, as she relived the terrifying ride they had endured that morning.

"I'm glad it all seems sorted out with Byron. You were right. I was really confused to start with but it slowly dawned on me what you were doing," Tasca yawned.

"Yes – he's been interfering with the rescue of Rory and Sarah. We witnessed it firsthand yesterday and goodness knows what he's been up to before that. Anyway, sussing him out like we did seems to have made him see the error of his ways. And I'm surprised about Napier. Goodness knows why he was in league with Byron. Let's put it all behind us, get a good night's sleep and give those children a really good send off in the morning. Night, night, Sis," and Camorra turned over and hoped that she would soon be drifting off into the land of dreams and make-believe.

After a short while, all was quiet in Boudicca's home, the three of them sleeping soundly, dreaming of riding on white swans, sailing in Roman galleons and fighting the Druids. It was around 1 o'clock in the morning when Camorra woke suddenly from a deep sleep. She lay there in her bed for a while thinking about the past events. She was desperate to get back to sleep but however hard she tried she just couldn't; something was niggling away at her subconscious. She tried to let her thoughts flow around randomly in her head to see if she could catch hold of the worry, but it just wouldn't keep still long enough for her to pinpoint it. Damn it, she thought to herself, what is it? I know something's troubling me but I just can't focus on it!

It was fluttering around like a butterfly, settling on one thought only to fly away the minute she tried to think too deeply about it. Its wings were so colourful and beautifully designed she couldn't read any logic into it. Suddenly a whole host of butterflies was flying around inside her head; she tried shaking them out but it was no use. She tried to focus on toads, lizards and even snakes, all predators of butterflies, in a vain attempt to get rid of them but that didn't help. She now had a whole reptile house roaming around and she thought if she didn't do something very quickly her head would explode.

She jumped out of bed and pulled her cape around her. She flapped her arms around her head to make the beasts disappear but that only made it worse. "Oh for goodness sake, why don't you all just go away!" she shouted.

Tasca, who had been in a deep sleep, was woken by the

commotion. "What's up Camorra, what's all this noise? Can't you keep quiet?"

"Oh Tasca, I don't know what's the matter with me. I've got this awful worry going around in my head but I just can't pin it down and now it's just getting worse and worse."

"OK, shhh, just sit down over here and let's talk it through together," Tasca said, calmly.

Tasca helped Camorra go through all the events of the day to see if it was something that had happened earlier which was niggling away at her. She thought of everything but no – nothing came to light, but at least the butterflies seemed to have settled down.

"OK," Tasca said wearily, desperately wanting to get back to sleep. "If nothing's worrying you about today, then what about tomorrow?"

"Well – how should I know? Tomorrow hasn't happened yet!" Camorra said, incredulously.

"Yes – but just have a go – for my sake. One last try and see if a little glimmer happens when you think of what you're planning to do tomorrow. Think about the children and what they are going to have to go through."

Camorra sat and thought for a few moments.

"Well – that's just it. I can't. It all seems a blank. In fact, as far as I can see nothing's going to happen to them tomorrow."

"Don't be silly – they've got to get back to ECH or else." Tasca was beginning to get a bit bothered. Why couldn't Camorra even imagine what would happen?

"No – there's nothing. Just a big dark tunnel." The butterflies and other reptiles had by now all disappeared leaving her mind a black void.

"You know what, Camorra? If what you are thinking is true, then they could be in big trouble. Try to concentrate a bit harder."

Camorra put all her cerebral energy into thinking about what the children should be doing the next day. She tried to imagine the boats they would be sailing and the journey down the river and then their real bodies lying in the hospital. Finally, just as she was about to give up yet again, she thought she saw a glimmer of a sparkly light in the corner of her mind. Focusing even harder, the glimmer became a tiny speck which began buzzing and flying around. The light became brighter and brighter as the noise inside her head became louder and louder and the bee got bigger and bigger. The bee began circling around and around until it metamorphosed into an enormous boa constrictor which was trying to squeeze all the light and the noise into a marble sculpture.

Now all Camorra could think of was butterflies, a bee and the boa constrictor. All beginning with the letter B. Then it dawned on her and a brilliant light dazzled the entire scene. She shouted out, "Byron – he's the snake in the grass!"

"What do you mean?" Tasca demanded.

"I shouldn't have believed him in the café. It's all so obvious now. He's not going to stop until he gets what he wants. Quick! We must tell Mum everything." Camorra's head had emptied itself of the creatures and she could see everything clearly now. "We can't waste a second. I think those children are in serious danger!"

They dashed into their mother's room and shook her awake and explained all their concerns and suspicions about Byron and Napier.

"We must warn Wellington straight away. We can't afford to waste any more time," Boudicca said, trying to bring Wellington up on the quadrisensor screen. There was no response.

"He's probably disconnected it all so that they can get a good night's sleep without any disturbances. We'd better go over to his place; we'll go in the carro." And with that the three of them pulled on some clothes and jumped into the chariot where the horses were ready and raring to go. They flew across St James's Park and Green Park and landed the chariot on the grass just beside Wellington's statue.

Boudicca leapt down and banged on the portal. "Come on," she urged. There was no answer. She banged again and the two girls joined in.

"They must be there," Tasca said. "Where else would they be?"

Eventually, Paddy opened the portal a fraction and looked out through the gap. The three women pushed the door wide open with such force that Paddy fell back, knocking his head against the wall.

"Hey, steady on!" he exclaimed. "What's got into you lot? Do you mind not disturbing us at this time of night?" He was sounding really groggy and his speech was slurred.

"Where are they? We've got to get to them?" Camorra demanded.

"Who?" Paddy said dreamily.

"Who do you think? Wellington and the children. We must speak to them now!" Boudicca shouted.

"Oh, do you have to shout so much, my head hurts!" Paddy replied.

"What's going on here?" Jock asked, as the three other soldiers roused themselves and gathered round the three women.

"He's got them, hasn't he? Weren't you lot supposed to be guarding them – how could you let him take them just like that?" Camorra was in a complete state now and wasn't thinking rationally.

Finally Bob came to the rescue, "Now, why don't you all just calm down, speak slowly and we'll try to help you."

"Yes, of course, sorry," Boudicca said, realising how they were overreacting. She started explaining calmly, "It would appear that Byron has got something in for your master and has taken him and the children to a secret location. We've got to find them tonight otherwise they won't get back into their own bodies."

"Now, why would Byron have taken them?" Jock asked.

"We don't know for sure but he's planning something evil, we're convinced of that," Tasca said.

"Well look, all we know is that Wellington gave us the evening off so we went to the pub. When we got back it was all quiet so we just had a final nightcap and then went to bed. We haven't seen Wellington since about 7 o'clock," Jock explained.

"Can we call up Victoria from here and see if she has any idea?" Boudicca asked.

"Sure, help yourselves."

Boudicca logged on to the system and quickly brought up Victoria.

"The kids have gone!"

"Now calm down, Boudicca, everything's fine."

"How can it be? They're not at Wellington's?" Boudicca replied.

Victoria reassured Boudicca saying, "Calm down. They're all safe in the *Welly*. I sent them there myself as I wanted them to be close on hand for tomorrow. But tell me - why did you think Byron had taken them?"

And so Boudicca repeated all the girls' concerns to Victoria, who sat patiently in silence taking it all in.

"Mmm – that's most interesting. I think we should be on our guard. Perhaps Camorra is right. I don't think he'll give up that easily. Let me speak to Arthur and warn him. He can put extra security around the boat. The best thing you three can do now is go back home. Try to get some rest but keep all the comms channels open just in case I need you urgently. Is that OK? Oh, and thanks." Victoria signed off and made an emergency call to Wellington.

It was with great relief that the carro took the three of them back to Westminster Bridge.

Chapter Twenty Three

Byron crept into the Evelina through the main door. He passed the Children of the World, the strange group of coloured clowns and dolls at the entrance, and gave them a wave. He was feeling a bit light-headed and not totally sure what he was doing here but his legs seemed to be on autopilot and he let them lead him along. He hadn't been in this new hospital before and what a place it was, he thought admiringly. I wouldn't mind being a sick child if I had to come to a place like this. It was all glass and colours and airy spaces. He noticed the names of the floors. Oh very clever – going from the Ocean to the Sky. Well, he didn't think it appropriate that they name a floor Heaven – it might not give the patients the right impression. He made his way up the stairs to the second floor, Forest, where Wellington had said the children were. They were supposed to be in PICU, paediatric intensive care unit. He tiptoed along the corridor, being careful not to disturb the karma of the place. He didn't want to cause any undue disturbances of the airwaves that might lead to humans sensing any strange presence. As he turned the corner into PICU he stopped suddenly.

Damn it, he thought, that looked remarkably like Florence Nightingale there. I'd better be careful.

The ward was a strange mixture of quiet intensity and the noisy, regular beeping and flashing of machines. Being night-time there was only a handful of nurses around, all the parents were either in the special hospital suites or the Ronald MacDonald House. He hung around waiting to see what Florence was going to do.

"Oh no – not her as well!" Byron stared in disbelief as Edith Cavell walked up to Florence and whispered in her ear.

"What are they both doing here? Don't they trust the human nurses to do a proper job?"

As Florence wandered over to the nurses' station and Edith checked the rota on the wall he saw an opportunity. Quickly, he needed to find where Rory and Sarah were. There were so many beds with different sized shapes under the covers he would have to look at each of them in turn. He discounted the first two as they were obviously babies, but for the next beds he had to look at the charts on the bottom of the beds. By the time he got round to the fifth bed he was getting a bit desperate but then he read the name *Rory Wheeler* on the chart and bingo! The adjacent bed was occupied by his sister, Sarah. The machines were working away rhythmically and methodically, the different coloured lines sweeping across the screens in perfect harmony.

Let's liven things up a bit shall we? Byron thought to himself mischievously. I wonder what will happen if I turn this dial ever so slightly to the right. And he turned a dial on Sarah's feeding pump. Nothing happened. The lines repeated the same patterns as before. OK, so what about if I move this one? He turned a dial on the breathing machine and all of a sudden alarm bells were ringing.

"Damn it! I may have done something too much," he said, as he slipped behind a screen.

It was mayhem! Nurses appeared like the cavalry out of every doorway and descended on Sarah's bed like bees around a honey pot. Everyone was speaking in urgent, hushed whispers, trying to make sense of what could have caused the bells to go off. Nurses were grabbing the charts, scrutinising them to check the doctor's instructions, wondering if a time delay had come into effect. But there was nothing obvious. Sister Bridge did a methodical check of each of the machines and it soon came to light. The oxygen level had been turned down; Sarah's brain was being starved of oxygen. She immediately turned it back to its rightful position and, sure enough, the alarms stopped beeping and all returned to some sort of normality.

"How did that happen?" she quizzed the night nurses.

"I'm not sure, Sister," Nurse Rose replied. "We were just filling in the sheets at the desk when the alarm went off, and no-one's been in as far as we know."

"Well – you'll just have to be a bit more alert won't you," Sister Bridge reprimanded the young girl. Honestly, she thought, the young nurses these days. They seem more bothered about filling in the on-line forms than actually looking after the patients. "Just make sure nothing untoward happens again."

Florence and Edith were annoyed with themselves. They had missed something but weren't sure what exactly.

***

Having drifted off to sleep with the tide of the Thames gently rocking the *Welly*, Sarah found herself suddenly gasping for breath. She felt as if a thousand ton weight was being pressed down on her chest and was crushing her so much that she couldn't breathe. All the air was being pushed out of her lungs and she felt really light-headed. She reached out for the light but as she did so she knocked a glass of water off the bedside table.

"Is that you Sarah?" Rory called out from the top bunk, the noise having woken him from a deep sleep.

"Oh my God," he cried, looking down from above at the sight below. Sarah was slumped face down hanging half out of her bunk.

"Wellington – quick! It's Sarah, something's the matter!" he yelled out and in next to no time Wellington was there helping Sarah back into her bunk.

"There, there – just take some deep breaths and you'll be fine."

Thankfully Sarah's breathing seemed suddenly to have returned to normal and her chest felt as light as a feather.

"Oh, that was awful. I woke up as I could hardly breathe but it's gone just as quickly as it came. How peculiar," Sarah said, as she settled back down into her warm bunk.

Wellington rushed straight to the comms office and called up Victoria.

"We've just had a situation with Sarah. Do you know where Byron is? I wouldn't put it past him to have gone to the hospital, he's a real loose cannon at the moment," he explained with some urgency.

"Right. Get a message to Florence and Edith. They must have seen something. But tell them to tread cautiously. If it was him we don't want them to scare him off. We need to catch him red-handed doing whatever he thinks he can get away with," Victoria instructed.

Wellington called up Florence.

"What's going on there? We've just had a major problem with Sarah?" he demanded.

Florence was embarrassed that neither she nor Edith had prevented the emergency in the ward.

"Just checking now, sir. Everything seems to be in order. We'll keep a closer eye on things from now on."

"Yes – make damn sure of it! I don't want you to take your eyes off those children for one second. Do you understand me?" Wellington ordered.

"Yes sir."

Byron had quite enjoyed that little escapade and was so obsessed with which other dials he could twiddle that he didn't notice the two nurse Malachis fast approaching Sarah's bed. He was just about to experiment with another dial when a voice rang out.

"Gotcha! Stay right where you are and don't move a muscle!" Edith shouted.

Byron turned round with clenched fists and swung his right arm to give Edith an uppercut under the chin.

"Oh no you don't," she said and as quick as a flash she grabbed his arm and twisted it behind and up his back.

"Let me go," Byron demanded. "Who do you think you are treating me like this?"

"Once you've explained yourself then we'll see if we can let you go," Florence joined in.

"I don't have to explain myself to you couple of no-hopers. Just look at the pair of you. Call yourself women? Huh – most men wouldn't give you the time of day, certainly not me."

If Byron was expecting a reaction from the two women he was disappointed. They knew better than that and they grappled with him to restrain him from doing any further damage to the children. He was strong though and also very angry. He was twisting and turning and eventually his strength proved too much for Edith and Florence. With a sudden spurt of force Byron yanked his arms free of their hold, raced down the corridor and was gone.

"Good riddance to bad rubbish!" Edith said.

"At least he didn't do any more damage. Can you call up

Wellington and put him in the picture? I'll stay here and then we'll keep watch over the two of them for as long as we have to," Florence instructed Edith.

"Of course."

***

Wellington debriefed Edith.

"I never imagined he would go for the human children. He's got a nerve. Anyway, they are all safe now. We're looking after Rory and Sarah here on the Welly and you two – don't take your eyes off them in PICU. Understood? I'll let everyone know here what's been going on in ECH. We'll speak in the morning."

Wellington organised a conference call involving Victoria and all the zonal chiefs and deputies. No-one was too happy to be woken up in the middle of the night but once they understood the reason they all calmed down. He let Boudicca explain it all to them.

Once she had finished there was a stunned silence.

Nelson said, "I don't know what's more incredible? The fact that Byron's done all this or the fact that Camorra and Tasca have unmasked him. Oh, and we mustn't forget Napier in all this. I'll speak to him in the morning."

"I agree," Gladstone said, nodding. "Boudicca – I want to congratulate your girls for their bravery and insightfulness. Jolly well done! Don't you agree, Anne?"

"Oh yes – absolutely! Incredibly well done; you must be very proud of your daughters, Boudicca," Anne concurred.

"Yes, I am," Boudicca said, wistfully. "They really are their father's daughters."

"I'm furious with Byron, I can't believe he's behaved in this shocking way, and all because of what happened all that long time ago. I was beginning to get quite fond of the old rogue you know. To tell you the truth I quite enjoyed our little chats in the park and his dog was quite sweet too," Wellington said, with a certain amount of despondency in his voice. "You can never tell what's going on inside peoples' heads can you – even Malachis' heads."

184

"Now you mustn't blame yourself, Arthur," Victoria said, sympathetically. "You could not have predicted this and you've done everything possible for those children. It's all clear now. Why they took so long solving the first clue, and why Camorra and Tasca had the problems they had with the second one. I want everyone to settle back to bed and get what rest they can. Something tells me it's not going to be all plain sailing tomorrow."

***

Meanwhile Byron had returned to his statue feeling absolutely furious. He gave Boatswain a surly greeting, just resisting the temptation to hit out at him. He was shaking all over he was so angry. He paced around his drawing room trying to calm down, but all he could think about was how those nurses had caught him red-handed. He couldn't let them get the better of him. Oh no – he would show them. After a while his thoughts slowly began to return to normal. He sat down at his desk and idly picked up a pen. Like an automaton he began to do what he did best. He let his mind wander and after a few moments his pen was flying over the paper which was soon filled with his flowery script. There, he thought, I can still pen a decent poem after all these years. Suddenly, another feeling overcame him and he screwed up the piece of paper, shoved it in his pocket and stormed out of his statue.

He strode over to Temple and gazed at the beautiful ships moored up against the embankment wall. He had to admit Brunel and his team had done a brilliant job of recommissioning the weather vanes. But he was determined that Rory & Sarah weren't going to get away that easily. He might just make their journey back up the Thames a little bit more of a challenge than they had bargained for. And so, checking that he was all alone, he jumped up onto the deck of the Liberty and had a good scout around.

Chapter Twenty Four

"What's that knocking?" Sarah asked as she reached up out of her bunk and looked out of the porthole.

It was a bright, sunny morning and the light was shimmering across the surface of the Thames. All she could see were two old-fashioned wooden boats moored at the pier whose shrouds were rattling in the light breeze. She had made a good recovery after her little escapade during the night and although her chest still felt a bit heavy she could breathe almost normally.

"Are those our boats, do you think, Rory?"

"Let's see," he said, as he climbed down from his bunk and followed Sarah's line of vision.

"Cool. They look pretty impressive, don't they? I've always wanted to sail in something like that. It makes my little Laser back home seem like a toy."

"I'm not sure I can handle such a large vessel. What if it's too much for me? I'm feeling really nervous about this whole thing now. There are so many things that could go wrong, and I do so want to get back into my proper body, and I do want to see Mum and Dad again. Oh, why do we have to go in separate boats?" Sarah was really anxious about what lay ahead of her. She wasn't sure if she would be up to it. It seemed like a fun thing to do yesterday but now it was the actual day she felt so nervous she was sure she wouldn't be able to steer. Her hands would be shaking so much the wheel would be going all over the place.

"Hey – what's happened to your trust now? Don't you remember it was you telling me I had to put my trust in Wellington? Come on; try not to think about it, just do it." It was Rory's turn to encourage his sister this morning. He thought back over the last few days. Normally, at home, he never had any time for his little sister and her giggling friends. All they were interested in was pop music, make-up and clothes and it drove him and his mates mad. Oh, and they were always hanging around him whenever he had his friends around – so annoying. But the more he thought about what they had both been through here in London, the adventures they had shared and the people they had met, he began to see Sarah in a different light. He couldn't have experienced this with anyone else.

She has been there for me so often, she's buoyed me up when I've been feeling really down and I've done the same for her. We've had some real laughs together with Wellington's soldiers; she even told me she fancied Paddy! I'll never let her down; she's part of me and I hope she feels that I'm part of her. And we'll keep this as a secret till the days we die (oh Lord, let that not be today), Rory thought.

Oh stop it Rory, he said to himself. You're getting too sentimental, get a grip and tell her to get on with it.

"Come on, Sarah. We'll be fine, just you see."

Sarah just hoped and prayed he was right; she didn't have any confidence in herself today at all.

After a hearty breakfast for Rory and just a glass of juice for Sarah, they had collected their things together and were ready to make their way to the ships.

"I just hope the journey back isn't as bad as it was here. I hated the feeling of being hurled along inside that tunnel of light. It made me feel so sick," Rory admitted to Sarah.

"As long as we get back into our real human dimension I think I could put up with anything," Sarah replied. "We will make it back, won't we?"

"Of course we will. I'll make sure of it," Rory replied, as confidently as he could.

Wellington had gathered together all the Malachis on the pier who had heard about everything by now. They were milling around in little groups anxiously waiting for the big send-off.

"Any sign of Byron?" Wellington asked Victoria.

"Not that I've heard. I've got all the half-Malachis on standby ready to tell me the moment anyone spots him. He's probably sulking somewhere. Just so long as he keeps out of the way today. And I've told all the Malachis to stand guard along the river on both sides forming an electrosecuroguard. With their combined powers that should keep the children safe from any rogue waves getting across to them." Victoria had thought of everything.

"And Florence and Edith are going to be the ones to give them their send-off. I've already briefed them on what they have to do but basically once the children get into the ward they give them a helping hand back along their medians of reverse visual energy – their morva. Then we just have to wait and see and hope the children regain consciousness. After that our job is done; more importantly, Arthur, your job as guardian angel is done."

"I must say I have enjoyed having them about the place, and I know the chaps did too. I shall miss them - they really livened it up," Wellington said, wistfully. "But I'm sorry about the *Turk*. Repairing that is going to be my first job on the list after all this."

"Oh – I think I may have overreacted – let's forget about it, shall we?" Victoria said, graciously.

"Of course. By the way, what are we going to do with Napier? I thought he enjoyed his role as a counter and I know that he had taken to the riding. How could he let himself down like that?"

"I know; it does seem rather out of character for him. Last night I sent Eisenhower over to his statue and he read him the riot act. He also put an osmoseal on his portal. Once the children are safely over to the other side you can go and have a little chat with him. See what you can get out of him."

"Sure. It'll be my pleasure." Wellington grinned at the prospect.

"Right. Why don't you get the children organised and I'll check everything's in place from our end," Victoria ordered, as she could see Rory and Sarah looking anxiously at their ships.

Brunel was tinkering with the *Temple*, making last minute adjustments to her rigging and compass. "You can never be too careful, Arthur," he said, as he waved his screwdriver at him.

"As long as this weather holds out, they'll be fine. I've just noticed those dark clouds over on the horizon. I hope they don't start coming over this way," Wellington replied.

***

It was approaching the time of the children's departure. Wellington and Brunel had shown them around the ships and explained how to use the controls. The navigation system already had the coordinates of their destination on the other side of the river programmed in. All Rory and Sarah had to do was to steer their ship to hold the course. The mast reduction system, the most vital piece of engineering, had been demonstrated. In order that the ships could navigate the bridges the masts had to be lowered and then raised again once they had gone underneath. It had taken them both a few attempts at mastering the system but Wellington had given them a mnemonic to remember in which order to operate the switches: MAST, which stood for Master, Auxiliary, Stop (wait for 7 seconds) Tertiary. They were both still feeling quite nervous about the whole trip but knew that they had no choice if they wanted to return to their proper dimension. Brunel had also given them both some other vital tools to be used in case of emergencies. The plasma screwdriver was an amazing piece of Malachi engineering which could be used for a variety of purposes when technology failed. An aerosol of Malachi Mist was another invaluable item the Malachis had developed. A short, sharp spray could transmit an immobilising force to the unlucky recipient.

Cook had been busy calculating their time of departure. It was vital they were sailing along this part of the Thames at high tide. The draft of their ships was several metres and with the Thames being tidal here they had to leave on a high tide so that the ships would have enough water beneath them, otherwise there was a real danger of them going aground. The wind was perfect – a light force 3 coming from a north-easterly direction. Newton had also calculated that there would be a rift in the plasma divide in the City of London at 12 noon. Rory and Sarah had to be in position to be flung down along the medians of reverse visual energy at this precise time to get back to their home dimension. The Malachis weren't quite sure what would happen if they missed this timeframe. A few years ago, when a similar thing happened to an elderly gentleman, they thought they saw him careering around the Earth in continuous circles in another parallel dimension. They didn't want anything like that to happen to Rory and Sarah. Getting the timing of the tides and the plasma divide aligned took a lot of complex calculations and it was vital they left at 11:30am precisely.

189

As the time was approaching 11:15am all was in order. Rory and Sarah had both said very emotional goodbyes to Wellington. They had had an incredible few days in his care. They would never forget him or his four men, and Sarah especially wouldn't forget Copenhagen either, or Paddy.

"Oh, Wellington, thanks ever so much for looking after us so well. I don't know what we would have done if you hadn't found us after the crash." Sarah was half crying at the thought of leaving this special person behind but the other half of her couldn't wait to get back to their real world. She gave him a big hug.

"Cheers, mate," Rory said cheerily. "I'll never forget you either," giving Wellington a more manly high-five.

"Now. Off you go and good luck!" Wellington said, with a brave face. He turned away quickly to wipe a tear away. He could be a real softie at times and he didn't want the children to have their last memory of him crying like a baby.

"Remember. You must get back into your world by 12 noon otherwise you could have a long wait," he warned them.

Suddenly the wind picked up and changed direction.

"Oh no!" Brunel cried. "We can't let this happen. Come on everyone. Use all your powers to change it back. It needs to be blowing from a north-easterly direction and it's just backed round to the west. They'll never sail against this wind."

All the Malachis focused on the wind and, using powers of deliverance, strength, protection and guiding, gradually the wind abated and they could feel it veering round to the north-east.

"Phew!" Cook said, as he breathed a sigh of relief. "That was close. They'd better cast off quickly now while they can."

Cook and Scott undid the ropes which were securing the ships to the pier and threw them onto the decks.

"Let's hope we've done our calculations correctly," Cook said. "We can't change anything now."

Suddenly, the sun grew brighter and brighter until a dazzling, shimmering glow spread across the whole of the London skyline. All at once the host of Malachis were revealed to Rory and Sarah.

Shielding his eyes from the bright light Rory shouted over to Sarah, "Crikey, look at the crowd on the pier, Sarah! Wellington said he had some mates helping him but I had no idea they would be like this!"

Sarah, who was busy at the helm, looked up. "There's Queen Victoria and James Cook! I remember them from our history lessons!"

Rory and Sarah waved at them all and shouted, "Thanks – we'll never forget you!"

"Right, come on, we need to concentrate on sailing these ships," Rory said, taking charge.

But Sarah's mind was on other things. She had found the little carved replica of her boat on the deck. She picked it up and marvelled at the intricacy of the carving. She turned it this way and that to inspect it all over and noticed some words underneath:

Buono viaggio, Sarah, da Christopher Columbus.

She was overcome with emotion and quickly put the carving safely away in the pocket of her jumper. She didn't notice a snake uncoil itself from the corner of the sunny deck and stretch out its body before settling down again to bathe in the warmth of the sunshine.

On the pier, Wellington leant over to Victoria, "I do hope they make it. It's the last leg of the journey and it's down to them now."

"Absolutely, Arthur. You've done all you can. Now you have to trust them to follow all the instructions they've been given. There's nothing more we can do."

Wellington knew that she was right but he still felt very nervous for them. What if they couldn't handle the ships or something went wrong with one of the systems on board? What if they couldn't find their way to the ward? Oh, there were still so many hurdles they had to overcome, and all he could do was stand and watch. He felt so helpless.

It was busy along this part of the river and for the first five minutes of the journey all the children had to do was concentrate on steering their ships safely out of harm's way. They made a zigzag course upstream as they tried to avoid all the cruise ships and river taxis that were steaming up and down the river. They were heading for the central span of Waterloo Bridge.

Rory was coping quite well and shouted encouragement across to Sarah.

"Are you OK? Are you ready for the first bridge? Remember the MAST routine!"

Sarah was a bit nervous but was gradually getting used to handling the *Temple*.

"Yeah – not too bad. I'll just follow you!" she shouted back. She was beginning to enjoy the sensation of the wind in her hair and the feel of the smooth wood of the wheel in her hands as she allowed the pre-programmed navigation system to take over.

"Right," said Rory, "activate MAST when I say!" and he carefully watched the buildings on the south side of the Embankment as he had been instructed to by Brunel to get to the right position before activating the mast-lowering mechanism. At last he reached the National Theatre, that modern concrete layered building he could see between the trees. He systematically counted the trees off, and as he got to the fifth tree before the bridge he shouted across to Sarah, "Now!"

Rory scrutinised the control deck and pressed the Master button, quickly followed by the Auxiliary lever. He heard the mechanisms whirring away. Good, something's happening, he thought. Now – count to seven. One, two, three, four, five, six, seven and then activate the Tertiary switch. Yes – the masts were beginning to lower themselves on to the deck. The sails folded neatly in on themselves and the sheets adjusted within the roller reefing. Soon the *Liberty* was ready to pass underneath Waterloo Bridge. The same success was not being enjoyed by Sarah, however. She had repeated the instructions on the *Temple* and had got as far as pressing the Auxiliary lever when she heard a grinding noise and knew straightaway that something had got jammed. She feared she had only counted to six before hitting the final lever.

"Damn it!" she cried. "Rory, the mechanism's stuck! What shall I do?"

Rory called across, "OK, just keep calm. What you should do now is release the automatic steering function. You're going to have to go about again and try to restart MAST whilst you are facing upwind. Can you do that?"

"I'll try!"

"Good girl, I'll stay here and wait." He put *Liberty* into a holding instruction. The little ship was able to stay in a given position for five minutes using this command. He watched nervously as Sarah manoeuvred the *Temple* back downstream.

A sudden noise distracted her. What was that? She turned round nervously expecting to see one of the Malachis in the ship. Nothing. She could have sworn it was something and she was certain she noticed a flicker of movement in the corner of the deck. It must have been the wind, she thought reassuringly, as she tried to stop feeling so nervous.

The Malachis looked on anxiously. They knew they couldn't interfere directly with either Rory or Sarah and the boats now. All they could do was watch and pray. It was a nervous time for them all.

As Rory waited he watched her over the stern of Liberty, his legs were shaking he was so nervous. His eyes caught sight of a crumpled piece of paper flapping in the breeze which was trapped under the cushions of the rear seats. He pulled it out. It was covered in flowery italic writing and looked very much like a poem. He started to read it:

An Apology

Young free spirits of a human kind,
Don't tarry on your journey, or else be blind.
Admirable is your strength of heart
And knowledge is liberty; oh thou art
The temple in which hope doth pray
That one day, you will return to make them pay.

Journey now across the water.
Each span has a story I have sought to
Enlighten your souls with stories of fact

To impart to your idols with haste a pact.

Oh wither thou sail in your wooden ships

Leste you forget your time, seal your lips.

Waterloo, the battle of your saviour soldier,

For once this span was a source of solder

For the physicist Faraday he did test

The effects of salt water on magnets;

And yet you have a stone of this older span

Resting in your home town of Wellington.

He couldn't quite understand what he was reading. He turned the paper over and looked at the last line: George Gordon Byron, 2010.

He re-read the first two verses very carefully. He'd never taken much notice of verse in his English lessons at school and struggled to get to grips with the messages the words were trying to give. He'd better leave it for now and concentrate on what Sarah is doing. It looked as though she might have restarted the MAST procedure successfully this time.

"How's it going, Sarah? You've got to hurry now!"

"Fine! I had to use the plasma screwdriver, like Brunel showed us but I got it sorted!" and she glided up alongside Liberty with the masts of the Temple all lying securely along the decks. She was regaining her confidence now and put all thoughts of strange noises and feelings out of her mind.

The two little ships made a swift, clean passage under the central span of Waterloo Bridge and both children let out a big cheer, which was echoed by the Malachis who by now had lined up along both side of the Thames. Their portent shields were fully active now to try to prevent Byron having a last ditch attempt at interfering. They had noticed some indentation just before the children had set sail but there had been nothing more since. They all assumed that Byron knew when he was beaten.

The two ships were back on track with a minute in hand.

"Hey, Sarah! Guess what I found on *Liberty*?" Rory called across to Sarah.

"How would I know? But I found a sweet little model of this ship. I'm taking it back with me," Sarah replied smugly, as she felt the outline of it in her pocket.

"Well, I found a poem, and it's been written by someone called Byron, by the looks of it. It's written in really strange writing but it seems as if he's trying to tell us something. I'll show you later."

Rory continued to read the strange verses as both ships carried on up the Thames:

Continue sailing if you can
Under the rail road and walkway span.
Brunel, the first one he did build
In 1845 for all to admire and be thrilled.
Suspend belief in your travels
You have succeeded in all your battles.

Westminster in livery common
A source of power and might; and for one
Poet who, much like me,
Wrote of this place of beauty.
Wordsworth, he did endow her with such qualities
As are revered by all us Malachis.

And so to your final resting place go.
Your hearts will be beating with slow
Rhythm and steady pulse
As you traverse the dimensions' space;

So return to your healer

Oh, Rory and Sarah Wheeler.

George Gordon Byron, 2010

He read it a few more times to take it all in. He didn't understand it completely. Some of the verses seemed to be describing the bridges they had to navigate on their journey along the Thames. And what about the title and the line about a pact? Was Byron trying to say sorry? But for what? Oh, it was all too much to think about now. He'd better just concentrate on sailing the *Liberty*. He must remember to recite it to Sarah when he could.

Both ships had now reversed the MAST command and were sailing along steadily upstream. They had to keep to the centre of the river and not get too close to the South Bank where tourist cruisers were moored up against the Festival Pier. Soon they were activating MAST again and this time both mechanisms went smoothly. They were beginning to get the hang of sailing these ships and had relaxed a little, although it has to be said that most of the navigation and manoeuvring had been pre-programmed by the Malachis. The main hazards the children had to avoid were the other craft on the river.

They were getting closer to their arrival point and both children were becoming ever so slightly more nervous. Their hands were getting sweaty so that they couldn't grip the wheels so well. They both tried to keep their concentration on the river ahead and tried not to look around too much. Suddenly looming up in the air in front of them was the London Eye.

"Crikey, look at that. It's huge! I hadn't realised it was so big. The views up there must be amazing!" Sarah shouted across to Rory. "I hope we can go on it when we get back!"

"Watch out, Sarah!" Rory yelled across to her as a barge narrowly missed the bow of *Temple*. The wash made the little wooden vessel bounce up and down with such force that Sarah had to hold on tightly to the rails as she nearly lost her balance.

"Whoa - that was close!"

"You must keep your eyes on the river ahead, Sarah!"

"I know, but there is too much to see!" she replied, as she steadied herself.

They were approaching Westminster Bridge now and they realised they were close to their point of disembarkation. Sarah looked over at Big Ben and just then she caught a glimpse of three women standing on top of a chariot their arms raised as they were all waving at them. Sarah recognised them at once – Boudicca and her two daughters.

"Look, Rory. There over by the bridge. It's Boudicca – one of the greatest women ever!"

Rory looked over at where she was pointing. He was more taken by the younger women and gave them a thumbs-up sign.

"Get ready for the last MAST action, Sarah," he yelled across to his sister. "And don't distract me anymore! Look at the time. We haven't got a minute to spare!"

"Sorry – I wish I could grow my hair like theirs."

"Let's just get back first, hey?"

They navigated through the central span as the minute hand on Big Ben was approaching five to twelve and then made their way over to the embankment on the south side. They needed to find a mooring to tie up the boats and quickly, they didn't have much time left. The arrangement was that they would leave the boats securely tied up and the Malachis would retrieve them later and return them to their aerial resting places once they had been thoroughly checked over and refitted. Rory made sure he had everything that he needed to take with him ready. He reached for the poem and stuffed it into his pocket. As he did so he felt something hard. He grabbed hold of the object and pulled out a perfect miniature replica of the Welly. Immediately his eyes welled up. How thoughtful of that old soldier. He must have slipped it into his pocket when they were getting ready to leave the Welly this morning. Wellington knew how much that boat meant to me, he thought. "I'd gone on enough about our family's connections to her back in New Zealand. He really is an old softie at heart, and so am I," he said, as he wiped away a tear with the sleeve of his hoodie. "Now, come on – let's get back to the matter in hand."

"Over here, Sarah, are you ready? Quick, we've got to hurry!" Rory directed, as he recovered his composure. He had spotted a flight of stone steps leading up to street level just the other side of the bridge. A perfect landing spot.

He expertly brought *Liberty* back up into the wind still with her masts lowered. Holding a rope, he jumped out onto the stone jetty and managed to secure her using a rusty ring in the wall.

"Sarah, throw me a line, make sure you've secured it to the ship first. Hurry!"

"What do you take me for? I can sail you know. Just not something as big as this!" and she threw out what she thought was a perfectly coiled line. But horror of horrors! Rather than the rope uncoiling itself ready to be caught by Rory the thing came alive. It was a snake and it was hissing and spitting and had its head held back proudly ready to strike at Sarah.

"Aaahhh!" was all Sarah could scream as she dropped it onto the deck of the ship.

"Oh my God! Sarah look out!"

Rory reacted instinctively. He grabbed the bottle of Malachi Mist and blasted it with all his force at the snake, holding the canister for as long as he dared. The snake writhed and hissed and eventually slithered over the railings and into the depths of the river below.

"Sarah, quick, now's your chance – you're just going to have to jump. But be careful here – it's really slipper..."

"Heeelp!!"

Before Rory could finish his warning she had already slipped and fallen into the cold, murky water of the Thames. She was being swept downstream in the current and there was absolutely nothing he could do to rescue her.

Chapter Twenty Five

Next he heard the most enormous roar! He staggered up the steps and climbed over the locked gates to street level to find the source of the noise. All he saw was the flash of a lion's small, bushy tail as it leapt down from the stone plinth on the opposite side of the road. Not quite believing what he was seeing he raced after it only to see the most beautiful white lion leaning over the barrier reaching a paw down into the water. The next thing he knew Sarah was being lifted out of the river, dripping wet, being held carefully in the biggest, furriest paw he had ever seen.

"Are you OK, Sarah? I thought you'd had it then," Rory said, as he rushed to her side to help her get her breath back.

"Me too. That revolting snake and then it all happened so quickly. I'm not sure how I got out of the water just then, but, boy, I'm glad I did."

"No, me neither. But you're ok and that's all that matters. Come on we've no time to lose!" was all Rory could manage to say. And they ran full pelt towards St Thomas' Hospital and the Evelina Children's Hospital.

Edoc, the lion, strode nonchalantly back to his plinth, shaking his mane and paw to get rid of the water. All in a day's work, he smiled to himself, as he stood proudly looking at the pair of them running towards the hospital and their final destination.

The Malachis all cheered and clapped as they saw that Rory and Sarah had made it across the river and were on their way to the Evelina Children's Hospital. Big Ben started to chime 12 o'clock. A sonorous 'Dong!' rang out across the water.

***

As the second dong rang out the children were racing along Westminster Bridge Road towards St Thomas' Hospital. They weren't entirely sure where they were going but had been assured by Wellington that they would be taken care of. A group of four

199

brightly-dressed children were hanging around on the pavement kicking a ball against a wall while a small spotted dog on a lead was trying to catch it. This was the gang known as *The Children of the World* who normally hang out at the entrance to the ECH. The leader, Amos, a tall, gangly boy wearing a baseball cap, called out to Rory and Sarah as they sped past.

"Here – you two! This way – quick! We've been expecting you, come on!"

Joy, flicking her long blonde hair out of her eyes joined in, "Yeah – you'd best hurry up, only 10 more rings to go!"

Rory and Sarah stopped suddenly, turned round and followed this group of strange beings into the hospital grounds. They ran along the pedestrian walkway, trying to keep up with Joy and Amos striding out with their long legs. Raggio, the dog, scurried along on his short legs yapping at the heels of the younger two ruffians, Felix and Spero, clutching the football, as they skipped along behind. Rory and Sarah were oblivious to everything they passed. Ambulances screeching to a halt with blue lights flashing, people in wheelchairs making their way to the outpatients department, relatives and friends visiting the sick – everyone passed in a blur. The only thing Rory and Sarah could focus on was getting onto the right ward in the hospital in time to be transported back to their own dimension before the twelfth chime of Big Ben rang out across the river. The gang of children led them up staircases and along more passageways until finally they came to a large set of glass doors.

"In here," Amos directed, as they all pushed their way into the massive atrium.

"Let's take the stairs," Joy shouted. "They'll be quicker than the lift." Another chime of the bell rang out.

Sarah was keeping a count in her head. "That makes 3, 9 to go," she called out breathlessly to Rory.

They ran past the café, and the main reception area where all they could see were pictures of sea creatures. They were both feeling the effects of their journey this morning and their legs were beginning to ache; their breathing was laboured and they were slowing down as they reached the bottom of the staircase.

"Come on, Sarah – keep going," Rory ordered, as he dashed up the stairs two at a time, whilst holding on to the banister to give him extra leverage. Sarah was panting and she could only manage a fast walk by this stage. Raggio was barking. It's no use – that won't make me go any faster, she thought, crossly.

Up the first flight onto Arctic level. Sarah shivered involuntarily. The sight of the blue tinted walls, the icebergs and polar bears made her feel freezing cold.

Another chime rang out, which they only just managed to hear through the glass walls. "Four down, 8 to go," Sarah called out.

Suddenly they were up another flight of stairs and the walls opened out into a refreshing forestscape. Sarah felt she could breathe again and the trees seemed to give her renewed energy.

Joy and Amos were already there at the top of the stairs waiting for Rory and Sarah and the others to catch up.

"Right – this is where we leave you. Have a good journey back and have a good life," and with that they turned abruptly and ran back down the stairs.

"Where do we go now?" Sarah asked, anxiously looking round at the doors which were covered in all sorts of different trees.

"Ah here you are, we've been expecting you," Edith Cavell greeted them warmly and took Sarah by the hand.

Dong! Another second ticked ominously by.

Florence Nightingale added, "It's good to meet you two. We've heard so much about you. I'm only sorry we're going to be saying goodbye now. How was the journey? Are you both ready?"

Rory and Sarah nodded, but looked very scared at the prospect of the return journey.

"Now there's nothing to worry about. You see your parents in the ward – they are keeping vigil by your beds. You are still in a coma but all the signs show that you could come out of it at any time," Florence informed them.

The children peered into the ward and sure enough there were their parents, each of them holding a hand of one of them. They wanted to rush up to them straight away and hug them but, of course, that was impossible.

Edith said, "Now, we're going to send you off into your dimension in a second so just stand still and we'll do the rest." And with that Edith and Florence took a couple of steps back and then stepped forward and gave the children a mighty shove in the back.

Rory and Sarah felt themselves falling forward through the doors and headlong onto the floor of the ward but instead of hitting the floor they felt themselves falling down and down, spinning round and round into a dark abyss where all they could see were trees, bushes, fish, seals , dolphins, penguins and a large polar bear. The polar bear beckoned them to follow him and a loud 'Dong' rang out, reverberating in their ears.

All Sarah could think of was 6, halfway and counting.

***

Mike and Liz had been sitting by the children's beds since 9 o'clock that morning, as they had done every morning since the children had been brought in from the accident. They had recovered from their own minor injuries and their only concerns were for the safe recovery of their children. It had been a very fraught few days with lots of ups and downs. Just when they had thought the children were making progress one of them would have a setback. The doctors had remained positive all the time. Of course, they had treated many similar cases and knew the value of time and allowing the body to heal at its own pace. Five days after the accident was a critical time and Liz was feeling particularly anxious this morning.

"Did you call the airline, Mike?"

"Yes – and they said not to worry. We can rebook once we have a definite prognosis from the doctors. They really were very sympathetic for a change."

"Well – that's something I suppose."

Liz was sitting by Sarah's bed and dreamt of the day she and Sarah could go shopping in London together. Their stay in the big city hadn't been exactly what they had all planned so many weeks ago. It seemed like a lifetime. She promised herself that when, and it was a 'when' and not an 'if', Rory and Sarah recovered then she would take them on the biggest day out in London they could ever imagine. They would do everything on their lists and not just the top three. She didn't care about spoiling them. They could do whatever they wanted.

She gazed out of the window and looked over into Lambeth Palace Gardens and heard the chime of Big Ben in the background. "Seven," she said to herself. She had performed this ritual every day since the children had been admitted. She loved to hear the bell ring out across the river, she felt calmed by its regularity and tone; she always made sure she was keeping vigil in PICU around midday so she could hear the twelve chimes.

She waited expectantly for the eighth chime when instead she heard a loud beep on one of Sarah's monitors. Her blood pressure had made an unexpected leap. Liz was jolted out of her reverie. What could that mean? Liz thought, hopefully. Sister Bridge scurried over.

"Well, little girl, are you going to say hello to us today?" She made a few adjustments to the monitors and dials and checked her notes. Just then the same alarm sounded from Rory's machine. Again, a few adjustments made and Sister Bridge was looking encouraged.

"This could be it," she said to Mike and Liz expectantly. "I'm going to call Dr Arnold."

Mike and Liz peered over the beds expectantly and stared into the faces of Sarah and Rory, scrutinising them for any signs of movement. They had waited so long for this moment – could they really be regaining consciousness?

Big Ben struck the ninth chime. It rang out so clearly this time, it was as though they were standing right underneath the clock tower. Everything else was silent. The machines were beeping in hushed tones and all the nurses had stopped and turned to Rory's and Sarah's beds.

Everyone waited. No-one made a noise. No-one breathed.

In her mind Liz started to count back, "Three, two..."

Silence.

As Liz said, "One," in her mind they all heard a slight rustling. Sarah's left arm was making slight jerking movements and then her eyes blinked.

No-one moved a muscle. No-one dared.

Liz bent forward slowly. Was her daughter really coming out of her coma?

Sister Bridge checked some of the readings and took Sarah's pulse.

Yes! Sarah's eyes were opening! This was it! The moment they had been waiting for after all these days of agony.

Liz was too afraid to say anything. All she could do was gulp back a sob and wipe the tears from her eyes. She turned to Mike.

He was staring at Rory. His right arm made a small movement. Mike took hold of his hand and gently rubbed his thumb.

"Hiya fella?" Mike said. "You've decided to come back to us then?"

Liz stroked Sarah's face and wiped a stray curl of hair from her forehead.

"Oh my little darling!" was all she could say. "Thank goodness, you're safe and sound." She wanted to grab her little girl and wrap her arms around her, nestle her face in her daughter's hair and never, ever let her go.

Liz and Mike stood there, overcome with utter joy and love and happiness and gratitude and relief.

Sister Bridge stepped in, "Now – this is fantastic! We're going to have to check them both out very carefully, a step at a time, to assess if there is any lasting damage. But it seems we have turned a corner. Welcome to the Evelina, Rory and Sarah!"

Second by second Sarah and Rory were slowly taking in their surroundings. They blinked and looked around, and were confused by the breathing masks over their faces. And then they smiled. They weren't sure what had happened since the accident but here they were back with their parents and that was all that mattered.

As their parents were straightening out their sheets and pillows to make them more comfortable they noticed that each of them was holding something. Rory and Sarah both unfurled their clenched-up fists and there were the models of the boats.

"I don't remember them having these strange models with them before the accident. Do you Mike?"

"No – I don't think I've seen them before. I wonder where they came from?"

Just then Dr Arnold came over and took over. He was busying around the beds of the two children and didn't notice a piece of paper flutter down from Rory's side and waft underneath to be lodged in the wheel of the bed.

***

Florence and Edith were looking on from the doorway.

"I love happy endings, don't you Edith?" Florence said.

"Usually, yes. Did you see something fall from Rory's bed? Looked like a sheet of paper?"

"Go and see what it is, can you?" Florence suggested.

So Edith went back into the ward and knelt under the bed and brought out Byron's poem.

The two of them read it over and tried to understand its meaning. "Well, well, well. I didn't think we had heard the last of him. Come on – let's go and report back to the others."

As they walked into the conference room at the Wellington Arch a loud cheer went up.

"Well done you two. We had the comms a few minutes ago. Both children are doing fine and it doesn't look as though they will suffer any long term effects from the coma," Victoria announced, proudly. "And well done to you too, Arthur; you did a grand job of looking after them and helping them find their way back home."

Wellington took it all in his stride; after all he was used to succeeding against the odds. Florence and Edith, however, allowed themselves to bask in the congratulations which were being heaped on them by their fellow Malachis as they went around the room. "We only played a small part in their journey. Lots of you did far more than us."

Nelson said, "We make a good team don't we? That's what it is all about."

Wellington turned to Victoria. "Florence said something about a poem by Byron. Have you seen it?"

"No. I'm not sure I want to have anything to do with that man. When he deigns to return to his statue then I will deal with him. I need to discuss it first with the MCC. See what punishment they feel is appropriate. As far as Napier is concerned, go and sort him out can you. I'm sure he's had enough time to think about what he did. He must be feeling quite sorry for himself."

Victoria clapped her hands to get everyone's attention.

"I just want to say a big thank you to you all. We did a good job with Rory and Sarah and I'm pleased to tell you that the prognosis from the hospital is that they are expected to make a full recovery." She paused to let the murmurs of congratulation quieten down. "As far as Byron is concerned, I will just remind you that no matter what grievances you have had with people in your human life they are left behind when you become a Malachi. He seemed to have forgotten that vital rule and got a bit carried away. Now, I want you all to go back to your statues and prepare yourselves for tomorrow. The contest will resume. Good luck everyone!"

Meridion Zone

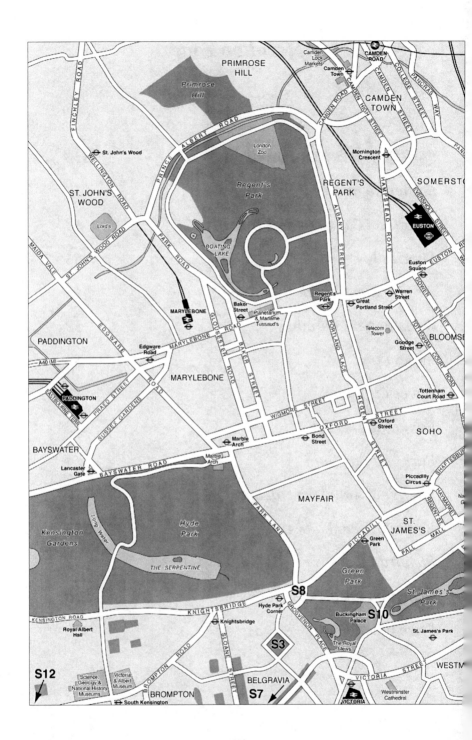

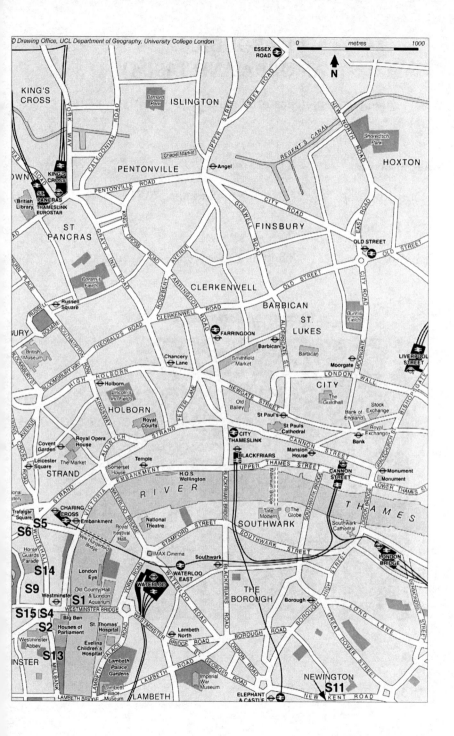

S1 – BOUDICCA,
(CAMORRA AND TASCA)

Queen of Iceni in Eastern England, 30 – 61 AD (approx)

Age at death:	31 (approx)
Statue Location:	Victoria Embankment, SW1
Date Erected:	1902
Sculptor:	Thomas Thornycroft

Deputy of Meridion Zone

Boudicca was the wife of Prasutagus, ruler of the Iceni people of East Anglia.

After the Roman invasion Prasutagus was allowed to continue to rule but after his death the Romans wanted to rule Iceni directly. They stripped and flogged Boudicca and raped her daughters, Camorra and Tasca. The Iceni rebelled, led by Boudicca, defeating the Romans at Colchester, London and St Albans.

Boudicca was finally defeated by a Roman army led by Paulinus but to avoid capture she poisoned herself and her daughters.

S2 – RICHARD I, COEUR de LION

Medieval king of England, 1157 - 1199

Age at death: 41

Statue Location: Old Palace Yard,
Houses of Parliament, SW1

Date Erected: 1851

Sculptor: Carlo Marochetti

Richard was the son of King Henry II and Eleanor of Aquitaine and was brought up in France. He was a great military leader and warrior and even fought against his father. After making an alliance with Philip II of France he overthrew his father and assumed the throne of England.

In 1190 he joined the unsuccessful third Crusades and on his way to the Holy Land conquered Cyprus. On his return home he was captured by Holy Roman Emperor Henry VI and held for many years. During this time his brother John formed an alliance with Philip II and assumed the throne. On his release in 1194 Richard defeated John and recaptured the land taken by Philip II.

He was fatally injured by an arrow while besieging the castle of Châlus in central France.

S3 – CHRISTOPHER COLUMBUS

Italian explorer, 1451 - 1506

Age at death:	54
Statue Location:	Belgrave Square, SW1
Date Erected:	1992
Sculptor:	Tomas Banuelos

Columbus was born in Genoa and spent his early years as a merchant seaman travelling extensively and acquiring navigation and map-making skills.

To avoid the threat of Islam to existing trade routes, Columbus eventually persuaded the King of Spain to sponsor his first voyage of discovery across the Atlantic Ocean to India. On 12th October 1492 he discovered land, mistakenly thinking it was part of the Indian subcontinent, but it was in fact a group of islands that we now refer to as the Bahamas.

His further voyages were not successful and he died a wealthy but disappointed man.

S4 – OLIVER CROMWELL

English soldier and statesman, 1599 - 1658

Age at death:	59
Statue Location:	Westminster, SW1
Date Erected:	1899
Sculptor:	Sir William Hamo Thornycroft

Cromwell was born in Huntingdon and studied at Cambridge University. He became an MP in 1628. He experienced a religious crisis and became a radical Puritan.

When Civil War broke out between Charles I and Parliament in 1642, Cromwell led the decisive victory over the King's forces at Naseby in 1645. He supported the King's execution in 1649 and became army commander. He then defeated Charles I's supporters, effectively ending the Civil War and made himself Lord Protector of the new republic in England in 1653.

After Cromwell's death the republic fell apart and the monarchy was restored. Cromwell's body was exhumed and he was hanged at Traitors' Gate in the Tower of London.

S5 – CHARLES I

King of England, Scotland and Ireland, 1600 - 1649

Age at death: 48

Statue Location: Trafalgar Square, SW1

Date Erected: 1633

Sculptor: Hubert le Sueur

Born in Scotland, Charles was the second son of James VI and became king as his elder brother had died. He was happily married to Henrietta Marie of France with whom he had five children.

He became an increasingly unpopular king, raising taxes and interfering with the English and Scottish churches.

Civil War began in 1642 which the Parliamentarians won. Charles refused to accept defeat but was eventually defeated and subsequently tried, convicted and executed in 1649. A republic called the Commonwealth of England (also known as the Cromwellian Interregnum) led by Oliver Cromwell, was declared.

S6 – JAMES COOK

Explorer and navigator, 1728 - 1779

Age at death:	50
Statue Location:	The Mall, SW1
Date Erected:	1914
Sculptor:	Sir Thomas Brock

James Cook was born in Cleveland, the son of a labourer and worked in the boat trade, transporting coal along the east coast. He joined the Navy in 1755 and learnt to survey and chart coastal waters.

He rose through the ranks of the Navy to Captain and made three voyages to the Pacific and was the first to circumnavigate New Zealand. He charted many of these newly discovered lands.

During his third voyage he landed on Hawaii where, during a struggle to take the local leader hostage, Cook was stabbed and killed.

S7 – WOLFGANG AMADEUS MOZART

Musician, 1756 - 1791

Age at death: 35

Statue Location: Orange Square, SW3

Date Erected: 1994

Sculptor: Philip Jackson

Mozart was born in Salzburg and from the age of 5 was composing music on the keyboard.

He began touring Europe performing at the age of 6 and learnt to play the violin. By the age of 13 he had composed his first opera. His family settled briefly in London before returning to the Continent, particularly Vienna and Prague. He wrote over 600 works during his lifetime.

He died of a mysterious fever and was buried in a common grave in Vienna.

S8 – ARTHUR WELLESLEY, DUKE OF WELLINGTON

British general, 1769 - 1852

Age at death:	83
Statue Location:	Hyde Park Corner, SW1
Date Erected:	1887
Sculptor:	Chantrey

Wellington was born into a noble Protestant Irish family and was commissioned into the British Army in 1787.

He fought in many wars in India before returning to the UK and buying a seat in Parliament. He led British expeditionary forces against the French and in 1815 returned to Britain a hero after famously defeating Napoleon at the Battle of Waterloo. He became Prime Minister in 1828 and again in 1834 and was equally loved and hated.

He had a state funeral and is buried next to Nelson, whom he met only once.

S9 – BENJAMIN DISRAELI, LORD BEACONS-FIELD

British statesman and novelist, 1804 - 1881

Age at death:	76
Statue Location:	Parliament Square, SW1
Date Erected:	1883
Sculptor:	Mario Raggi

Disraeli was born into a Jewish family but baptised a Christian. He originally trained as a solicitor.

He lost money on a publication supporting South American mines and so became a novelist. Eventually he went into politics becoming MP for Maidstone in 1837 as a Tory. He became Prime Minister in 1868 taking over from the then ailing Earl of Derby. He became PM for a second term in 1874 and his legacy was social reform with the introduction of the Public Health Act and Education Act.

He had an aggressive foreign policy culminating in Queen Victoria becoming Empress of India in 1876. He retired from politics in 1880.

S10 – QUEEN VICTORIA

Longest reigning British monarch, 1819 - 1901

Age at death:	81
Statue Location:	Buckingham Palace, SW1
Date Erected:	1911
Sculptor:	Sir Thomas Brock

Chief of Meridion Zone and Malachi Chief

The only child of the Duke of Kent, she was born in London and succeeded her uncle King William IV in 1837 at the age of 18. She married her first cousin in 1840 and she and Albert spent a happy marriage of 20 years with their nine children.

Albert became her political adviser but died from typhoid in 1861. Victoria mourned him for the rest of her life. She was monarch of a vast empire and oversaw great changes in British society throughout her long reign.

She was the first monarch to reside in Buckingham Palace and died on the Isle of Wight.

S11 – CATHERINE BOOTH

Wife of the founder of the Salvation Army, 1829 - 1890

Age at death: 61

Statue Location: Denmark Hill, SE5

Date Erected: 1929

Sculptor: G E Wade

Catherine Booth was born in Derbyshire, the daughter of a coach builder. She was brought up in Brixton, South London and was a devout Christian.

She married William Booth, a Methodist minister, and together they began the work of the Christian Mission, which later changed its name to the Salvation Army.

Catherine was a renowned preacher and was known as the Mother of the Army.

S12 – LORD ROBERT BADEN-POWELL

Lieutenant General in the British Army and founder of the Scout movement, 1857 – 1941

Age at death: 83

Statue Location: Queen's Gate, SW7

Date Erected: 1961

Sculptor: Donald Potter

Baden-Powell was born in London and educated at Charterhouse.

He joined the army aged 19 and served in South Africa, becoming a hero of the Siege of Mafeking (1899 – 1900). He wrote books about military scouting and wrote Scouting for Boys in 1908. This led to the formation of the Boy Scouts and Girl Guides movements. He married in 1912 and his wife Olave supported the Scouting movement. At the first Scout Jamboree in Olympia in 1920 Baden-Powell was acclaimed Chief Scout of the World.

He and his wife moved to Kenya in 1939 where he died in 1941 and was buried there.

S13 – EMMELINE PANKHURST

Leader of the British women's rights activists, known as the Suffragettes, 1858 - 1928

Age at death:	69
Statue Location:	Victoria Tower Gardens, SW1
Date Erected:	1930
Sculptor:	A G Walker

Emmeline (known as Emily) was born into a political family in Manchester. She married Richard Pankhurst, a lawyer and supporter of the Women's Suffrage movement, in 1879. He died in 1898 and Emmeline went on to found the suffragette movement, the militant Women's Social and Political Union (WSPU).

Her daughters, Christabel and Sylvia, were both activists and the suffragettes were renowned for their hunger strikes, demonstrations and window smashing as they protested at the government's continued failure to grant women the vote. The First World War intervened but afterwards in 1918 women aged 30 and over were granted the vote.

Shortly before Emmeline's death women were granted equal voting rights with men (at 21).

S14 – EARL DOUGLAS HAIG

British commander, 1861 - 1928

Age at death: 66

Statue Location: Whitehall, SW1

Date Erected: 1937

Sculptor: Alfred Hardiman

Douglas Haig was born in Edinburgh, into a wealthy whisky family. He was educated at Oxford and Sandhurst and served in the cavalry in India.

At the outbreak of the First World War Haig was appointed Commander-in-Chief of the Army and was responsible for ordering the Somme offensive during which 20,000 soldiers were killed on the first day. Under his leadership the Germans were gradually weakened leading to victory in 1918.

Haig served as a commander in the British forces until he retired and also helped establish the British Legion.

S15 –SIR WINSTON CHURCHILL

Politician and war-time Prime Minster, 1874 - 1965

Age at death:	91
Statue Location:	Parliament Square, SW1
Date Erected:	1973
Sculptor:	Ivor Roberts-Jones

Born at Blenheim Palace to a Tory MP father and American mother, Churchill attended Sandhurst and embarked on an army career.

After seeing action in India and the Sudan he went into politics in 1900. He served as both a Tory and a Liberal MP and held a number of military-oriented posts in cabinets. Churchill warned about the Nazi uprising and took over as PM from Neville Chamberlain. He refused to surrender to Nazi Germany and he inspired the country building strong relations with America to win the war effort.

He lost power in 1945 but returned as PM in 1951. He was awarded the Nobel Prize for Literature and was given a state funeral. He is regarded as a national hero.

Occidental Zone

Queen Alexandra	*W8*
Lord Byron	*W5*
Charlie Chaplin	*W14*
Dwight D Eisenhower	*W15*
Queen Elizabeth, the Queen Mother	*W17*
Sigmund Freud	*W10*
Charles de Gaulle	*W16*
Admiral Lord Horatio Nelson	*W3*
Quintin Hogg	*W9*
David Livingstone	*W6*
General Sir Charles Napier	*W4*
Florence Nightingale	*W7*
Sir Joshua Reynolds	*W2*
Captain Robert Scott	*W11*
Franklin Delano Roosevelt	*W13*
Sir Ernest Shackleton	*W12*
William Shakespeare	*W1*

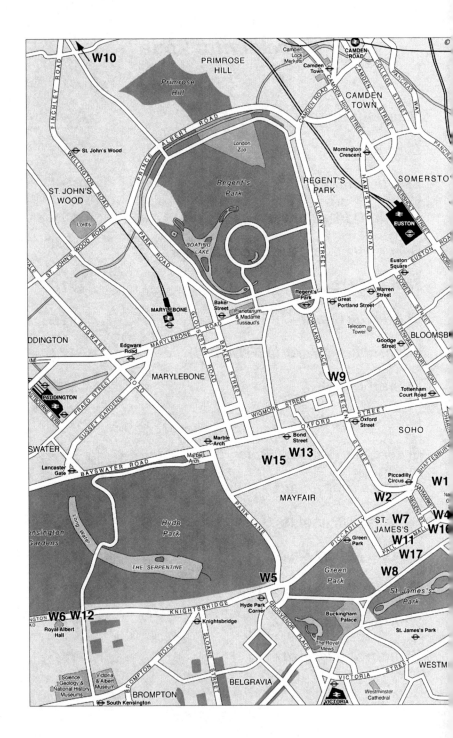

W10

PRIMROSE
HILL

Primrose
Hill

London
Zoo

Camden
Lock
Markets

Camden
Town

CAMDEN
ROAD

CAMDEN
TOWN

St. John's Wood

ST. JOHN'S
WOOD

Lord's

Regent's
Park

Mornington
Crescent

REGENT'S
PARK

SOMERSTO

BOATING
LAKE

EUSTON

Euston
Square

EUSTON

MARYLEBONE

Baker
Street

Planetarium
& Madame
Tussaud's

Regent's
Park

Warren
Street

Great
Portland Street

Telecom
Tower

Goodge
Street

BLOOMSB

DDINGTON

Edgware
Road

MARYLEBONE

MARYLEBONE

W9

PADDINGTON

Tottenham
Court Road

SWATER

WIGMORE STREET

OXFORD

Oxford
Street

STREET

SOHO

Lancaster
Gate

BAYSWATER ROAD

Marble
Arch

Marble
Arch

Bond
Street

W15 W13

Piccadilly
Circus

W1

MAYFAIR

W2

ensington
Gardens

Hyde
Park

THE SERPENTINE

PARK LANE

ST.
JAMES'S

W7

W11

W17

W4

W10

Green
Park

W5

Green
Park

W8

St. James's
Park

W6 W12

Royal Albert
Hall

KNIGHTSBRIDGE

Hyde Park
Corner

Knightsbridge

Buckingham
Palace

St. James's Park

The Royal
Mews

Science,
Geology &
National History
Museums

Victoria
& Albert
Museum

BROMPTON

South Kensington

BELGRAVIA

VICTORIA

VICTORIA

Westminster
Cathedral

WESTM

0   metres   1000

N

ESSEX
ROAD

KING'S
CROSS

Barnard
Park

ISLINGTON

Shoreditch
Park

HOXTON

Chapel Market

Angel

PENTONVILLE

REGENT'S CANAL

TOWN

KING'S
CROSS

British
Library

ST
PANCRAS
THAMESLINK
EUROSTAR

PENTONVILLE ROAD

CITY ROAD

ST
PANCRAS

GOSWELL ROAD

FINSBURY

OLD STREET

Coram's
Fields

CLERKENWELL

BARBICAN

ST.
LUKES

LIVERPOOL
STREET

Russell
Square

FARRINGDON

Bunhill
Fields

Barbican

Moorgate

British
Museum

Chancery
Lane

CLERKENWELL ROAD

Smithfield
Market

Barbican

LONDON WALL

Holborn

HIGH HOLBORN

HOLBORN

Lincoln's
Inn Fields

NEWGATE STREET

CITY

Old
Bailey

The
Guildhall

Stock
Exchange

St Paul's

St Pauls
Cathedral

Bank of
England

Royal
Courts

STRAND

CITY
THAMESLINK

Royal
Exchange

Covent
Garden

Royal Opera
House

ALDWYCH

Mansion
House

Bank

Leicester
Square

The Market

Temple

BLACKFRIARS

CANNON STREET

Monument

14 W1

STRAND

Somerset
House

EMBANKMENT

H.Q.S.
Wellington

UPPER THAMES STREET

CANNON
STREET

Monument

LOWER THAMES ST

National
Gallery

RIVER

Millennium Bridge

THAMES

4 W3

CHARING
CROSS

National
Theatre

Tate
Modern

The
Globe

SOUTHWARK

Southwark
Cathedral

6

Trafalgar
Square

Embankment

Royal
Festival
Hall

STAMFORD STREET

SOUTHWARK STREET

Horse
Guards
Parade

New Hungerford
Bridge

IMAX Cinema

Southwark

LONDON
BRIDGE

London
Eye

WATERLOO
EAST

WATERLOO

THE
BOROUGH

Westminster

Old County Hall
& London
Aquarium

Borough

WESTMINSTER BRIDGE

Big Ben
Houses of
Parliament

St. Thomas'
Hospital

Lambeth
North

LONG LANE

Westminster
Abbey

Evelina
Children's
Hospital

BRIDGE
ROAD

BOROUGH ROAD

GREAT DOVER STREET

MINSTER

Lambeth
Palace
Gardens

Imperial
War
Museum

NEWINGTON

Lambeth
Palace
Museum

LAMBETH BRIDGE

LAMBETH

ELEPHANT
& CASTLE

NEW KENT ROAD

W1 – WILLIAM SHAKESPEARE

Elizabethan playwright and poet, 1564 – 1616

Age at death:	52
Statue Location:	Leicester Square WC2
Date Erected:	1874
Sculptor:	Giovanni Fontana

Born in Stratford-upon-Avon to gentry, Shakespeare is one of the greatest playwrights, poets, actors and dramatists of all time. He wrote 38 plays and 154 sonnets, all published posthumously.

He married Anne Hathaway in 1582 and they had three children. He moved to London in the 1580s to become an actor and playwright and was instrumental in building the Globe Theatre.

He is regarded as Britain's national poet and known as the "Bard of Avon".

W2 – SIR JOSHUA REYNOLDS

Artist, 1723 - 1792

Age at death:	68
Statue Location:	Royal Academy, W1
Date Erected:	1931
Sculptor:	Alfred Drury

Born in Devon, one of 11 children, he went to Rome to study art.

He travelled extensively in Italy and returned to England in 1752. He established his home and studios in Leicester Square and soon became a successful portrait artist. He founded the Royal Academy with Gainsborough in 1768 and is considered one of England's most important painters.

He was the first president of the Royal Academy and was knighted by George III in 1769. He painted more than 3000 portraits, never married and lost his sight in 1789 having already lost his hearing whilst in Rome. He is buried in St Paul's Cathedral.

W3 – ADMIRAL LORD HORATIO NELSON

English admiral, 1758 - 1805

Age at death: 47

Statue Location: Trafalgar Square

Date Erected: 1843

Sculptor: E H Baily (statue)

Chief of Occidental Zone

Born in Burnham, Norfolk, he was a sickly and slender child and joined the Navy aged 12.

He was promoted to captain, then commander and finally admiral and was an inspirational leader.

He lost the sight of his right eye at the Battle of Calvi and his right arm at the Battle of Santa Cruz in 1797.

As a British naval commander and national hero, Nelson is famous for his naval victories against the French during the Napoleonic Wars. His last victory was the Battle of Trafalgar in 1805 when he also lost his life.

W4 – GENERAL SIR CHARLES NAPIER

British army general, 1782 - 1853

Age at death: 71

Statue Location: Trafalgar Square, SW1

Date Erected: 1855

Sculptor: George Cannon Adams

Napier was a British General and Commander-in-Chief in India. He was born into a military family and served as a soldier in the Napoleonic Wars.

He was Governor of Cephalonia 1822 – 1830. He was an advocate of Greek Independence and was a friend of Lord Byron.

In 1842 he was Major-General of the Indian Army and followed a brutal policy to defeat ruling emirs. He is famous for capturing the Indian province of Sindh.

W5 – LORD GEORGE GORDON BYRON

Romantic Poet, 1788 - 1824

Age at death: 36

Statue Location: Hyde Park Corner, SW1

Date Erected: 1880

Sculptor: Richard C Belt

Byron is regarded as one of Europe's greatest poets. Brought up in Aberdeen he inherited the family estate of Newstead Abbey in 1798 and when not at school lived with his mother at Burgage Manor, Southwell, Nottinghamshire.

He published his first book of poetry in 1809 and then travelled extensively across southern Europe. On his return to England he assumed his seat in the House of Lords, using his position to argue for radical causes. He went into exile from Britain in 1816 following pressures of a failed marriage, scandalous affairs and debts. He served as a leader of Italy's revolutionary organisation and travelled to fight against the Ottoman Empire in Greece's War of Independence in 1823, where he is regarded as a hero.

He wrote many poems, plays and novels. He died of fever in Greece. His statue features his dog, Boatswain.

W6 – DAVID LIVINGSTONE

Missionary and explorer, 1813 - 1873

Age at death: 60

Statue Location: Royal Geographic Society, SW7

Date Erected: 1953

Sculptor: T B Huxley-Jones

Livingstone was a Scottish missionary and one of the greatest European explorers of Africa. He studied medicine and theology and was posted to Africa in 1841 as a missionary doctor to introduce Africans to Christianity and to free them from slavery.

He was the first European to see the Victoria Falls which he named after Queen Victoria. He also discovered the source of the Nile. Henry Stanley was sent by the New York Herald Tribune to provide vital supplies to Livingstone.

He died from malaria. His heart is buried in Africa and his body in Westminster Abbey.

W7 – FLORENCE NIGHTINGALE

Nurse, 1820 – 1910

Age at death:	90
Statue Location:	Waterloo Place, SW1
Date Erected:	1915
Sculptor:	Arthur Walker

Florence Nightingale was born in Florence, Italy, where her parents were on a tour of Europe. She was a gifted mathematician and against her parents' wishes entered nursing in 1844.

Known as "The Lady with the Lamp" she was a pioneering nurse and is particularly remembered for her work in the military hospitals in the Crimean War, in 1854. Using statistical analysis she improved hygiene in the war hospitals.

She returned to the UK in 1857 and set up the Nightingale Training School in St Thomas' Hospital in 1860. She became the first female member of the Royal Statistical Society. She died in her sleep aged 90.

W8 – QUEEN ALEXANDRA

Queen Consort of King Edward VII, 1844 - 1925

Age at death: 80

Statue Location: Marlborough Road, SW1

Date Erected: 1926

Sculptor: Sir Alfred Gilbert

Born in Copenhagen, Denmark, she was consort to Edward VII. She married Edward, Queen Victoria's heir, in 1863 and was known as the Princess of Wales. She was very popular and very stylish.

She was Queen-Empress consort from 1901 – 1910 and was a devoted mother, putting up with her husband's affairs. She enjoyed social activities including dancing, skating and hunting but rheumatic fever left her with a permanent limp.

She founded the Queen Alexandra's Nursing Corps during the Boer War. She died at Sandringham House, Norfolk, aged 80.

W9 – QUINTIN HOGG

Philanthropist, 1845 - 1903

Age at death: 57

Statue Location: Langham Place, W1

Date Erected: 1906

Sculptor: Sir George Frampton

Hogg was educated at Eton where he became an accomplished sportsman and played football for Wanderers Football Club.

He started his philanthropic work by teaching poor children in the street and he opened his first school near Charing Cross in 1864. He was also a successful businessman dealing prosperously in tea and sugar. In 1882 he founded the Young Men's Christian Institute to provide for the athletic, intellectual, social and religious needs of young men, which was renamed the Regent Street Polytechnic, now the University of Westminster.

As an alderman of the first London County Council he encouraged the founding of other polytechnics, helping to establish 12 by the time of his death.

W10 – SIGMUND FREUD

Austrian neurologist, 1856 - 1939

Age at death:	83
Statue Location:	Belsize Lane, NW3
Date Erected:	1970
Sculptor:	Oscar Nemon

Freud was born to Jewish parents in Moravia, now part of the Czech Republic. He was brought up in Vienna and studied medicine.

He specialised in psychoanalysis, developing many controversial theories concerning sexuality, ego and repression which greatly influenced this field. He developed a method of treating psychological problems through analysis.

As a Jew he was forced to flee Nazi Austria in 1938 and spent the last year of his life in London. He was diagnosed with throat cancer in 1923, (he was a heavy cigar smoker). After more than 30 operations he eventually succumbed to the disease.

W11 – CAPTAIN ROBERT SCOTT

Explorer, 1868 - 1912

Age at death: 43

Statue Location: Waterloo Place, SW1

Date Erected: 1915

Sculptor: Lady Scott

Scott was born in Devon and followed the family tradition of serving the armed services and entered the navy as a cadet aged 13.

He served on many Royal Navy ships and led the National Antarctic Expedition of 1901-1904. Scott organised an expedition to reach the South Pole but was beaten by a team of Norwegians led by Amundsen. The team headed back but perished in the bitter conditions.

Their bodies and Scott's diary were found eight months later and the bodies were buried at the spot.

W12 – SIR ERNEST SHACKLETON

Antarctic Explorer, 1874 - 1922

Age at death: 47

Statue Location: Royal Geographic Society, SW7

Date Erected: 1932

Sculptor: C Sargeant Jagger

Shackleton was born 30 miles outside Dublin but brought up in South London and attended Dulwich College. He went to sea at the age of 16 against the wishes of his father.

He was chosen to accompany Captain Scott to the South Pole on the famous Discovery Expedition, when they came within 400 miles of the pole, in 1902. In 1907 he set out on his own expedition coming within 97 miles of the pole before running out of food. He commanded a second voyage on Endurance to circumnavigate the South Pole in 1914 but the ship became trapped in ice forcing Shackleton to travel 800 miles to South Georgia to get help.

Shackleton embarked on his third expedition to circumnavigate the Antarctic. On the way he suffered a heart attack in Rio de Janeiro and subsequently died of a fatal attack in South Georgia after failing to seek proper medical attention. He is buried in South Georgia.

W13 – FRANKLIN DELANO ROOSEVELT

US President, 1882 – 1945

Age at death:	63
Statue Location:	Grosvenor Square, W1
Date Erected:	1948
Sculptor:	Sir William Reid Dick

Born in New York state to a wealthy family, Roosevelt attended law college but went into politics in 1910.

He contracted polio in 1921 but with the help and support of his wife returned to work and was elected 32nd President of the USA in 1932, as a Democrat. With the New Deal he successfully combated the problems of the Great Depression.

During his third term as president he provided financial support to Britain and her allies in the Second World War. After the Japanese attacked Pearl Harbour Roosevelt brought America into the war and took the lead in establishing a grand alliance among the countries fighting the Axis powers. He died a month before Germany's unconditional surrender.

W14 – CHARLES CHAPLIN

English comic actor and silent film director, 1889 - 1977

Age at death: 88

Statue Location: Leicester Square, WC2

Date Erected: 1981

Sculptor: John Doubleday

Chaplin was born to actor parents and raised in South London. He spent time with his siblings in the workhouse when his father abandoned them and his mother suffered with mental illness.

Chaplin started performing as a young child and was soon touring America. He began appearing in silent movies from 1913 and started writing and directing his own films. He declined to support the Second World War effort which led to public anger and after the war he was accused of "un-American activities" and of being a communist. Chaplin left the USA in 1952 and J Edgar Hoover, who was head of the FBI, successfully revoked his re-entry permit, effectively exiling Chaplin.

He settled in Switzerland where he continued to make films. His health began to fail him and he died in his sleep on Christmas Day in 1977.

W15 –DWIGHT D EISENHOWER

World War II general and US president, 1890 - 1969

Age at death: 79

Statue Location: Grosvenor Square, W1

Date Erected: 1989

Sculptor: Robert Dean

Deputy of Occidental Zone

Born to a family of farmers, Eisenhower attended military college. He led military operations in Europe during World War II and led the successful invasion of Europe in 1944.

He retired from the army and was Supreme Commander of NATO before becoming the 34th US president in 1953, for two terms. During his presidency he ended the Korean War and built the interstate highway system.

He continued to be very athletic during his retirement frequently playing golf. He died of heart failure.

W16 – CHARLES de GAULLE

French general and president, 1890 - 1970

Age at death: 79

Statue Location: Carlton Terrace, SW1

Date Erected: 1994

Sculptor: Angela Connor

De Gaulle grew up in Paris and was the son of a teacher. He joined the army and was decorated during World War I.

After the war he wrote books and articles on military topics and campaigned for the modernisation of the French army. In 1940, after German forces had overrun France, he refused to accept the French government's truce with Germany and he fled to England to become leader of the Free French. He flew into Paris after the liberation of France to a hero's welcome.

After the war he became disillusioned with politics and retired but re-emerged after the revolts in Algiers. He founded the Fifth Republic and was elected president in 1958. After surviving much political controversy from socialists he resigned in 1969 after losing a referendum and died of a heart attack. He is regarded as a national hero.

W17 – QUEEN ELIZABETH, THE QUEEN MOTHER

Queen Consort of King George VI, 1900 - 2002

Age at death:	101
Statue Location:	The Mall, SW1
Date Erected:	2009
Sculptor:	Philip Jackson

Elizabeth Bowes-Lyon was born in Scotland and married Albert, Duke of York, the second son of King George V and Queen Mary. They had two daughters, Elizabeth and Margaret.

Albert unexpectedly became King in 1936 when his brother Edward VIII abdicated to marry the American divorcée Wallace Simpson. During the Second World War Elizabeth provided much moral support to the British public, notably visiting the bombed areas of the East End of London.

She was widowed at the age of 51 in 1952 and assumed the role of matriarch of the Royal Family, as her eldest daughter Elizabeth became Queen. She was immensely popular and continued with her royal duties until a few months before her death.

Oriental Zone

Queen Anne	E3
Sir Francis Bacon	E1
Isambard Kingdom Brunel	E11
Robert Burns	E8
Edith Cavell	E13
Michael Faraday	E9
Mahatma Gandhi	E14
William Gladstone	E12
Sir Henry Havelock	E10
Dr Samuel Johnson	E5
Sir Isaac Newton	E2
Joseph Priestley	E7
George Washington	E6
John Wesley	E4

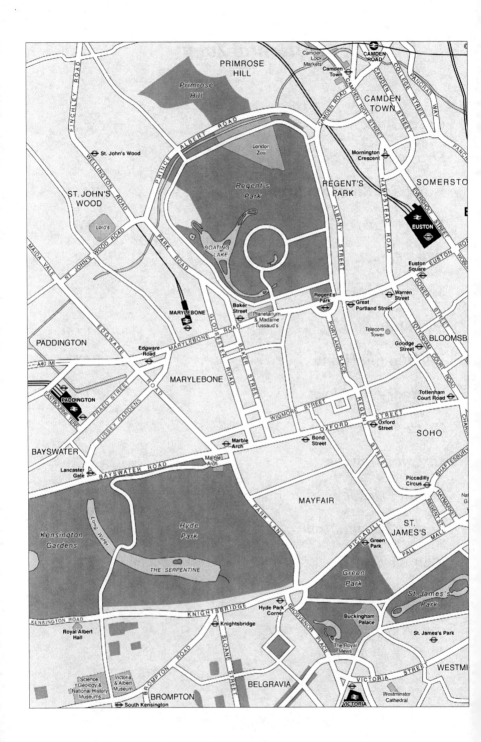

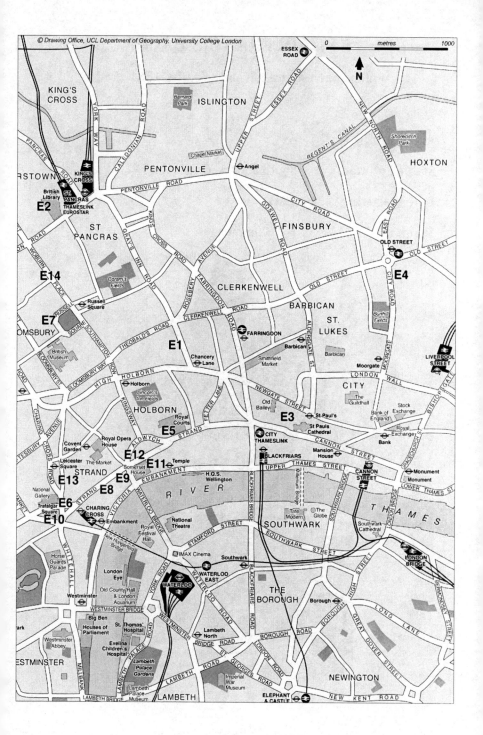

0   metres   1000

N

KING'S
CROSS

ESSEX
ROAD

YORK WAY

Barnard
Park

ISLINGTON

ESSEX STREET

UPPER STREET

REGENT'S CANAL

Shoreditch
Park

NEW NORTH ROAD

HOXTON

PANCRAS ROAD

CALEDONIAN ROAD

Chapel Market

Angel

PENTONVILLE

CITY ROAD

GOSWELL ROAD

EAST ROAD

RSTOWN

KING'S
CROSS

British
Library

ST.
PANCRAS
THAMESLINK
EUROSTAR

PENTONVILLE ROAD

FINSBURY

OLD STREET

CITY ROAD

OLD STREET

E2

ST
PANCRAS

KING'S CROSS ROAD

GRAY'S INN ROAD

E4

E14

Coram's
Fields

ROSEBERY AVENUE

FARRINGDON ROAD

CLERKENWELL

OLD STREET

ALDERSGATE ST.

ST.
LUKES

Bunhill
Fields

GOSWELL ROAD

BISHOPSGATE

LIVERPOOL
STREET

WOBURN PLACE

Russell
Square

RUSSELL SQUARE

E7

OMSBURY

British
Museum

BLOOMSBURY ST.

SOUTHAMPTON ROW

THEOBALD'S ROAD

CLERKENWELL ROAD

FARRINGDON ROAD

FARRINGDON

Barbican

Smithfield
Market

Barbican

Moorgate

MOORGATE

LONDON WALL

E1

Chancery
Lane

CITY

The
Guildhall

Stock
Exchange

Bank of
England

Royal
Exchange

Bank

CHARING CROSS ROAD

HIGH HOLBORN

KINGSWAY

Holborn

Lincoln's
Inn Fields

HOLBORN

FETTER LANE

NEWGATE STREET

Old
Bailey

E3

St Paul's

St Pauls
Cathedral

GRACECHURCH ST.

SHAFTESBURY AVENUE

Royal
Courts

E5

STRAND

CITY
THAMESLINK

CANNON STREET

Mansion
House

Monument

Monument

Covent
Garden

Royal Opera
House

ALDWYCH

E12

Somerset
House

E11   Temple

BLACKFRIARS

UPPER THAMES STREET

CANNON
STREET

LOWER THAMES ST.

Leicester
Square

The Market

STRAND

E9

EMBANKMENT

H.Q.S.
Wellington

BLACKFRIARS BRIDGE

THAMES STREET

Millennium Bridge

SOUTHWARK BRIDGE

STRAND

National
Gallery

E13

E8

VICTORIA

RIVER

Tate
Modern

The
Globe

THAMES

Trafalgar
Square

E6

E10

CHARING
CROSS

Embankment

WATERLOO BRIDGE

National
Theatre

STAMFORD STREET

SOUTHWARK

Southwark
Cathedral

LONDON
BRIDGE

WHITEHALL

Horse
Guards
Parade

New Hungerford
Bridge

Royal
Festival
Hall

IMAX Cinema

Southwark

SOUTHWARK STREET

HIGH STREET

BOROUGH HIGH STREET

BERMONDSEY STREET

LONG LANE

Westminster

London
Eye

Old County Hall
& London
Aquarium

YORK ROAD

WATERLOO
EAST

WATERLOO

WATERLOO ROAD

BLACKFRIARS ROAD

THE
BOROUGH

Borough

GREAT DOVER STREET

National
Gallery

Westminster
Abbey

WESTMINSTER BRIDGE

Big Ben

Houses of
Parliament

St Thomas'
Hospital

WESTMINSTER

Lambeth
North

BRIDGE ROAD

LONDON ROAD

BOROUGH ROAD

ark

ESTMINSTER

MILLBANK

Evelina
Children's
Hospital

Lambeth
Palace
Gardens

LAMBETH PALACE ROAD

Lambeth
Palace
Museum

LAMBETH BRIDGE

LAMBETH

LAMBETH ROAD

GEORGES ROAD

Imperial War
Museum

ELEPHANT
& CASTLE

NEWINGTON

NEW KENT ROAD

E1 – SIR FRANCIS BACON

Philosopher, statesman and scientist, 1561 - 1626

Age at death: 65

Statue Location: South Square, Gray's Inn, WC1

Date Erected: 1912

Sculptor: F W Pommeroy

Bacon was an eminent philosopher, MP, scientist and lawyer. He established a scientific methodology for conducting scientific enquiry which is known as the Baconian method.

He was made Lord Chancellor by James I in 1618 but was dismissed for corruption in 1621. Barred from office he spent the last years of his life writing.

He was a keen gardener. Whilst trying to preserve the carcass of a chicken in snow he contracted pneumonia and died.

E2 – SIR ISAAC NEWTON

Mathematician and physicist, 1642 - 1727

Age at death: 84

Statue Location: British Library, NW1

Date Erected: 1995

Sculptor: Eduardo Paolozzi

Born in Lincolnshire and brought up by his grandparents, Newton studied mathematics, physics, optics and astronomy at Cambridge University.

In 1687 he published his greatest work, Principia Mathematica in which he showed how a universal force, gravity, applied to all bodies in the universe. He defined the basic laws of motion.

He was appointed Warden of the Royal Mint in 1696 and was knighted by Queen Anne in 1705. He was prone to depression and was an argumentative man. He is regarded as one of the greatest physicists and mathematicians ever.

E3 – QUEEN ANNE

First sovereign of the United Kingdom, 1665 - 1714

Age at death: 49

Statue Location: St Paul's Cathedral, EC4

Date Erected: 1886

Sculptor: Richard Belt

Chief of Oriental Zone

Anne was born in London but spent her early years in France and was brought up a Protestant in spite of her father being Catholic.

She married Prince George of Denmark in 1683 and they lived a happy marriage. Although she had 18 pregnancies, none survived beyond 11 years. She was ill with gout and rheumatism and was carried to her coronation in 1702. Anne was Queen of England, Scotland and Ireland, and became first sovereign of a united England & Scotland, under the Acts of Union in 1707, reigning for 12 years, and was therefore the last Queen of England and the last Queen of Scots.

She had a liking for spirits and died of gout. She had no surviving heir.

E4 – JOHN WESLEY

Founder of the Methodist movement, 1703 - 1791

Age at death:	88
Statue Location:	City Road Chapel, N1
Date Erected:	1891
Sculptor:	J Adams Acton

Wesley was an Anglican cleric and Christian theologian who with his brother Charles founded the Methodist Church. He was raised in a pious family, one of 19 children, and went to Oxford University. There he established the "Holy Club" and advocated a methodical approach to studying the bible, hence the name Methodists.

He travelled with his brother, Charles, to Georgia, USA, to preach but soon returned to England where he gave sermons in the open air. A network of Methodist Societies soon became established, and the City Road Methodist Church was built in 1777 receiving financial support from the monarch George III.

He lived a simple life, travelling and preaching on horseback.

E5 – Dr SAMUEL JOHNSON

Author, 1709 - 1784

Age at death:	75
Statue Location:	St Clement Danes, WC2
Date Erected:	1910
Sculptor:	Percy Fitzgerald

Born in Staffordshire to a bookseller, Johnson spent a brief period at Oxford University.

He worked in London as a journalist and gradually acquired a literary reputation. He was commissioned to compile *The Dictionary of the English Language* which was completed after 8 years and brought Johnson popularity and success. Despite this success Johnson was continually short of money but in 1762 he was awarded a government pension.

He travelled extensively in Scotland and was an important literary figure in London.

E6 – GEORGE WASHINGTON

Revolutionary and first president of the USA, 1732 - 1799

Age at death: 66

Statue Location: Trafalgar Square, SW1

Date Erected: 1921

Sculptor: Jean Antoine Houdon

Washington was born in Virginia into a family of farmers. He trained as a surveyor and joined the army, fighting for the British during the French and Indian Wars.

He led the American army during the War of Independence and forced the surrender of the British soldier Cornwallis at Yorktown. He became the *first* president of the United States of America in 1789 and served two terms as president.

When he retired from politics in 1797 he returned to Vermont to farm his family estate. He had false teeth and red hair, which he powdered white. He died from a throat infection.

E7 – JOSEPH PRIESTLEY

Chemist, 1733 - 1804

Age at death: 71

Statue Location: University of London, Russell Square, WC1

Date Erected: 1914

Sculptor: Gilbert Bayes

Priestley was born in Leeds and brought up by his aunt after the death of his mother. He was a brilliant student and studied the sciences, philosophy, maths and languages.

He became a Presbyterian minister and was a non-conformist, travelling around the country teaching and preaching. He wrote books on science, religion and politics and began experimenting with electricity and gases. He discovered oxygen in 1774.

He met Benjamin Franklin, a future Founding Father of the United States. His support for the American colonies and the French Revolution caused much unrest and he was forced into exile in America in 1794 where he spent the rest of his life.

E8 – ROBERT BURNS

National poet of Scotland, 1759 – 1796

Age at death: 37

Statue Location: Embankment Gardens, WC2

Date Erected: 1884

Sculptor: Sir John Steel

Burns is regarded as the national poet of Scotland. He was born in Ayrshire to tenant farmers, the eldest of seven children, and was educated at home.

He enjoyed writing poetry and songs and had his first book of poetry published as a means to raise enough funds to pay for his passage to the West Indies. However, his book was so successful he decided to stay in Scotland where he continued to write. He supported his family by working as a tax collector. His radical political views led to his becoming the Peoples' Poet of Russia and he supported the French Revolution.

He died suddenly of heart disease and more than ten thousand mourners attended his funeral.

E9 – MICHAEL FARADAY

Chemist and physicist, 1791 - 1867

Age at death:	75
Statue Location:	Corner of Savoy Place, WC2
Date Erected:	1988, (copy of original)
Sculptor:	John Foley

Faraday was the son of a blacksmith and became an apprentice bookbinder in London. He worked for Humphrey Davy as his assistant and travelled throughout Europe with him.

He published his first work on electro-magnetic motors in 1821. After Davy died, Faraday's reputation as a leading scientist was firmly sealed. He is responsible for establishing the principles behind the electric motor, batteries, generators and transformers. He was a great public servant and assisted with planning the Great Exhibition in 1851.

It was only after his death that the first electric light was installed.

E10 – SIR HENRY HAVELOCK

British general, 1795 - 1857

Age at death: 62

Statue Location: Trafalgar Square, SW1

Date Erected: 1861

Sculptor: William Behnes

Havelock was born near Sunderland but educated in Kent where his family moved to when he was a child.

He trained as a lawyer but his studies were interrupted and he joined the army at the age of 20. He participated in the Afghan Wars and as a British General he is renowned for the capture of Cawnpore from rebels during the Indian Rebellion of 1857. He became a Baptist in 1826 and was responsible for the distribution of bibles to all soldiers.

He died of dysentery after being held by a blockade after a siege on Lucknow in India.

E11 – ISAMBARD KINGDOM BRUNEL

Civil Engineer, 1806 - 1859

Age at death: 53

Statue Location: Victoria Embankment, WC2

Date Erected: 1877

Sculptor: Baron Carlo Marochetti

Brunel was born in Portsmouth to a French engineer father and was brought up in both England and France.

He worked for his father and together they built the Rotherhithe Tunnel under the Thames in 1843. He was responsible for the design of many tunnels, bridges, railway lines and ships, including Paddington Station, the Great Western Railway and the Clifton Suspension Bridge. He also designed several steamships.

He was a heavy smoker and needed only 4 hours sleep a night. He died of a stroke.

E12 – WILLIAM GLADSTONE

Politician, 1809 - 1898

Age at death: 88

Statue Location: The Strand, WC2

Date Erected: 1905

Sculptor: Sir Hamo Thornycroft

Deputy of Oriental Zone

Gladstone was born in Liverpool and educated at Eton and Oxford and entered politics at the age of 23.

He was one of the dominant political figures of the Victorian era and a passionate campaigner on a huge variety of issues. He was originally a Conservative but became a Liberal with Robert Peel when the Conservative Party split in 1846. He had an intense rivalry with Disraeli and was also at odds with Queen Victoria. He supported Irish home rule. In a career lasting over sixty years, he served as Prime Minster four times and Chancellor of the Exchequer four times.

He died of cancer and is buried in Westminster Abbey.

E13 – EDITH CAVELL

Nurse, 1865 - 1915

Age at death: 49

Statue Location: St Martin's Place, WC2

Date Erected: 1920

Sculptor: George Frampton

Edith Cavell was born in Norwich. Her father was a priest. She was educated, amongst other places, at Laurel Court, Peterborough. She trained as a nurse in London and worked in Brussels where she launched a nursing journal and became the training nurse for three hospitals.

At the outbreak of World War I her hospital was taken over by the Red Cross. After the German occupation of Brussels she started sheltering Allied soldiers and helped to guide them out of Belgium to neutral Holland. The Germans accused her of harbouring Allied soldiers and after a court martial she was shot by a German firing squad. The British did little to save her; it was the US who tried to intervene.

Her body was brought back to the UK where a memorial service was held in Westminster Abbey. She is buried in Norwich Cathedral.

E14 – MAHATMA GANDHI

Leader of India's movement for independence, 1869 – 1948

Age at death: 78

Statue Location: Tavistock Square, WC1

Date Erected: 1968

Sculptor: Fredda Brilliant

Gandhi was born in India and trained as a lawyer in London.

He returned to India in 1891 and practised law. He became increasingly involved in politics and rose to become the leader of the Indian nationalist movement against British rule in India with a doctrine of non-violent protest to achieve political and social progress. He was against the partition of India, proposed by the Mountbatten Plan of 1947, and fasted in protest.

He was shot by a Hindu fanatic in Delhi after only six months of independence.

Lightning Source UK Ltd.
Milton Keynes UK
UKOW030606250212

187891UK00001B/94/P